BLITZKRIEG TOMMIES

BLITZKRIEG TOMMIES

JAX SINGH TAAK

BLITZKRIEG TOMMIES

ISBN: 978-1-7384491-0-1 (Paperback)

ISBN: 978-1-7384491-1-8 (Hardcover)

ISBN: 978-1-7384491-2-5 (Ebook)

Cover Design by Jax Singh Taak

Published by Jax Singh Taak

First Edition:

For inquiries or permissions, please contact:

jaxsinghtaak@outlook.com

Author's website: www.jaxsinghtaak.co.uk

Dedication

In profound respect, I dedicate this book to the pillar of inspiration in my life. I dedicate this book to my late father, whose legacy of compassion and integrity continues to illuminate my path. My father lived to do 'Sewa', the selfless service that involves acting selflessly and helping others. Through my father's teachings and example, I learned the values of kindness, empathy, and honesty, which have guided me in writing and my interactions with the world. This dedication is a tribute to my father's enduring influence and the profound impact of his wisdom and love on my life and work. It is something I have instilled within my twins growing up; now, they are young adults, and it warms my heart to see my father's principles and memory live on.

Additionally, I dedicate it to the fallen souls of the two World Wars, whose bravery and selfless sacrifice have left an indelible mark on history. Their unwavering courage and dedication are a touching reminder of the human cost of conflict and the enduring importance of honouring those who have given their lives to serve others. Not forgetting the millions of victims of tyranny and genocide within any conflict.

Lest We Forget.

Acknowledgements

I extend my heartfelt gratitude to all those who have supported me throughout my journey in crafting Blitzkrieg Tommies. First and foremost, I express deep appreciation to my wife, Ravindar, and my twins, Meru and Josh, whose unwavering love and encouragement have sustained me through the trials of chronic pain and the pursuit of my creative endeavours. Your patience, understanding, and belief in my abilities have been invaluable support pillars.

I also wish to sincerely thank my uncle, Biant, who has remained a stalwart supporter of my writing talents and whose continual encouragement has been a source of inspiration and motivation. Furthermore, I acknowledge the profound influence of my late father, whose legacy of ethical principles, moral integrity, and selfless service continues to shape my life and work. Through my father's teachings and example, I have learned the importance of compassion, kindness, and integrity, which characterise my writing and interactions with others.

Foreword

In Blitzkrieg Tommies, Jax Singh Taak embarks on a journey through the violent landscapes of World War II, weaving together a blend of courage, sacrifice, and resilience. Through the eyes of Private Singh, a Sikh soldier serving in the British Army, and Major Watkins, a seasoned officer leading a covert mission, Jax Singh Taak uses his literal skills to transport readers to the heart of Nazi-occupied Europe.

Jax's narrative expertise shines as he delves into the intricacies of identity and duty, drawing parallels between historical events and contemporary struggles. From the harrowing experiences of soldiers navigating the horrors of war to the quiet moments of unity amidst the chaos, Jax makes it captivating through authenticity and depth. As the narrative unfolds across various theatres of conflict, Jax skilfully navigates the complexities of human relationships and the moral dilemmas individuals face amid the chaos of war. Through triumph and tragedy, he paints a vivid portrait of the indomitable human spirit, resilient in the face of unimaginable adversity.

But he makes Blitzkrieg Tommies more than a tale of wartime heroism; it is a testament to the enduring power of hope, compassion, and solidarity. His exploration of themes such as identity, sacrifice, and loyalty resonates deeply, inviting readers to reflect on the timeless lessons of history and the enduring legacy of those who dared to defy tyranny. In writing this gripping narrative, Jax draws inspiration from his own experiences and cultural heritage, infusing the story with authenticity and empathy. Through meticulous research and vivid storytelling, he brings to life the untold stories of Sikh soldiers and their contributions to the Allied cause, shedding light on their often-overlooked role in shaping the course of history.

As we embark on this journey through the pages of Blitzkrieg Tommies, Jax wants us to learn from the lessons of the past and honour the sacrifices of those who came before us, whose bravery and selfless sacrifice continue to inspire generations to come.

With gratitude, Jax Singh Taak.

Prologue

I'm Albie George-Hunter, known as 'Foxy' to my army chums. Not because of my foxy good looks, nor do I have any cunning or sly notions of deceit. It is all due to my surname and the toffs, who loved fox hunting, where my old mum worked. You know the sort, Daimler driving, quaffing champagne, wearing stout brogues, shouting "Tally-ho," and are normally potless. How great are childhood names? Like crap, they stick to you. I'm big and ugly enough, though, to take it on the chinny-chin chin. Saying that, 'Old Lordy-Lord Augustus' of this gaff we talk of, that loveable rogue, used to cop an eyeful, when I used to wear short trousers, so maybe 'Foxy' is an apt name for yours truly.

Sorry, look at me getting carried away, engaging in this very British of pastimes, of having a natter, chewing the fat or partaking in a chinwag, depending on which side of the river you're from. So, I have a tall tale to tell you regarding a turkey shoot in Provence; well, it started off there. So here goes, us Tommies are pushing hard within this war we find ourselves in, with that oh-so-true British steadfast mentality and tenacity. The Nazis are being driven back slightly in different theatres of this war, but we are still finding the most fanatical resistance we have ever faced within this conflict.

Jerry is going for it; the German war machine is on overdrive as we see no let-up within the fighting. We all know eventually the Führer will give the order for 'Total War' to every man, woman, and child to fight. Pick up arms against the foreign invaders. Defend the Fatherland with everything they have, from garden forks, harsh words to sticks, and stones. The Germans have nothing to lose as the Red Army is doing their damnedest, and our boys have a few tricks up their sleeve, too. They have landed in Sicily; our aim is to eventually reach Rome, then Paris; after that falls, hopefully Berlin should be next. Why don't they just give up and wave a white flag, and that will be that? No more unnecessary devastation, and certainly no more death. It is shocking what one man can do to another.

It will make your fucking toes curl - what humans are capable of if their mere existence is under threat. I have seen many things in life, but the horrors of this war are something else. When you witness a blokes skin being melted off his body due to being on the receiving end of a flamethrower or his limbs having been blown apart by an explosion. His guts spewed all over the terracotta due to shrapnel ripping open his stomach. This is just the tip of a sharp bayonet, which we Tommies experience daily. Most of us have a good grasp of life and what this war entails. You'll be buggered if you don't, but you'll soon get your noggin around the trepidation as you approach the front.

My old mum was in service in some posh gaff, as I said earlier. So, I know the difference between a Gainsborough, being blooded and a jam sponge. I often went to work with her, roaming around the gaff, making a bloody nuisance of myself. Mostly, spending time within the grand-looking library, reading those dusty old 'First Editions' and encyclopaedias, leather bound, of course. Would you have it? I know of fine English art, classical composers and even French champagnes, not forgetting pukka-looking grub, you know, silver service and all that. All from hanging around that place, so you can take me anywhere as I'm fully house-trained. Look at me getting carried away again; sorry, back to Jerry.

One thing about Jerry is that he is not like the Japanese. Now they are a different kettle completely, with their honour in defeat bollocks, which us Gaijin Rockers will never comprehend. How many of our boys have been killed due to their Kamikaze attacks? Sikhs like Private Singh are serving in Burma, fighting against this formidable foe in the Pacific conflict, too. Like his cousin Balnoor Singh, who is serving in the Chindits. They are officially known as 'Long Range Penetration Groups', who deep behind enemy lines wage a guerrilla warfare campaign against the Japanese. Their objective is a simple one: to kill, maim and attack the Jap lines of communication all within the cloak of darkness. The challenges confronted by soldiers in their theatre of war, characterised by high humidity, frequent heavy rainfall, and the dense tropical jungle, present formidable obstacles. Amidst these conditions, the presence of venomous snakes, relentless mosquitoes, and the risk of fever further heightens the precarious nature of combat for every soldier involved. At least Europe is more like Blighty, with its grey skies and weather conditions.

I could not be doing with all that palaver, sweating your Bristol's off while watching out for snakes, and lastly being blown-up by some mad Jap Geezer, not on your Nelly, me old China. Fuck that for a game of soldiers, if you ask me. The Japanese have brought it on themselves by waking up the sleeping giant. The Yanks are pouring soldiers into the war effort in the Pacific conflict, Africa and now Europe, all sparked by the attack on Pearl Harbour. We needed the Yanks to join, with their deep pockets, an abundance of boots on the ground, and metal, which they have done eventually. We caught Jerry off guard in French North Africa with his pants around his ankles. Yeah, we got proper fucked, royally shafted, done over like a day tripper at Southend-on-Sea, at Dunkirk though. It was like daylight robbery on the battlefield, seeing how the Krauts robbed us of the ground we fought over. But saying that, we've had numerous successes too, which often resulted in Jerry certainly being on the back foot. After these small victories, we thought if this did not swing things our way, nothing else would.

We had banked heavily on the French, but Jerry waltzed into France and did a hatchet job on them, easy-peasy, earlier on in the war. Then, the little German Geezer had the audacity to make the French sign the armistice in the same bloody railway carriage as in 1918. The sheer balls of the man before he shipped the 'Compiegne waggon' off to some museum in Berlin. Hat's off, or visor cap, in this case, to the deranged bloke; proper mind games, if I say so myself. This was long before the Yanks joined the fighting, which is now definitely helping us drive Jerry back into that dark, dirty little rat hole where he popped his head out in the first instance.

The Allies are a mixed bunch from around the globe. I do not give a monkey's if the fella next to me is pink with yellow spots, as long as this fella has got my back. You do not fight for yourself; you fight for the bloke next to you. Yeah, neither skin colour nor appearance should make any difference, as we are all fighting a common enemy. Unfortunately, it does.

Due to the British Commonwealth, we have soldiers who are from different ethnic backgrounds fighting alongside us, Tommies. Most of the Sikh soldiers wear a turban and have a full beard; this should not make them a worse soldier than the next bloke. They fight for King George VI under the Union Jack. Why should they be treated differently because of their identity, skin tone, or heritage? These Sikh soldiers, letting loose some lead at Jerry, should be no different from a Tommy. It makes my fucking blood boil, to the extent that yours truly is going to bust a blood vessel or two. They are labelled as Sepoys; why can't they be treated the same as the Tommies? When the crap flies over no man's land, guess what? They will be the poor sods who'll be left out there dealing with it.

Unfortunately, those tasked with sending soldiers into danger often prioritise their own comfort, opting for lunch while others face the imminent risks. Some officers just want the fight, whatever the human cost. The Sepoys are treated as expendable pawns, sacrificially deployed like lambs to the slaughter, without the need for any mint sauce. As they climb that rickety wooden ladder into no man's land, or often are the first wave of attack in most battles, their fate is seemingly sealed.

It is a grim reality that, considered 'cannon fodder', their worth to the higher-ups is close to nothing. Why can't they see the valour and fortitude displayed by these men, often refusing to hide within their trenches. They opt to attack the enemy instead, till death. Just ask the Aussies, what happened at Gallipoli? While many soldiers understand and appreciate the bravery of their Sikh comrades, there are a few among the Tommies who, regrettably, show a lack of regard. These individuals would leave a Sikh soldier stranded in no man's land, indifferent to their fate, often under the thunderous rhythm of enemy shell and machine gunfire.

Let the Krauts shoot them down in flames. Take potshots at them; call it target practice. It is funny, as when Sikh soldiers do come face-to-face with Jerry, the look on their 'boat-races' when they clap eyes on them. I've been told there is always a slight pause, an element of "where did you come from", before they start shooting. Some Sikhs have been taken in as prisoners of war by Jerry. I hope they get treated fairly, as long as they have not been captured by the SS. These Nazi scoundrels will definitely take target practice at your noggin, which always means your ultimate demise. Oh well, that is a tall tale for a different day. Where was I before I rudely interrupted my own train of thought? Oh yeah, the fucking Nazis, that's it, and that little deranged Geezer called Adolf.

Contents

Chapter One: A little stroll in the woods

Private Singh grips the stock of his army-issue Enfield rifle for dear life as he creeps through the woods in some part of France. He and his fellow soldiers have been scattered all over the place due to high winds, and the fact that Jerry was taking pot shots at the aircraft he was travelling in. He doesn't even know where the rest of his unit is, let alone where the hell he is. He looks scared shitless to put it politely, probably due to the fact he's just been dropped out of an aircraft. I do not think he looks like someone who has a good head for heights. Jumping like some crazy Geezer thousands of feet up there, to his certain demise, hitting the old French terracotta doesn't do wonders for anyone, let alone a British soldier.

Suddenly, there is a noise, and his head snaps around to have a butcher's at what it could be. His rifle cocked and ready to spit out some lead, just in case Jerry is closer than he thinks. He looks like someone who is not too keen on taking human life, but this is the hand he has been dealt with due to that little deranged Geezer called Adolf Hitler and his bunch of brown shirts.

On moving forward slightly, he suddenly hears a noise. Private Singh is ready and willing to engage any Kraut who thinks he's hard enough to have a ruckus with him. Tension consumes him as he looks slightly nervous at facing the enemy firsthand on French soil. His hand trembles slightly as he moves slowly towards the dense hedgerow where the noise is coming from. He swallows his non-enthusiast spit, as he knows this is it. Beads of sweat form on his brow as he wipes them away with his sleeve. Thoughts of what he is going to encounter rattle around his noggin. His stomach is in knots as he slowly creeps forward.

All that training, all those drills, and all that shouting by some loud-mouthed drill Sergeant suddenly evaded him. The adrenaline kicks in. This is it, now or fucking never, he thinks to himself. On slowly making his way around towards the edge of the dense hedgerow, he springs into action and lunges his rifle forward. It is pointing to where the noise originated from. To his relief, it is an old bicycle, semi-buried with its front wheel sticking upwards out of the soil. Due to the wind, it is spinning intermittently, striking a twig from the hedgerow, which in turn is making the offending noise that caught his attention.

The look on Private Singh's 'boat-race' is priceless; I like to say just the word "boat" normally instead of the whole Cockney rhyming slang thing. Saying that, I will still say "face", too. It just depends on my mood, so you'll have to bear with me regarding this. Often it's Estuary English, with an element of Received Pronunciation and a mere sprinkling of Cockney banter. I'll come to that in a minute. This should highlight how relieved he is feeling due to not finding some Kraut who is ready to fight. Even though we feel we might be nearing the end of this conflict we all find ourselves fighting in, according to London, he thinks to himself. We all know if things do not go Adolf Hitler's way, he will give the order for an all-out attack for men, women, and children to pick up arms.

The reports indicate that we are finding the most fanatical resistance we have ever encountered. This is not a German war machine in retreat; it is far from it. These people are obedient to their Führer, and their defiance grows further. Reports have it that groups of children roam the European countryside, wearing oversized Nazi uniforms with weapons. A child using a shooter or lobbing a Stielhandgranate has the same desired effect for the recipient.

I hope no Tommies or other Allied soldiers have been on the receiving end of one of these kindergarten killers. It is a bloody shame when you have to gun down one of these Hitler Youth little bastards; if you do not, they will kill you. It is as simple as that, so it is all about the self-preservation society nowadays. Back to Private Singh, who sits down as he takes in the view and takes his pack off in an attempt to rest. His back is screaming due to the weight of the damn thing and with the extra equipment attached to it. On opening his water bottle, he takes a sip and closes the cap. He remains seated as he takes in the view of this hedgerow, which disappears into the distance. It looks like Blighty, the English countryside to which he has become accustomed. He wipes his brow once again, as his skin is leaking, and the front edge of his turban is now soaked in sweat due to how nervous he really is.

The air grows still, a hush broken only by the whispering rustle of the wind as it sweeps through. He appreciates the silence, as he looks around, in contrast to the noise of war. With an outstretched hand, he beckons the breeze, guiding the long grass to dance upon his palm. The gentle caress on his face is akin to the satisfaction of a chilled beer and the embrace of a cherished companion or a right rotten tart. This soldier, far from home, feels a surge of relief wash over him in this moment.

Private Singh is a Sepoy serving within the King's army, as some would say. A turban-wearing Sikh from the Punjab, in Northern India, he is many miles away from his native shores. Here, serving King and Country under the Union Jack. He is in his mid-forties, a true masculine soldier, with his stature that stands six feet in height. He is a caring individual who displays principles and empathy for his fellow man. Someone who has battled adversity throughout his life, from childhood to now adulthood. This only fuels his will to succeed and not fail. He is an emotional man who wears his heart on his sleeve but displays a gritty exterior, as this can be perceived as weakness within the military.

He served in the Great War at the tender age of seventeen. Would you have it? He fought in the battle of Gallipoli on the Turkish coast. As a young runner, he ferried messages between the front line and Anzac Gunners. The 14th Sikhs held the trenches around Gully Ravine for months after losing a significant percentage of their men due to the attacks from the Turks. Thousands of Sikh and Indian soldiers lost their lives fighting as loyal Sepoys as they defended the Suez Canal and the theatre of war, which was Gallipoli.

After being wounded, Private Singh spent time within Australia before returning home to Blighty, where he continued his military career until being called up for duty to fight once again. His injuries on the fifth day of the Gallipoli campaign meant spending time within a military hospital within Melbourne.

Private Singh underwent elements of hostility, as they had not seen a turban-wearing Sikh before. You would think the Australians would recognise these men from another shore, taking into consideration that their boys were within the same trenches next to them, fighting the same foe daily. This must have been a challenging time for him, being in a foreign country and being treated like a second-class citizen. To top it off, he had been injured, and all this at this tender age.

Private Singh has been within Blighty for many years now, since he was a child, to be exact. Due to his schooling within Blighty, his communication skills, both written and verbal, were quite unique. This made him an excellent candidate for the runner's position in the battle of Gallipoli. His family had been instrumental within the British war machine for many years now, from iconic theatres of war like Somme to Gallipoli, fighting side by side with the British, like he had. Unfortunately, many were killed, gassed, and maimed. Sikhs are a warrior race but peaceful and respectful of other beings, too. The British army has been reliant on Sikh soldiers to swell their ranks and march into battle under the guise of freedom one day for many years now. Many Sikhs hoped this day would come when India would gain its independence from the foreign invader. The Sepoy soldiers are disposable; they are 'cannon fodder'. As the British officers march them in, let them take heavy casualties.

"Balderdash, it's collateral damage, friend or foe", is what one officer called it.

The Gallipoli campaign is evidence of this, whoever cares, mentioning the thousands of Sikh soldiers who died throughout the campaign. The ANZACs who fought side by side with these warriors know different. Look at me getting carried away, getting on my soapbox again. Where were we? Oh yeah, Private Singh taking in the view, which he knows he shouldn't be doing.

Private Singh takes another sip of water and contemplates finding the closest town, as he remembers seeing a church steeple. So, this should be the place to head too, he thinks to himself. Suddenly, he hears a whistling noise, like some air raid siren, the noise screaming down towards him. It's a 'Junkers Ju 87', more commonly known as the 'Stüka' dive bomber; he must have spotted him sitting here in the open. What a prize plum, sitting here in broad bloody daylight. On scrambling to his feet, he grabs his Enfield rifle and runs towards some undergrowth. He can hear the siren getting closer, its menacing tone screeching to instil terror within its target. His heart is in his mouth as suddenly the bullets rain down, whizzing past him as his legs do their damnedest to carry him at speed towards the undergrowth for cover. His legs feel like lead weights as he powers towards the undergrowth. Sweat pours down his boat as the nerves kick in too.

The aircraft swoops over him, gaining height for another attack. He grabs his rifle and fires a volley of shots towards the direction of the aircraft. What good is small arms fire against a dive bomber thousands of feet in the sky? He thinks to himself. Private Singh readies himself for another attack, and the screeching starts again, getting closer and closer. By now, he is sitting up taking aim, like some professional soldier would do. Trying to calm himself down, limiting his breathing.

BANG! BANG! BANG! BANG! His rifle sounds.

He frantically tries to reload as this Red Barron of the skies is soon upon him once again. The bullets rain down, and his only reply is his trusted Enfield rifle. To his horror, the pilot releases a bomb; this distant dark object suddenly starts to fall towards him.

"Bloody hell, this Geezer is taking liberties," Private Singh calls out.

He gets to his feet and frantically runs for much-needed cover. On seeing what looks like a drainage ditch, he hurls his body into it. The aircraft swoops over him, making that whining noise that our boys had become accustomed to as he ducks for cover. Seconds later, the explosive device goes off. This thunderous sound shatters the silence which is followed by his retreat towards the skies. This split second of calm and silence which, is immediately followed by carnage. His ears start to bleed instantly, and he can feel something wet on his face. On touching his face, he looks at his hand, which is now covered in the red stuff.

In the aftermath of the explosion, blood trickles from his ears, and a sudden jolt of pain shoots through his lower leg. With a dawning realisation, he notices his trousers are torn and soaked in blood. Amidst the chaos, the aircraft plunges once more, its deafening roar intensifying. Private Singh remains motionless, hidden amidst the swirling dust and debris, escaping notice. Shots ring out towards the billowing cloud as the pilot ascends, disappearing into the distance. Relief washes over Private Singh, yet he remains still, ensuring the aircraft's departure. Perhaps the pilot assumed he was dead, hence flying away. His sense of relief falters, replaced abruptly by searing agony. Clutching his injured leg, he bellows in pain, a shard of shrapnel embedded deep within.

He scrambles, trying to grab hold of his rifle, which he eventually gets hold of the strap and pulls it towards himself. On using the rifle to stand upright, he limps over towards his pack. He is dazed and confused, ears still ringing, some form of shrapnel lodged in his leg, and he knows in the back of his mind that Jerry will soon be sending a patrol. He needs to get the hell out of here before he gets his collar felt by the Gestapo. On hobbling over towards his pack, he falls to the ground. On grabbing at the pack, he pulls out his water bottle and pours water onto the wound.

"ARRRRRGGGGGHHHHH!" he calls out.

The pain is unbearable as he wraps a handkerchief tightly around the wound to help with the bleeding.

"Come on, boy," he calls out.

"Pull yourself together," he adds.

His manner is aggressive, in some form of attempt to get his arse down the road a bit before Jerry shows up. He stumbles to his feet again as he places his pack back on and uses his rifle butt as a walking aid. He walks along the dense hedgerow so he is camouflaged from the roadside, as this is where Jerry will be coming from, he thinks to himself. His nerves have gone; they have been replaced with a mixture of pain and adrenaline by now. He has nothing to lose now, as he is alone in Nazi-occupied France, and fuck knows where the rest of the boys are. He is leaking the red stuff, and Jerry is imminent at any time now.

On seeing a hole within another hedgerow, Private Singh slowly climbs through it, and to his surprise, he can hear a river or some form of flowing water, even though his ears are still ringing. Thoughts of apprehension wash over him at what he might discover, but the adrenaline has taken over. As Private Singh slowly moves down the bank, he loses his footing and falls arse over tit, as he goes tumbling down the bank. His final resting place heaped and impaled in a bramble bush.

Without feeling sorry for himself, he pulls himself free of these little spiky bastards, which tear into his uniform. On picking up his rifle, which lies to the side of him, he gets to his feet once again.

"ARRRRRGGGGGHHHHH!" he calls out.

Private Singh wipes blood away from his face, which is leaking into his beard too. He immediately grabs at his leg before slowly inspecting it. One part of him does not want to look, but he knows deep down that he needs to get it strapped up so he can move to safety and avoid capture. He notices the shrapnel had embedded further by the fall into his leg. He tries to pick at the edge of that metal that still protrudes from the wound, but this increases the pain he endures. Private Singh decides not to attempt removing the shrapnel, but instead, he pulls the handkerchief tighter around the wound, which only aggravates it further.

"Hells fucking bells!" he calls out.

He clutches his leg once more, wincing from the intense pain surging through him. Private Singh reclines, desperately seeking relief, and eventually succumbs to unconsciousness. A brief respite is shattered by the cacophony of rushing water, jolting him back to awareness. As he gingerly sits up, he rubs his eyes, only to be confronted by the sight of his blood-soaked uniform. With a touch to his fevered forehead, he senses the heat radiating from his body. His turban and uniform are drenched in sweat. Grasping his water bottle, he takes a prolonged sip, splashing cool water on his face to rouse himself from the grogginess.

On looking around, he is still in the same position where he had fallen earlier, and there is no sign of Jerry, much to his relief. His mind starts to race, thinking about Jerry catching him and what they will do to him. He suddenly becomes quite anxious and scrambles to his feet. On looking around, Private Singh realises that he is closer to the river than he originally thought. The noise of the water breaking onto the rocks is far louder than before, so he decides to have a butcher's. As he makes his way towards the noise of the flowing water, he is still apprehensive of Kraut patrols. He is not feeling a million British pounds and knows the Krauts could turn up at any moment. With these thoughts rattling around his noggin, he moves slowly towards the water. His rifle is now a walking aid, as the red stuff still leaks from his wounds.

Suddenly, he hears shouting; it is a male voice, and it sounds like German to him. It is certainly not the King's English he can hear, he thinks to himself. As he slowly approaches the area where the shouting is coming from, he prepares himself for an altercation of sorts. As he goes to lay on his stomach, he slowly moves towards a clearing in stealth mode, like all that bloody training he underwent. He winces in pain as his wound makes contact with the ground as he moves forward, leaving a trail of blood.

Private Singh sucks it up and continues as the shouting becomes louder. He notices a German military truck parked in a clearing near the edge of the water. A German soldier who is doing all the shouting has his back towards him, and he does not notice him approaching. To his horror, the German soldier who is wearing a black uniform is standing over a group of young children who are kneeling on the floor, looking up at him. He is barking something at them as the children look distressed, with a few of them crying. They look like refugee children to him. The German soldier pushes one little boy to the floor with his foot before he pulls him up and slaps him in the face. The little boy starts to cry before he grabs him by his shirt and shakes him violently while screaming at him.

His face is right up close and personal for Private Singh's liking. He knows he must stop this bloke as soon as he produces a small handgun. It is not a Luger, as it is far too small, but a shooter is a shooter. Any small firearm or shooter in question here will do these little skulls much damage if lead is let loose.

He points the gun at a young girl who is clutching a raggedy doll against her chest. He grabs the doll and yanks it away from her before he throws it to the floor. Private Singh slowly stands up; tension consumes him as he continues to slowly move towards the German soldier. His only concern is that one of the children will give him away. He knows he must take this chance, as he'll regret this for the rest of his days if any of these little buggers end up brown bread on his watch.

On standing up, he slowly creeps forward; he raises his finger towards his mouth in some form of attempt to keep the children from giving him away. The German soldier is far too preoccupied with playing Führer to notice him. His heart is going like a good'un as he approaches him from behind, poised for attack even though he is in agony due to his leg. On feeling for his bayonet, he soon realises that he must have dropped it when he went for a tumble earlier. So, he decides to use the butt of his rifle to give this Geezer a good licking to his noggin.

Private Singh is consumed by adrenaline and nerves as he is right on him by now and steps on a bloody twig or something. The German soldier goes to turn slightly, and he strikes him to the side of his head. He goes down like a sack of spuds, out for the count like he has just gone a few rounds with the heavy champion in the blue-ribbon division. The children start to scream, even though they have just been saved. He tries to calm them down. Private Singh produces some chocolate he has. On seeing this, the children soon gather around him, beside the little girl with the doll.

"There you go, have some chocolate; plenty to go around," Private Singh calls out.

"Jude?" he asks.

They do not respond, but the look on their tiny faces answers his question. Suddenly, he hears a noise from the back of the truck and moves the children aside. He picks up his rifle and hits the deck. Just imagine it is more Germans as these thoughts rattle around his noggin. Private Singh lies on the floor near the rear wheel of the truck. He notices blood trickling downward onto the axle and then onto the grass. Instantly, he knows there are no Germans within this vehicle, but something he probably does not want to discover. The children, by now, have huddled within a small group, away from the truck. They are near the German soldier, who is lying on the floor still unconscious. The children look down at him, before they suddenly start to kick and punch him.

Private Singh gets to his feet and hastily hobbles over towards them and stops them from doing this; the anger is plain to see.

"Go to the next town; where's the church?" he calls out.

"You will be safe there; follow the river."

"Find the French, they're pukka," he adds.

The children gaze at him, but one of the boys appears to grasp what Private Singh is conveying. He gestures towards the river, sketching a cross in the soil with his rifle, hoping to illustrate his message for the children to comprehend.

"Go before the Krauts come," he calls out.

"Come on, kids, just go and hide."

"Go to church; you understand church, don't you" he adds.

Private Singh puts his hands together in a praying-hands gesture so the children would understand. Suddenly, a shell explodes nearby; the children start to scream while others run away. He hits the deck as the little girl does not move; she is shocked and just stares at Private Singh as she starts to cry. He knows she wants his help but is too frightened to move. On jumping to his feet, he grabs her and gets to the tree line for safety. The other children are near the riverbank by now, calling out for them to follow, he thinks. He does not fully understand them, but he can tell from their hand gestures that they are beckoning the little girl over. The little girl starts to wince and whine, and he soon realises her doll is still on the floor, where the German threw it. On going back for it, he collects it and walks back over before kneeling to pass the doll back to her. She embraces it at once and smiles at him. To his surprise, she suddenly embraces him tightly, too. Her dirt-covered, innocent little face shows a million emotions. Emotions run high as Private Singh thinks of his own family at this time. He knows they must leave, but the little girl has tugged on his heartstrings with her innocence and helplessness. Private Singh just looks at her small face, which is covered with dirt, and smiles back at her.

"You must go now, quickly, with the other children," Private Singh calls out.

"Please go, sweetheart," he adds.

As the other children call her, she makes her way towards the rest of the group. Private Singh watches anxiously as they slowly follow the river as it snakes into the distance. Suddenly, he can hear further shelling within the distance, which only becomes closer with time. On walking over towards the truck, he pulls the canvas back to reveal the dead bodies of men and women. They lay there lifeless, all intertwined with one common denominator: they had all been brutally murdered by the Nazis. Nearest to him is a young lady; she must be in her late teens, with her plaited brown hair soaked in dried blood. It dawns on him; they are all wearing a yellow star, which has been crudely sewn onto their clothing, the mark of the Jew. The yellow star was the moniker, used by the Nazis to identify Jewish folk.

In an instant, his heart plummets at the sight before him. How could one person inflict such horror on another? The thought weighs heavily on his mind. With trembling hands, he retrieves a small chrome hip flask and takes a prolonged, fortifying sip. But as the liquid touches his lips, a wave of overwhelming emotion hits, causing him to lose his balance and collapse to the floor. The magnitude of his discovery becomes unbearable.

His face contorts in a mixture of agony and incredulity, witnessing the atrocities committed under the guise of war. After a few moments, he wipes his brow with his sleeve as beads of sweat trickle down his boat. He must be developing a fever; he thinks to himself. The shelling continues, only getting closer towards his position. He hears a groan from the German soldier, who is coming too. Private Singh makes his way over to him and readies his rifle. He pokes the lifeless Kraut with his rifle; he slightly moves his head and faces Private Singh. He is surprised that he has been bleeding from his head wound, as his mop of blonde hair is now soaked in blood.

The other thing Private Singh had not noticed is that this Nazi he had within his custody was quite young too and his black uniform with its insignia is different from what he had previously seen. Private Singh decides to search the young Kraut on the off chance he may be carrying papers. All he discovers are a packet of cigarettes, some boiled sweets and oh yeah, a Hitler Youth knife. The young soldier slowly comes to and holds his head in pain.

He looks to be in his late teens if that.

"Are you okay?" Private Singh calls out.

"Yes," he replies, in a thick German accent.

To Private Singh's surprise, he can speak English, so he offers him water to start with. He pushes Private Singh's hand out of the way at first quite rudely, and the water bottle falls to the floor.

"Suit yourself, fella," Private Singh calls out.

"Don't have any bloody water then; see if I give a monkey's," he adds.

The aggression is slapped across Private Singh's boat about how rude he feels this young German Geezer is being. He picks up the water bottle off the floor and dusts it down. The German soldier is quite defiant at first and then reluctantly puts up his hand to take the water bottle. Private Singh lowers it towards his outstretched hand. He takes a drink from it and suddenly grabs his head, as he must be in pain. Private Singh produces a field dressing and unfolds it before he moves forward towards the injured Kraut.

He pushes his hand away to start off with. On holding up the field dressing, Private Singh gestures at what he is going to do with it. The young German pauses and then points towards his head with his hand. The hatred is so clear to see; the body language and mannerism of this young man tells the story of a nation. Suddenly, the soldier changes his mind and gestures for help. Private Singh presumes he now wants him to attend to his wounds. So, he wraps the dressing around his head and helps him up to his feet. The young German is quite defiant about accepting any help at first, but he soon realises that Private Singh is only trying to help him.

"You help?" The German asks in an accent.

"It was the humane thing to do, fella," Private Singh replies.

"You take me to camp?" The German asks.

"You hurt me," he adds.

"No, Geezer, the shelling started, and you got injured," Private Singh replies.

"You've copped an unfortunate one to your noggin," Private Singh adds.

"Your Kraut chums did that; you probably don't understand the banter?" he adds.

He just looks up at Private Singh as they both speak to one another. The last thing any British soldier is going to do is walk into some German camp, whistling as he walks into the gaff. It is every man for themselves. Private Singh is not going to shoot this young man of the Aryan race he has in front of him. Nor is he going to let this young Geezer shoot him dead once his back is turned, either. Private Singh has already pocketed his small sidearm, and Private Singh cannot see any other weapons of choice within the truck. Unless he is going to use sticks and stones or harsh language to inflict any bodily harm. Private Singh thinks he should be pukka, seeing he has no weapons on him and has a busted wing of sorts, or head trauma in his case.

Suddenly, more shells drop, but this time, they are much closer, which throws soil into the air. They explode with force; another and another hail down thereafter. Smoke and debris fill the air, which makes it difficult for Private Singh to see. He decides to pull the young Nazi away from the truck, as this could be seen as a target. Private Singh walks over towards him; the young man thinks he is going to hurt him in some way. He wears a look of vulnerability for someone who was aggressive only moments ago.

"Nein, nein," the young German calls out.

"Geezer, I'm only pulling you outta harm's way," Private Singh replies.

He soon realises that he is trying to help him again. Private Singh places his arms under his shoulders to pull him aside as soil and flying debris strike them. Suddenly, one shell lands to the side of the truck and explodes near the rear tyre, which turns the vehicle onto its side. The truck explodes too; its fuel tank ignites, causing a fire and thick black smoke. They are both thrown with force away from the explosion, landing on the ground. Private Singh slowly comes too; his head is throbbing, and he can feel pain in his back. On rubbing his eyes, it is hard to visualise due to the thick smoke and debris that are still in the air.

As a thick plume of black smoke billows into the air, it swiftly blankets the surroundings in an eerie shroud of darkness. Private Singh straightens himself, his gaze scanning for the young German soldier. Spotting him near a tree stub, Singh cautiously approaches, searching for his missing rifle amid the obscured terrain. With a small handgun drawn as a precaution against any potential threat, he moves closer to the motionless soldier. The German lies inert, sprawled on the ground by now.

Singh, noticing additional bruising on the soldier's head, gently turns him over, revealing the solemnity of his lifeless form. Private Singh puts the handgun away. As the young Kraut is in no fit state to be any trouble, he thinks to himself.

"Oi, Geezer, wake up," Private Singh calls out.

"Come on, boy, let's be having you now."

"This is no time to rest your weary head," he adds.

There is no response from him, so he checks to see if he is still within the land of the living. To his relief, he is. So Private Singh decides to lift him up and carry him. Private Singh's ears are still oozing blood, which had only been made worse by this second wave of shelling. His leg wound is killing him, and he is walking around with a lifeless Nazi in his arms, which does not help. The young German's head has taken the brunt of the explosion, going off near him by the looks of it. As he slowly walks, carrying him towards the main road, Private Singh knows deep down that he is going to be in hot water if he comes across a Kraut patrol. A cloud of dense black smoke still covers the whole area due to the shelling and the truck fire. This acts as a background to the eerie silence after all that noise, which has suddenly stopped. The plume of black smoke will give away their position, so he tries to distance himself between them and the scene of the crime as he can.

For some reason, the young German Geezer he is carrying seems to weigh a tonne. Even though he is of slim build, it just seems to be this way. Maybe it is due to Private Singh being injured himself with the loss of blood. Private Singh harbours the notion that he cannot let this young man die; on the other hand, he is asking for trouble by saving him. He wrestles with his conscience, but he is a good bloke, and he does the right thing, even though that is what the Nazis are doing. Many Tommies would have opted for a straightforward resolution, put a bullet in his head and move on. Private Singh, grappling with the incongruity of holding a lifeless German soldier in his arms while contemplating a peaceful parlay, wonders how he can navigate this delicate situation without risking his own safety or arrest. With these perplexing thoughts swirling in his mind, he halts and gently places the man on the grass verge.

"ARRRRRGGGGGHHHHH!" he calls out.

He notices fresh blood trickling down his leg but knows he needs to get the young man seen by a medic. Drawing from his water bottle, he takes a contemplative sip, his gaze shifting to the motionless young German. Observing the boy's fair features - blonde hair, blue eyes - Private Singh reflects on the irony that this seemingly youthful figure, likely in his late teens, could harbour intentions of harm towards innocent children. The paradox perplexes Private Singh, leaving him unable to fathom why a young man of such tender years would be driven to such violence.

He picks up the lifeless man again and starts to walk, which aggravates his back. Holding it somewhat, he continues walking down the road. He walks for another mile or so, and as sweaty beads roll down his boat due to the sheer weight he is carrying, he stops once again to rest up. Suddenly, he hears a vehicle approaching from behind them; he does not even have the energy to hide due to being exhausted. Private Singh knows that walking behind the dense hedgerows was the safer option, so he would not have been as easily discovered. It is far easier to walk on the road when you are carrying a lump than it is to walk along an uneven grassy area.

He is still struggling with his conscious of leaving him in the middle of the road and doing one behind the bushes. Private Singh attempts to pick up the lifeless soldier; by this time, the vehicle approaching has now pulled up behind them, with its brakes screeching to a stop. Suddenly, Private Singh hears German being spoken.

"Halt," a man calls out in a stern voice.

He hears a gun cocking at the same time and realises he should go steady with his reaction towards what has been said. On slowly turning around, he sees a grey Mercedes saloon car parked up next to them. The driver is holding an MP-40 submachine gun which is, pointed in his direction. The passenger is an officer who opens the rear door and exits the car before he walks over towards them.

"Hands up," the officer calls out in a thick German accent.

"We will shoot," he adds.

Private Singh has no idea what is going to happen next, who this young soldier is, or what ramifications it will have on him.

"Listen, fella, I'm going to slowly place him down," Private Singh calls out.

"Tell Geezer over there not to get trigger-happy," he adds.

On saying this, he bends down slightly and slowly places the young soldier onto the grass verge. The driver moves forward and thrusts the gun into his boat with vigour. He senses he means business by the look in his eyes. The officer, on the other hand, looks more intrigued, to be honest with him. Maybe these boys in grey have never clapped eyes on a Sikh Geezer before, he thinks to himself. The officer approached the young soldier lying on the grass to assess his condition. However, the driver, uncomfortably close to Private Singh, waves his gun carelessly. With his MP-40 submachine gun now pointed towards him, Private Singh felt compelled to kneel with his hands raised. As the driver advanced aggressively, lifting his hands, Private Singh feared an impending strike.

"Nein," the officer calls out.

To the surprise of the driver, who just stares at the officer in protest. His body language settles down slightly, but he decides to spit on the floor next to Private Singh instead. He must feel that Private Singh had hurt his fellow countryman in some way or another, by the looks of it. The fact remains: why would a British soldier carry this injured Kraut, breaking his already aching back, when Private Singh could have easily left him within the undergrowth in the dark with the mushrooms, playing dead?

"You are a prisoner of the Third Reich," the officer calls out.

"We will ask you questions," he adds.

Suddenly, the officer stops in his tracks as the young soldier moves his face to the side as he comes too. He recognises him and calls the driver over, back towards where the car was parked. They stand and talk, looking over at Private Singh on a few occasions. The officer calms the driver down and barks some form of order at him. The driver does not look too pleased with what is being discussed, given the dirty look he gives Private Singh.

They both walk back over towards them; the young soldier is still unconscious. The driver carefully picks him up and takes him to the car, where he places him in the rear seat. Private Singh has ample opportunity to run, have it away on his toes, and get away, but for some reason, he does not. Suddenly, the officer realises that they have left him to his own devices and rushes around. He produces his Walther P38 handgun and points it at him as Private Singh is still kneeling on the floor with his hands behind his head.

"You not run, Herr English," he calls out.

"Nah, it's been a long day, Geezer. I just need a cuppa, a jam tart, and a sit down," Private Singh replies.

"Plus, I've got this hunk of metal sticking out of my bloody leg," he adds.

Private Singh turns his leg slightly, which highlights his wound. The officer looks at him sternly, slightly confused at first, but then he smiles as he understands part of what is being said. The driver takes his seat, and the officer points his handgun towards the car so as to lead the way.

"You sit!" he calls out.

"Trouble Herr English, I shoot," he adds.

Private Singh slowly gets into the front passenger's seat. The driver looks at him in disgust or contempt after he helps the young soldier into the rear seat. The officer enters the rear and sits down, placing the young soldier's head on his lap. The driver starts the car, and they start to drive, with the officer holding his handgun at the back of Private Singh's noggin. Tension fills the air as apprehension washes over Private Singh. What is going to happen next as his mind races to where they are taking him?

They drive down narrow country lanes towards a small town; the smoke disappears in the distance as they reach the town. It reminds Private Singh of East Anglia within Blighty. An area he had visited on days out towards the coast. Green fields, winding country roads, and bramble bushes are the same wherever you are, he thinks to himself. This brings a momentary smile to his boat as he thinks of the fond memories before the war, which has brought only death and carnage.

On arriving at a checkpoint, the car screeches to a halt. Private Singh soon realises this could be the town he flew over before he jumped out of the aircraft. His thoughts go back to the children of earlier; he wonders if they made it to safety, or did these fuckers capture them?

The officer leaves the vehicle and enters the checkpoint building, where he winds up a telephone before picking up the receiver. He continues to speak as Private Singh watches him through the window. The driver soon puts a small handgun into Private Singh's side forcefully as he notices him looking around at their fortifications. They look well dug in here, with machine gun nests and snipers on rooftops.

He can just make out military vehicles within the distance; they look like tanks from their silhouettes, but they are covered over with camouflage netting. Suddenly, a military ambulance arrives, and two medical staff carry the young soldier onto a stretcher and into the vehicle. The officer oversees this before speaking to the ambulance staff, Private Singh hears 'Berlin' being mentioned within the conversation. Suddenly a military escort appears, to follow the ambulance. Private Singh thinks, this young man must be of significant importance for all this palaver. It drives off, at speed sounding its siren, with military vehicles in front and behind it. The officer turns to Private Singh and just stares at him.

"Herr English, we talk," he calls out.

"They take him to Berlin, by air, he is important" he adds.

Two soldiers suddenly arrive to escort Private Singh towards a makeshift hospital to his surprise. It is an abandoned-looking building that resembles a school hall to him. The Germans have made it into a medical facility of sorts, by the looks of it. Injured soldiers lay on metal beds, some wearing bandages over their injuries, others with glass bottles of blood attached to them. A palpable sense of urgency fills the room as a doctor races against time to rescue an injured soldier.

Despite the doctor's frantic efforts to staunch the bleeding from the soldier's neck wound with fresh bandages, a haunting air of defeat lingers. The disappointment etched across the doctor's face is unmistakable, yet unwavering determination propels every action taken to salvage the soldier's life. Abruptly, the soldier convulses as if seized by a sudden fit. Reacting swiftly, the nurse swiftly delivers a syringe into the doctor's hand, who administers it to the patient. The convulsions subside, but the relentless flow of blood from the wound persists unabated.

Death and despondency fill the air as more stretchers are brought in, with injured German soldiers upon them. This is the true face of war; Private Singh thinks to himself. After all the speeches and the promises of victory and greatness, is this really what it is about? Death is death, whichever colour uniform you wear and whatever your ideals are, Private Singh thinks.

A second female nurse walks over to where Private Singh is standing and asks him to sit down with a hand gesture. On sitting down, she wipes the blood from his ears as he looks at her. She just glances at him momentarily, and as she continues to clean the blood, she does not try to make eye contact with him again. She is of the true Aryan race, with blonde hair and crystal blue eyes. She looks slightly nervous to Private Singh for some reason; maybe it is his identity, he thinks to himself.

Many Germans have not seen a traditional turban-wearing Sikh, maybe on film, let alone up close like this. She wipes away dried blood from his beard and discovers small fragments of what looks like shrapnel. She walks away and talks to the doctor; they both look over at him a few times while they converse. Private Singh presumes they are talking about him. He should be used to this by now, but unfortunately, within Brightly, many people whisper among themselves about seeing him. Some bigots will even shout out abuse due to his traditional Sikh identity and his turban.

He tried explaining this to one of the Tommy's once, who could not get his noggin around it. You only understand once you have experienced something like this, for example, being an apple in an orange tree. The nurse shows Private Singh to his bed; he sits on the edge for a moment before laying down. She walks away and he watches her from his bed. She first picks up a bowl and fills it with water, which is warm due to the steam coming off it.

On walking back, she places the metal bowl next to him and opens a new field dressing, which she soaks in the water. On ringing it out, she brings it towards his face before she slowly wipes away the dried blood from his beard. On repeating this, she removes a percentage of the dried blood; the water has now changed colour to a hint of rouge. The doctor walks back over, drying his hands. He leans in to take a closer look at his facial wounds, which are partly concealed under his beard, which Private Singh was not aware of.

"We do face, and then your leg," he calls out.

As he picks at the first facial wound, Private Singh flinches due to the pain he is experiencing. He lowers his hand, knocking the tweezers onto the edge of a metal dish the nurse is holding. He sees a small black piece of what he thinks is metal fall into the dish. The doctor repeats the process a few times; fresh blood oozes from the small wounds. The doctor then removes the handkerchief from around his leg wound and inspects it. On producing forceps, he pulls the piece of shrapnel from his leg and places the piece of blood-covered metal down onto the tray and examines it.

"ARRRRRGGGGGHHHHH!" Private Singh calls out.

"Fucksake, doctor," he adds.

"This is good size," the doctor replies.

"Look at the bloody size of that hunk of metal," Private Singh replies.

The doctor just looks at him, as to say, take the pain as he starts to mop up the blood after removing the shrapnel. Private Singh is in agony and shakes his head due to this excruciating pain.

"Staff will do stitching; we cannot give you medication only for German soldiers."

"Orders of Mein Führer," he adds.

"Thank you, Doctor; you're a proper gentleman," Private Singh replies.

He pauses for a minute and turns to see another patient. The nurse talks to him and prepares a small silver tray with dressings on it. She walks over and places it down next to him; she then suddenly produces a cutthroat razor and raises it towards Private Singh's face. He abruptly moves back, knocking the metal tray, which crashes to the floor. The whole room stops and looks over; suddenly, silence fills the air, compared to the noise of chaos that is created when you are frantically trying to save lives. Two soldiers rush forward, and one thrusts an MP40 submachine gun into Private Singh's boat.

"Don't shoot," he calls out.

"I'll come quietly," he adds.

He raises his hands to reflect that he does not want any trouble in a slightly jovial manner. The doctor walks back over; he makes a hand gesture for the soldier to lower his weapon.

"Nein," he calls out.

"What is this?" He asks.

"I'm a Sikh; we don't shave our facial hair," Private Singh replies.

The doctor initially appears slightly puzzled by the statement. When Private Singh explained that Sikhs do not shave their facial hair nor cut their hair, the doctor seemed to be taken aback. Using a hand gesture mimicking scissors and shaking his head, Private Singh illustrates this practice. The doctor, intrigued, switches to German with his staff, expressing genuine interest and inquiring about the reason behind this Sikh tradition. Private Singh elaborates, providing an explanation to the doctor. The medic is recommending just bandaging up his facial and leg wounds without the need to shave him.

He also produces what looks like morphine, to Private Singh's surprise, and he passes it to the nurse to administer. As soon as she injects him, it takes the edge off the pain. He feels this warm sensation within his chest and suddenly feels drowsy. He awakes sometime later to find himself within a side area of the makeshift hospital. A white screen had been pulled across his bed. He notices his wounds had been dressed, and he has a drip attached to my arm. He is now wearing a white pyjama suit, and his turban has been removed too. His 'Kesh' or head hair have been tied up with a white bandana or scarf. Maybe he mentioned his 'Kesh' must be covered hence they have done this before he passed out.

After he was wounded previously, his arm hair was shaved, when he was unconscious to his horror on awakening. Private Singh is not a baptised Sikh but follows the Sikh religion the best he can, within wartime. Sikh soldiers were also allowed to pray to their holy scriptures and make 'Langar', which the officers felt kept up morale within the ranks. Us Tommies loved the 'Langar', the hot vegetarian holy food they made compared to eating our army rations. I know they don't eat beef either, as I once read there was a disturbance, a ruckus and proper hoo-ha over cow fat being used to grease the cartridges for the Enfield rifle, back in the day which led to a bloody rebellion by the Indian soldiers.

So back to Private Singh, he cannot really remember these bits, as they were patchy after the morphine was administered. He remembers being blown off course and helping a young German soldier when the shelling started. Being arrested and brought here to this field hospital. This is when they gave him the morphine; he must have passed out, he thinks to himself. On looking around, he sees his British uniform neatly folded, sitting on a chair next to him. His turban, and nunchucks, sit on top of his neatly folded uniform. Suddenly, he is consumed by panic, too, as to where his boots had gone. On sitting up, he feels excruciating pain in his leg, which makes him lie back down again.

"ARRRRRGGGGGHHHHH!" he calls out.

"Fuck!" he screams.

As he lies back down, he turns his head to the side, and to his relief, he sees his British army boots sitting to the side of his bed with his military pack on the floor, too. He wonders what the Germans made of him with his turban, beard, and Kesh, his uncut hair. At least they have been respectful, he thinks to himself. His thoughts go back to the young German soldier he helped earlier; who was he? It's just the look on that officer's boat when he clocked the Geezer. He clearly knew who he was; maybe he was the son of someone important.

He cannot grasp why they are treating him this way; it seems unusual for a prisoner of war to end up in a private room like this in any hospital. As the nurse draws the curtain aside and steps in, she first tends to the hanging drip on the metal stand before carefully examining his bandaged leg.

"Where am I?" Private Singh asks.

At first, she does not speak; it is like she does not understand what he is saying. She puts her hand up as a gesture for him to wait, and she suddenly leaves, pulling the screen back. Private Singh continues to call out, as he needs some answers.

"Nurse, nurse ARRRRRGGGGHHHHH!" he calls out.

Suddenly, the doctor, whom he had seen earlier, pulled back the screen and entered the space. He explains to him that he is still in the field hospital where he was arrested. Private Singh does not fully comprehend what he is saying, as his English is not brilliant; well, it is far better than his German, he thinks to himself. He tells him that his wounds look good and that they should be able to move him to another hospital. He asks why he is being treated like this. The doctor stops and just looks at him; suddenly, an air of tension fills the room. He looks slightly nervous, and as he pulls back the screen to see if anyone is looking before, he pushes it back. He moves closer towards Private Singh with an element of concern.

Private Singh moves slightly backwards because his face is right up close and too personal for his liking. The doctor whispers near his ear that he is going to Berlin. Why would Private Singh be going to Berlin, he thinks to himself. So, he questions him: why and for what reason? The doctor just repeats himself that he is going to Berlin. He talks about giving him some painkillers, which he will need to take and get the dressing changed, as he hears someone approaching.

Suddenly, the doctor seems to be changing the subject matter. He tells Private Singh he must see other patients and produces a small brown glass bottle of medication. He leaves them on the small bedside table and acknowledges him with a smile and a nod of his head. He turns and leaves, pushing the screen back to shield Private Singh from the hustle and bustle that is still taking place on the other side of this screen.

Private Singh just lies there, staring at the ceiling with its flaking paint and cobwebs. The fan rotates, making a swirling noise as the blades spin round and round. What is bouncing around his noggin is the fact that he is going to Berlin, but for what? The Nazis still have power in Europe. Then it dawns on him: what if they are going to make a show of him to the German people? Show him off before he is executed, probably on camera, if Goebbels could have his way. His head is all over the place, thinking stupid thoughts about why he is going to Berlin. Suddenly, these thoughts turn to anger; whatever the Germans are going to do, bring it on, he thinks to himself. He knows he has fought for King and Country with valour and has no remorse for what he has done in the line of duty.

He is a principled Sikh, committed to aiding others with kindness and consistently showing humility and respect towards everyone. As Private Singh rests, memories transport him back to his beloved home in London, vividly recalling his upbringing in this bustling city. Despite being raised in a land far from his family's roots in India, it has not been without its challenges. He reminisces about navigating the complexities of growing up as the sole Sikh child in his school, where diversity was scarce, and he and another brown-skinned peer were conspicuously different. Their distinctness often resulted in unfair treatment, and they were subjected to ridicule simply because of their ethnicity.

His topknot would intrigue his fellow classmates, which all changed when he started to wear his turban. All the bullying started again because they had something new to poke fun at. All the new names under the sun, he was called. It was not just him; the Jamaican boy called Arley Clifford got the brunt of it, too, as he was called an assortment of names as well. Singh met Arley again, to his surprise, in the military training camp. He, like Private Singh, could speak dual languages, so he could be deemed useful. They sat and spoke of their childhood, how they were often alienated and of the few good times they had. Arley told Singh he had requested a transfer to covert operations but had not heard anything, maybe due to his skin colour? Private Singh lived and was raised in the East End of London, near the Bow Bells. They say you are only a proper Cockney if you were born within earshot of St Mary-le-Bow Church in Cheapside. Well, within reason, seeing he was only a nipper when he arrived here in Blighty, he might get away with it. Private Singh loved going to the docks with all those ships arriving from around the world with their bounty. All those different 'boat-races' or faces from shores across the globe.

As I said earlier, I like to use the word 'boat', sometimes the proper word, like face, so you'll have to bear with me. Like the King's English states. When I can't be bothered to say the whole word, like butcher's instead of the complete Cockney rhyming slang, 'butcher's-hook'. You'll get used to how commoners converse down Mile End. Sorry, look at me getting carried away again. Where were we? Oh yeah, the boozers would be heaving with sailors, crew, and Navy men alike. They would often have fisticuffs after a few too many rums. The East End was the life and soul of London.

Those were the days when you had no care in the world. He always thought of hiding on one of these ships and returning to India one day. After grammar school, he enlisted in the army, as Sikhs have been an integral part of the British armed forces since before the Great War, fighting in some of the most iconic theatres of any war. He had to enlist and follow in the footsteps of these real warriors, who fell defending the crown. Why did the British build the Suez Canal so they could move soldiers, goods, and ammunition to and from India? It was the gateway to the Empire. India was classed as the jewel in the crown of the British Empire. How did this little island rule nearly a quarter of the world at one time?

Joining the army was what Private Singh always wanted. When he first enlisted, it was difficult being a recruit and the only turban-wearing Sikh. He wasn't typically a Sepoy as he was raised in Blighty. But was branded a Sepoy, an Indian soldier fighting under the British flag. The training was rather stressful; he had to do everything twice as well as the next recruit. Only because everything was scrutinised, and he was asked to do tasks repeatedly. Certain officers were fine; they understood how Indian soldiers played their part within the British army. It was the others, the ones who thought you were crap on their boot heel. The ones that referred to you like you were some form of servant from the Old Empire or other. It was the ones with the bigoted comments and rude remarks, which were made in front of the other soldiers, vulgar insults with derogatory comments. A proper bunch of racist cunts, if you ask me.

Luckily for Private Singh, Brigadier Williams, who had served in India, took him under his wing. He helped him pass his studies and aided him in his military career, warding off the racist fuck's away with his sharp tongue. This is not before he experienced beatings, lack of supplies and even being kidnapped one night and left tied up soaked in petrol on the Moors.

This incident alone has shaped Private Singh into the person he is today, according to old William's. He was sound asleep in his barracks when a group of masked men burst in and started to beat on him with clubs and fists. The odd boot heel was added into the mix just for clarity's sake. Singh tried to fight back, but when you've got a bloke sitting on your chest while others hold you down, what sort of defence is one supposed to muster up?

A hood was placed on his head too, and his lifeless body was dragged away to a waiting vehicle, where he was manhandled into the boot. Singh could hear muffled voices as they drove into the night. After a while, they stopped. On opening the boot, Singh swung a tyre wrench he had discovered, hitting one man in the head. This must have really pissed the others off, as the fists rained down on him while he was still within the boot. On being dragged across the frozen ground, he could hear farm animals, so he sensed he was in the countryside.

After a short while of being dragged, they stopped, and his hood was removed. On looking upwards, a selection of other privates and two Sergeants stood over him. As he rubbed his eyes, he could not believe what he was witnessing. His fellow soldiers disliked him that much. One of the soldiers was holding a cloth up to his head wound as he lent inwards towards Private Singh. On spitting on him, he continued to kick him in the sides for the injury he had sustained due to Singh's attack. Nothing was said, but the looks were enough. Water vapour clouds appeared as the men breathed out of their mouths in the cold. One of the Sergeants produced a Jerry can and slowly opened the cap while making eye contact with Singh. He started to pour petrol on Private Singh, who was being held down as he violently struggled to free himself. The Sergeant threw the empty Jerry can to the floor and glared at Singh. The now drenched Singh looked up at the men, still ever so defiant in his manner.

"You've been warned, leave," the Sergeant called out.

"The British army is no place for darkies like you," he added.

Within seconds of him saying this, the men all suddenly left, back into the darkness. Private Singh looked up at the full moon, which flooded the whole area with an eerie light. This was a simple message so he would leave the army at the training stage. He never reported the incident, but Brigadier Williams eventually found out what had taken place that night of the full moon on the Moors.

Private Singh was often threatened due to his long hair being cut off while he slept. It was the same few recruits who delivered this racial abuse, but they soon changed their tune when, on the battlefield, he came to their aid. It is funny how people change their views when you show them humility.

Touch wood, since he has been deployed, he has not experienced too much racism besides the one-liners from some of the Yanks and French soldiers. After experiencing it firsthand in Australia, you would think he had become accustomed to it by now. The problem is the French have an issue with religious headwear anyway, and the Yanks can be an uneducated bunch of bigots, too. These people need to travel or get an education that highlights other religions and beliefs. The US is not the world; there are plenty of creeds and cultures if you venture outside Dixie Noir. See the world and appreciate other cultures through the windows to your soul, your bloody eyes.

Look at me getting carried away again, back to Private Singh who helps himself to a glass of water, which sat on the bedside table next to where the doctor had left the bottle of medication. It hurts as he stretches; the leg wound must be deeper than he originally thought. On lying back down he looks for where the doctor had gone. He is still waiting, considering that he is off to Berlin soon. His thoughts turn to the young children from earlier, within the woods.

He wonders what may have happened to them; suddenly, it hits him like a slap across the kisser. What if the Germans had apprehended them? What if they had been shot dead? Rage suddenly consumes him whole. If only he had escorted them to safety, he thinks to himself. Hopefully, they may have made it to the church. Why did he mention the church? Normally, the priests or nuns who are in service would help anyone, let alone a group of young children who are escaping monsters.

If only they had found a hiding place within the church, away from Jerry, who was inexplicably rounding everyone up. Why was the young German soldier gathering children in the first place? Suddenly, his thoughts shift to himself and his own identity. His mind is scattered, perhaps due to the medication they had administered, he speculates. His heart races and an unsettling sense of unease envelops him. What if they intend to execute him in Berlin? He wonders to himself.

He suddenly feels panicked. His heart is pounding in his chest, ten to a dozen. Stupid thoughts start rattling around in his noggin about what is going to happen. What if the Gestapo arrested him for questioning? What if the children are dead? He will have their blood on his hands if only he would have helped them. His head starts to spin; he feels hot and clammy with these thoughts rattling around in his noggin. His heart is beating faster and faster. Private Singh goes to sit up but finds it difficult to do. So, he tries to grab the bedside table to aid him in getting up. He ends up knocking the white enamel water jug, crashing to the floor. He tries to call out but cannot; for some reason, it is like someone is sitting on his chest. Panic consumes him at what is happening to him. He tries to scream once again, with all my might, but his voice is subdued.

“Doctor, Doctor,” Private Singh calls out.

"Doctor?" he adds.

Suddenly, the doctor and nurse both rush into the room, pushing the screen aside. He looks concerned and tries to calm him down. The nurse holds him down as Private Singh starts to thrash around with my arms. The doctor fills a syringe with clear white liquid and injects him. Within seconds of this happening, Private Singh slowly stops thrashing and eventually stops. Suddenly, he feels drowsy, and his eyelids feel heavy. He tries to keep his eyes open but cannot. He knows whatever the doctor has injected him with is the cause. He endeavours to keep his eyes open but passes out with his head falling to one side.

Meanwhile, back in town, the children hide in a derelict café building. This has been blown to smithereens by our boys, the Angels of the skies, our Spitfires, like some of the Tommies called them. They would escort our Lancaster bombers as they levelled most towns and cities like this one. The children hide in various places within the café from the German soldiers who still patrol the area. They are unaware they are less than a few miles away from the makeshift hospital Private Singh is within. They wait for the soldiers to walk by and listen out for the sound of the vehicle tracks to disappear into the distance. They slowly venture out of their hiding places and gather behind the piano.

One of the older boys rallies them together, trying to calm the younger children down. The little girl with the raggedy doll is crying as she clutches the doll against her chest tightly. They talk among themselves; they should make their way towards the church, where they would be safe. They are apprehensive at first, as you can imagine a group of young children in the middle of a battleground. The older boy kneels on the floor and carefully holds the little girl by the arms to reassure her that everything will be okay. She continues to cry; he tries wiping her tears away with his shirt cuff. Another girl calls out that they should be going before another German patrol comes along soon. The children decide to head towards the church, with the older boy leading the way through the ruins.

Moving quietly, they navigate the challenging terrain marked by massive craters due to the shelling. Hazardous debris is scattered everywhere, and dust swirls into their small faces. Attempting to link arms for support, they slowly progress towards the imposing church that dominates the small town. While passing through what used to be an open terrace resembling a town square, they encounter a tragic sight: a lifeless body. Reacting swiftly, the older boy shields the other children, redirecting them away from the unsettling scene. They opt for a different route, strolling down a narrow, cobbled alleyway towards the rear of the church, hopeful to avoid any encounters with German forces.

Tension fills the air as they suddenly hear a mechanical noise, like the metal tracks of a tank or armoured vehicle approaching. The older boy makes them all stop. He raises his finger towards his mouth to gesture to the younger children so as not to make any noise. They all stop and hide behind an outbuilding. The rubble and part of the metal roofing camouflage them. The noise becomes louder as the vehicle gets closer towards them. The older boy is nervous but knows he must show courage so the younger children will not give them away. He knows any noise made at this stage will alert the Germans. Trepidation consumes him, as what will they discover as the noise of grinding metal becomes ever so closer?

He can see the anxiety on the little girl's face and is fully aware she can no longer conceal her fear. He slowly moves and cradles her against his chest to calm her down. He whispers something in her ear, and she immediately covers her ears with her small hands. The noise is deafening; he again gives the remaining children a look of reassurance in the face of adversity. What sounds like a tank must be on the other side of the alleyway they are hiding in; luckily for them, due to the sheer size, it will not fit down the cobbled alleyway within which they are hiding.

The grinding and mechanical noise suddenly stops, but the revving of an engine continues intermittently, like the roar of a lion. They hear male voices as if someone is shouting orders in German. The boy knows this is it; they will soon be captured once again, like earlier, when they were near the river with that young German soldier. This was before that strange-looking man came to their help. This man looked like no man they had ever seen before, but they know now that this kind, caring man saved them from what they believed was death. Death at the hands of that young German soldier who was hell-bent on doing something harmful to them all.

The male voices get closer; they know they will be captured again within minutes. They all huddle closer together as the voices get closer towards them. Tension fills the air as the engine continues to rev loudly. The soldiers will soon be upon them. The fear is clear to see on the older boy's face, too, let alone the younger children's. Suddenly, a lone Spitfire unexpectedly flies over, followed by a volley of machine gunfire. The soldiers start to shout, and the vehicle starts to move again as per the grinding and mechanical noises.

The children start to cry due to the crescendo of noise but, luckily, remain hidden. The German soldiers move away from where they are hiding, returning small arms fire at the Spitfire overhead. The vehicle also starts to drive away from the children as the noise becomes fainter. The older boy gestures to the group to remain calm with a hand gesture.

Within minutes of the Spitfire turning up, the focus has shifted towards this aircraft. Anti-aircraft guns sound as the soldiers so desperately try to shoot down this foe of the skies. Luckily, this gives the children a window to run under this cloak of confusion towards the church. The older boy gestures for the children to get up and make their way towards the church. The group of children are apprehensive at first, but the older boy explains that the Germans are far too busy to be looking for them now. He picks up the little girl in his arms and begs the remaining children to follow him towards the church to safety. With the grace of God, the children follow him as they all make their way down the alleyway till it bottles necks into a narrower space. As he walks, he continues to look back towards the rest of the children who are following.

They all reach a small outbuilding with a window through which he sees the German soldiers frantically trying to shoot down the Spitfire. The anti-aircraft gun spits out the empty shell casings as it fires. They make a clunking noise as they hit the floor and fire repeatedly.

BANG! BANG! BANG! BANG!

He notices the fear on the face of a young German soldier, who momentarily looks over and makes eye contact with him. The boy suddenly ducks under the window ledge in fear of being captured again. He begs the children to hurry up, and they start to walk again, reaching the edge of the buildings. They know they will have to run across a grass verge towards the rear of the church. The older boy tells the children they must run when they get to this part. The fear is all too clear to see on their small faces.

They all group up before they all decide to run under the cloak of bullets and bombs exploding around them. As they run, he looks towards the anti-aircraft gun and notices the young German soldier has now been killed, and his lifeless body lies slung over the rear of the gun mount. The group of children continue to run in desperation, with this taking place around them, terrified as they are. On reaching the rear door of the church, they all gather, breathing heavily as some of the children are crying by now. The older boy places the little girl on the floor and knocks on the door. After a few moments, they hear metal bolts being undone, and the heavy wooden door slowly starts to creak open.

Trepidation once again fills the older boy as he anticipates what they are about to discover. Fortunately, a young nun opens the door. The little girl rushes forward and embraces her around the waist. The nun bends down, reciprocating the embrace. She quickly ushers them all in, closing the door behind herself discreetly, ensuring no one is watching. A look of concern is evident on her boat, possibly due to the fact that Jerry is scattered all over the place.

She ferries the group of children through the church to safety. The children look around in amazement at the huge wooden beams and the stained-glass window where light floods into this dimly lit space. Stone walls and floors adorn the church with its dark wooden pews. The nun leads the group of children towards a side door behind the vestibules. Tension fills the air as the bombing starts outside again. It must be the RAF doing their damnedest to beat down Jerry. Suddenly, they all stop and look up as dust falls downwards from the huge stone walls. The noise of the explosions seems to be right above where they stand. They all stop for a moment before the nun twists the iron handle, which opens this dark wooden door, and she walks through, with the children following her.

She lets all the children through, counting them as they walk past her. Once they are all in the room, she walks towards a bookshelf. She stops again, rushes back to the door she just closed, and bolts it. The heavy iron bolt makes a screeching noise as it slides into the closed position. The children watch her in silence as they look around the room. It looks like an office but also resembles a storage area. Boxes with paperwork sit stacked up against the wall near a bookshelf. A desk sits near a small window on the opposite side of the room. Spare robes hang from hooks on the wall beside a hand-carved wooden crucifix. The nun smiles, takes the little girl by the hand, and walks towards the bookshelf. She pushes the bookshelf slightly to reveal a gap within the wall.

On lighting a candle, she again takes the little girl by the hand and asks the children not to be scared and to trust her. She assures them they will all be safe here and away from the German soldiers. The candlelight only highlights the dark, eerie space as they slowly walk down what looks like a corridor. Once again, the nun whispers softly for the children not to be afraid. The little girl squeezes her hand ever so tightly as they continue down this corridor with its stone walls. She turns and points the candle towards the group of children who are following, which only highlights their small faces, which are wearing expressions of fear. The little girl makes a squirming noise as the corridor in front of where she is standing suddenly becomes pitch black due to the candle being moved. Quickly, the nun moved the candle back, which lit up the little girl's face to her relief. They slowly continue to walk, which seems forever. They can still hear the subdued noise of the bombs exploding overhead. Finally, they arrive at another solid wooden door adorned with ornate ironwork.

The nun knocks on the door twice, pauses, and repeats the sequence. After a brief interval of her knocking, they discern the sound of metal bolts being slid open, emitting a screeching noise. The door slowly begins to open, intensifying the anticipation among the children: who will be the one to welcome them? All the while, the children look on anxiously, sensing the tension that fills the air.

Uncertain of what lies ahead, they contemplate the possibility of a trap by the Germans. To everyone's collective relief, the door reveals another nun who warmly smiles at the children. The sheer relief on the children's faces is palpable. She guides the group into the room, illuminated by candles, casting a warm glow that accentuates the space where a gathering of nuns awaits. To the children's surprise, these nuns appear distinct from the ordinary, though they cannot quite put their finger on why.

Suddenly, the first nun rips off her veil to reveal a huge mane of blonde hair, to everyone's surprise. She shakes her head and runs her fingers through her hair, to the children's shock. The remaining nuns, too, remove their veils and robes. They are all dressed in black leather catsuits underneath, all wearing bright red lipstick. Was the lipstick the one thing that made them look slightly different from a normal God-fearing nun to start with? One of the ladies' smokes very provocatively. She suddenly produces a black beret hat and places it on her head. She adjusts it slightly to get the right look she desires.

What surprises the children is that this group of kind, caring nuns suddenly resembles a group of kick-arse band of vixens. What the children are not aware of is that this particular group of young ladies is a precarious group known as the 'The Society of Eradicating Nazis'. They are a band of hot-looking vixens of death, especially if you don a Nazi uniform. These ladies took it upon themselves to use the gifts of beauty God gave them after they followed his path for several years till, he did not respond to their cries for help when the Nazis showed up doing their worst.

So, as I was saying before being rudely interrupted by myself, these ladies use their beauty as a weapon to seduce the enemy into a false sense of security before they rip their bollocks off and shove them down their gobs. They are highly trained assassins nowadays, who have all lost loved ones to German boot heels or rifle butts. So, the aim of their particular game is to kill these Jackboot wearing cocksuckers and send them all to hell. Straight to hell, do not pass the Brandenburg gate and certainly do not collect two hundred Reichsmarks as you pass go. 'The Society of Eradicating Nazis' has brought these ladies much attention nowadays from Jerry, who refers to them as 'The Fräuleins of Death'.

Before this notoriety, they would pretend to be intoxicated ladies of society or even the odd brass, far too drunk to function. This is where a German officer normally would show his chivalrous side and escort them to his bed. Normally, this would pan out slightly differently than Fritz thought it would. What Fritz is not aware of is this night of passion would normally end with his demise in the most gruesome of ways possible. The ladies have a wager on who would kill the most Nazi cocksuckers before the war ended. Let's say the ladies collected trophies of this so-called past time of theirs. Whatever body part the Nazi was willing to give up, or in this case have cut off, to save his life became the property of the Fräuleins.

What these un-expecting Nazis' victims were not banking on is that after losing their bodily parts, they would still end up on the sharp end of a knife or thud of a bullet for their troubles. These vixens all have a different skill set, which they apply when carrying out these sensitive missions of lust. Fritz did not know what hit him normally; simply, just shooting them was not enough for the ladies anymore. Stabbing, impaling, dismembering, burning, removing bodily organs, the list goes on, as I've just said. The more imaginative the ladies got, the more the myth of the 'Fräuleins of Death' spread among the German ranks.

The German soldiers would often bet on the next victim's rank, the way they would be done over and in which town or city they would meet their demise. Obviously, the Fräuleins became aware of this, so they upped the stakes here. They dug deep to surprise the most cynical within the Nazi hierarchy with what would happen to them. The Führer even became aware of what was becoming of his foot soldiers of evil under the sexy blade of these gals. He ordered these ladies to instant death due to the brutality of what his boys were going through, but what he did not know was that soon, another band of killers would be feasting on Nazis' flesh. This is not before the Nazis started to hunt down this bevy of beauties, but they just vanished into the night air without a trace.

Sorry, look at me getting carried away with this tall tale about these vixens of death we talk of. There are seven formidable women comprising this deadly squad, each with unique qualities. Leading the pack is Coco, the captain of this striking group. In her late thirties, she possesses a mop of blonde hair and a captivating Persian allure that could be lethal. Once a loving mother who opened the door to any children who needed sanctuary from the Nazis.

Her tragic past involves the loss of her own family and the ones she harboured. Apart from her heartbreaking history, she is an adept hand-to-hand combatant, displaying a particular fondness for gleaming cold steel. Knives and any stabbing implements are her specialities, making her the commanding force as the governor of this alluring yet lethal Jerry death squad. She has a fiery temper and has an inner rage against the Nazis for what they did to her family; this is what drives her.

So, as I was saying earlier, Coco instigated 'The Society of Eradicating Nazis'. This all took place after, the Gestapo questioned her friend Pierre, within their unique way. They had only used a machine which peeled back a thin layer of skin without killing you on him. The pain Pierre must have endured at the hands of these callous bastards must have been inconceivable, to say the least, as he lost his left forearm due to this. He was originally from Lyon and had a small cabin in the snow near the French Alps, which Coco had been invited to visit one day. He runs a small café in Paris now; the Gestapo officers had taken a liking to it and started to hang out here.

Most nights, the gaff was crammed to the rafters with Gestapo, drinking, singing, and partying with French women of loose morals. But this all changed one fateful day when normally only a handful of Gestapo officers would be frequenting the establishment within the daytime. Coco walked into this typical French café, with its black and white tiled floor and dark wooden furniture. The main bar again was dark wood with a brass foot rail. The back bar display was mirrored with glasses stacked up against it with bottles of spirits lined up next to them.

The walls were adorned with posters of classical French cinema, with a grand piano sitting at one end of this venue we talk of. She was dressed like a God-fearing nun, wearing red lipstick, of course, and walked over to the piano. The handful of Gestapo officers looked at her but continued with their drinking. Coco glanced over at Pierre, who was behind the bar, with his arm still in a sling after what had happened. Coco sat down and opened the lid to the piano, which was against the back wall facing the café floor, so all the patrons could see was the back of the piano. The men all stopped, one placing down his book interested in what she was going to play. Coco started to play a scale to start with before she played 'La Marseillaise'. She began to sing along to the horror of the Gestapo officers and a few enlisted men present.

Suddenly, the Gestapo officer reading stood up, flinging his chair backwards in protest of this outrage. Another called out to Pierre for this to stop immediately before they were both arrested. What Coco did next was the inception of 'The Society of Eradicating Nazis', or as the Nazis eventually called them, 'Fräuleins of Death', which cemented her position within the French Resistance too. Without me spoiling this anecdote, let's just say Coco 9 – Gestapo 0 if this was the beautiful game. Just imagine the film version of these events in glorified 'Technicolor'. Look at me getting carried away again; this is definitely a tall tale for another day.

Back to the gals, her second-in-command is Prada, a brunette with a fringe hairstyle and is of a similar age to Coco. She wears a beret hat very sexually and loves all things that go bang. We are not talking about German officers' nut sacks within a vice here, either. We are talking about things that go bang-like and explode. She could easily shoot you but chooses often to wire you up to a hand grenade and watch you paint the walls a tinge of rouge. This is especially true when it is strapped to your wedding tackle.

Which often leads to this individual's demise in the most gruesome fashion possible. As I said, she wears a beret hat and is very Parisian in her intoxicating looks. She loves to chain smoke, especially when she's preparing explosives. The lipstick-covered cigarette butts were the only evidence she was ever there. Oh yeah, besides the Nazi, swine's wedding tackle which is normally plastered all over the ceiling.

She has often used the old trick of sending Nazi officers gifts, like a fine bottle of French cognac within a wooden presentation box. I can hear you say there is nothing more innocent than that. What the recipient is not aware of is that this rather innocent-looking bottle of fine French cognac is a Trojan horse masquerading as a rather innocent-looking bottle of fine French cognac. No, I hear you say, but guess what happens next? Oh yeah, they normally have to redecorate his office. She is loud when she needs to be and is a happy soul.

Then we have Gucci, she is the baby of the bunch. She is in her early twenties and is quite petite with mousey brown hair. Gucci comes across as very shy and innocent but can be the loudest in the room. Her skills are commutations and anything mechanical, as she is a proper grease monkey. She can often be found tinkering with armoured half-tracks or Nazi trucks. This all leads to failed brakes and results in dead Nazis, of course. She can turn her hand to anything mechanical. Gucci wears think-rimmed glasses and has tattoos on her arms. She has a sense of fashion, wearing garments like a boiler suit, but jazzing it up with accessories and her hair tied up is her thing. Gucci is also a card shark, often winning a few Franks or Reichsmarks here or there. Her party trick is cutting the deck of cards with her soon-to-be-dead victim, which could save their lives, potentially. Unfortunately for them, she always has lady luck on her side, so they end up brown bread every single time. Gucci has even mastered the art of flicking cards at such a killer pace she can impale you from a distance.

Then we have Stella, she is an ex-pat who now resides in France; she is in her early forties and has blonde hair. She is a caring individual and highlights her feelings often due to wearing her heart on her sleeve. Stella's dress sense is sharp, wearing trouser suits and killer heels. She fell in love with the country at some art exhibition or other before the war started. She is a scrounger and can lay her hands on everything one desires, from fine French perfume, Beluga caviar, fresh lobster to vintage Dom Pérignon champagne if the party requires it. She can even put her finely manicured fingers on designer clobber, Coco Chanel and Christian Dior if one desires. This, of course, took a lot of backhanders and parting of the folding stuff. This is probably why our Stella looked a million Francs, dressed to the nines in her haute couture clobber, we talk of.

She liaised with the French underworld, which is rife with quality merchandise if you are willing to part with the folding stuff. Her contacts normally hijacked shipments meant for German officers. These French bandits relieved Jerry of any goods that were required off this shopping list of choice for our Stella. The German soldiers transporting the goods also got a good seeing too for their troubles. Often, they would receive a few black eyes, broken hooters, nothing too harsh as Stella's contacts cannot afford for Jerry to hunt them down. If these soldiers were too savagely beaten or, worse still, even killed, that is not good for business.

Next, we have Vivienne, another blonde who is in her early forties. She is tall and leggy, with sass, one would say. Her crystal blue eyes are enough for any Geezer to fall in love with. She is quiet and keeps her thoughts bottled up. Viv, as the girls like to call her, should be the captain of the group, but due to being shot by Jerry previously, she likes to take it slightly easy on the 'I'm in charge bollocks.' She is an expert forger and can make fake permits, passports, and other documents, which you may need to get past any of the German checkpoints. She is your gal. Viv loves horses and cares for an old nag they have tied up within the church grounds. Pre-war, she was a skilled equestrian; she owned her own stables and was quite wealthy. Her family owned a historical château near Lillie, northern France, with its lake, rolling fields and stables. This was before the Nazis showed up and took it over, using it as a form of headquarters.

Then we have Louis, who is in her early thirties and has short blonde hair and brown eyes. She is petite and is an ex-ballerina, so she is very supple. Louis looks like a sweet young gal, but she is a proper bruiser and is always up for a punch-up. She can be loud to say the least, often getting into arguments with the other girls. She can drink her own weight in booze and gets all emotional.

Louis is rather a good cook and can knock up something flavoursome from odd ingredients and anything she can kill with her crossbow. Oh yeah, she is a skilled marksman, too, a proper William Tell if you ask me. Often rabbits, pheasants and even bloody squirrels are on the menu for the girls to dine on, like royalty when she's been out hunting. She normally works closely with Prada to blow things up. Due to her size, she can crawl through air ducts and other spaces to setup any explosive devices. They are normally found together when trouble is brewing.

Lastly, we have Chanel, who is the madam figure of the group, with brown mousey hair and brown eyes. She is in her late fifties and is quite refined. Chanel is an educated socialite who moved within all the right circles before the war started. Her dress sense is very classical, even though we are in the middle of a bloody war. She is intelligent and hides her inner emotions due to what the Nazis did. Chanel is a caring soul; she often lends an ear or a shoulder to cry on if any of the group desires.

Being married to a Jewish filmmaker did not do her any favours. They were stripped of anything of monetary value, and he was shot dead by the order of Joseph Goebbels. He wanted to show French-Jewish cinema that he was the new kiddie in town, so he lined up the most important Jewish directors, producers and even certain cinematographers and shot them all dead. Some Jerry officer took possession of their luxury Paris apartment and all that went with it.

All she has is an elegant Cartier diamond ring, a gift from her loving husband, which she hid on her person so the Nazis would not plunder it. She often looks at the ring and memories of her beloved Nathaniel come flooding back to her. The life they shared together and the loss of their child at birth. Heartache normally turns to a smile when she thinks of the previous lifestyle, with all the dinner parties, champagne receptions, the glitz and glamour of the film industry and her love for her Nathaniel.

Chanel brings stability to the ladies, as she offers them her wealth of knowledge and life skills, especially while they try to navigate killing Nazis and helping the French resistance in striking a blow at the heart of the fascists.

There you have it, ladies and gentlemen of the jury, the full line of 'The Society of Eradicating Nazis'. The girls loved the notoriety they had, which only fuelled their passion for killing more Nazis in compelling ways. Beauty is a cruel mistress, especially if you're a cocksucking Nazi who is willing to die for his Führer, Adolf Hitler. Whatever tickles your fancy Geezer, as these ladies will pander to your every need before they box you up. These rascals, these scallywags, these bad girls, these hotties are off to provoke the country's Nazi bumpkins of occupied France into a life of hell, death and debauchery. This band of beauties who disguise themselves as peaceful, Godfearing nuns throughout the day and in the evening become this killer elite organisation of sexy bitches they are, so be aware, you Nazi cocksuckers.

Look at me getting carried away; well, any red-blooded Geezer would be hot under the collar chatting about these gals. Sorry, back to the children. They are astounded by the true identities of these nuns, but deep down, they feel reassured that this is a safe haven, just as the peculiar-looking man had promised them. The nuns assist the children in settling down for the night. The little girl clutching her doll smiles for the first time as Coco embraces her, providing assurance that they are all now in a safe and secure place away from the Nazis.

Chapter Two: A right Rum Bunch

Two British soldiers are seated within a prototype of the Austin Champ jeep that is driving through the English countryside. The two men do not talk; the one in the passenger's seat is an officer from the Pips. The driver is the younger of the two men and keeps his eyes on the road, not trying to make any eye contact with him after the stare he just gave him over his driving ability. The officer is in his late forties, has mousey brown hair and is of stocky build. He looks like a bulldog of a man; someone you would not want to mess with. He resembles someone with a dogged determination for success and displays a granite exterior. He definitely looks like a gentleman of principals and someone with a short fuse, taking into consideration his response towards the driver mere seconds ago.

He carries quite a distinct six-shooter strapped to his waist within a tan leather holster. The stock of the six-shooter in question has a picture of a pin-up girl wearing a red swimsuit on it. Maybe this is a tall tale for another day. The jeep snakes its way through the country roads, its engine whining as it accelerates up a hill towards a small quintet English village. It drives over a small stone bridge, which crosses a flowing stream. The officer looks over as they reach a crossroad at the young driver but does not say anything. They stop for a moment at the junction within the road before driving off towards the village, which is sign posted on a white wooden sign with black text.

Upon entering the village, they navigate towards the main high street, passing by an old church and crematory. The scene unfolds like a picturesque postcard one might purchase on a seaside holiday. The jeep emits a characteristic whining noise as the driver shifts through the gears once more. A few locals observe, engaged in conversation near a red telephone box, their attention captured as the vehicle rolls past. The wheels bounce over the cobbled high street, creating a distinctive sound, and the jeep's reflection dances within shop windows adorned with taped-up white crosses. The village looks semi-deserted beside the jeep driving through; it resembles a ghost town. The jeep drives through water collected due to a dip within the road, the wheels only throwing it upwards as they drive through it. The officer turns and looks at the driver once again. He does not say anything, but the look is enough to highlight the disproval of this manoeuvre. On reaching the edge of the village, we see a huge brick wall running alongside the open countryside, with its reddish bricks with yellow flagstones only reflecting the height of this gargantuan thing.

The jeep continues to drive as it follows this huge wall we talk of before reaching an entrance that two British Military Police officers guard. The brakes are applied, screeching the jeep to a stop. One of the Military Police officers moves forward towards the driver and salutes the seated officer with conviction. The officer salutes back and taps a brown leather satchel he is holding. The soldier acknowledges this and signals the other soldier to raise the barrier. The jeep drives through and up a gravel driveway towards a stately, home-looking building. This huge gaff looks like some museum, which is set within these landscaped grounds.

Trees line the gravelled driveway towards the building as the jeep wheels make that noise of driving over loose gravel. On reaching the building, they drive around a water fountain display and park up outside the front entrance. The jeep grinds to a halt as the front wheels dig into the loose gravel as they stop. The officer glares at the young driver once again because of how abruptly they had stopped. The driver tries not to make eye contact again, as you can see the fear plastered across his boat.

The officer exits the jeep and walks over towards the front entrance, which again is guarded by two Military Police officers. The two men are quite burley and of stocky build. They both salute the officer, and in return, he salutes them back, but much softer in his hand action. One of the men opens the door and he walks through into the building. The two men return to their original stance. As he walks through the hallway, huge antique gold-framed oil paintings adorn the walls. His boots make a loud knocking noise against the polished parquet flooring as he makes his way towards a reception area. A young soldier who is seated behind a desk jumps to his feet. He is in his early twenties, with combed-over dark brown hair and wears thick rimmed black glasses. He looks like a bookworm, very studious in his manner, and is nervous looking.

"Morning, Sir, I'm Private Ward. Welcome to Headquarters," he calls out.

"Private," the officer replies.

He salutes the officer slightly nervously as he tries not to make eye contact with him. The officer salutes him in return before he removes the leather satchel from under his arm.

"Sir, they are waiting for you in the drawing room," Private Ward replies.

Private Ward points the way with his hand as if to gesture to the officer where to go. The officer looks towards a narrow corridor, which is slightly cloaked within darkness due to being in shadow, as light flooded in through a large window at one end.

"This way, Sir," Private Ward adds.

The officer and Private Ward both walk down the corridor till they reach what looks like an unmarked doorway. Private Ward tries not to make eye contact with the officer; maybe his reputation precedes him. This unmarked doorway resembles the English Oak wooden panels that lined the walls, virtually making it invisible at first glance. This type of English oak panelling is only seen normally within period buildings and in gaffs of this calibre. A small side table with an antique lamp sits to the side of it. Unless you were aware of this doorway's existence, you probably would not have guessed it was there from merely looking at it. Private Ward stops and presses a certain part of the wall, which pops open a door. The officer stops and looks at Private Ward, slightly surprised at all the spy bollocks that are being employed here. The officer pauses and then enters this space of hidden espionage. The Private acknowledges the officer with a subtle nod of his head. The officer proceeds into a narrower corridor, dimly lit by metal ceiling lights. This brick-built passage, characterised by whitewashed walls, exudes a chilly atmosphere. Two Military Police officers are stationed on either side of a doorway and stand vigilant on duty. As he approaches, both officers salute him with unwavering conviction.

"Sir," they call out.

"At ease, gentlemen," the officer replies.

The officer salutes the men in return and, with an outstretched hand, grasps the metal doorknob. The metal door is painted black; does it resemble a door to a bomb shelter? He twists it slightly and pushes the door open. Tension fills the air at what he is going to discover. As he walks through to his amazement, he realises that the room inside is not what he expected. It is a traditional study, with a large, roaring open fire that burns and floods the room with an eerie glow. An oil painting of King George VI hangs from the wall, which is lined with the same English Oak wooden panels as earlier.

Two bookshelves sit on either side of the desk, and a deep buttoned dark green leather chair is centre stage on which an older man sits. He is wearing a British military uniform and smokes a pipe; he looks particularly important. He must be in his late fifties and is a portly-looking gentleman with a receding hairline. He does not say anything and looks at the officer. He looks quite the authoritarian, with a stern look on his face. Someone who doesn't mince his words and is quite direct and to the point by the looks of it. Back to the room, which looks out of place compared to the cold, brick corridor from which the officer had just entered from. The officer stops for a moment to take in his new surroundings and the man sat before him.

"You made it, good chap," the old man calls out.

"Whisky?" he asks.

The officer salutes the older man with vigour, holding his salute position slightly longer than he normally would.

"Morning, Sir," the officer replies.

"At ease, whisky?" he asks.

"Yes, Sir, I'll have a drop of the good stuff," the officer replies.

"It is the good stuff," he adds.

"Yes, my dear boy, it's from the Highlands of Bonnie, Scotland."

"Here you go, throw this down your throat," he adds.

"I know, normally you would savour it, appreciate it's subtle tones, but needs must and all that," he adds.

"I'd offer you the Johnnie Walker Black Label, but I like to save it for my Indian chum," he adds.

"He likes a good old drop of the fine stuff," he adds.

The older man pours a decent-sized measure into a crystal tumbler from a crystal decanter. On replacing the stopper, he holds up the tumbler. The officer moves forward and accepts the drink; on taking hold, he takes a drink from the glass.

"Bottom's up," the old man calls out.

"Chin-chin, Sir," the officer replies.

"Another, old boy, as this is certainly the elixir of choice," the old man replies.

The officer finishes his drink and places the empty tumbler down on the desk; the old man pours another drink from the crystal decanter. They both raise their glasses to one another and finish the drink in one time.

"To that madman's bad health," the old man calls out.

"Yes, Sir, too, that madman's bad health," the officer replies.

"Where are my manners? I'm Colonel Smith."

"You're Major Lenny Watkins's, AKA Big Len, to your friends?"

"Am I correct?"

"We know all about you and how you've infiltrated the enemy throughout this and other conflicts," he adds.

"Like some cheap brass who's been knocking around for 99 years down the Old Kent Old, your reputation precedes you," Colonel Smith adds.

"Thank you, Sir, for this kind moniker," he replies.

Silence fills the air momentarily before Colonel Smith opens the desk drawer and retrieves a brown paper file, forcefully placing it onto the desk. The words 'Top Secret' are prominently stamped in red across the front. It lands alongside the brass desk lamp, its green glass shade casting a focused light that illuminates the entire desk space and its surroundings. Silence envelops the room again, the only audible sounds being the hissing and crackling of the open fire. Neither Major Watkins nor Colonel Smith utters a word, creating an eerie and tense silence.

Suddenly, someone clears their throat, which cuts the atmosphere. This someone had been within the room throughout the conversation. Major Watkins snaps his head around to see who it may be, taking into consideration they are within a secret room within this building for a reason. The noise comes from a Queen Anne-style armchair, which cloaks the occupant from the others within the room. It faces towards the roaring open fire but is within shadow; hence, the person seated was not apparent to Major Watkins when he first entered the room.

Who could this be? It is a male voice due to how deep it is. This man's conduct slightly takes Major Watkins's aback. He turns towards Colonel Smith again. His body language changes. He suddenly looks slightly annoyed by the man's conduct. He stares at the Colonel like he is owed an explanation of what is going on here.

"Oh yes, where are my damn manners again?" Colonel Smith calls out.

"This is, well, let's say Mr X for now."

"He's from that department. Well, what do I say?"

"You know, all that cloak and dagger goings on," he adds.

"Major Watkins, this is Mr X."

"I like to refer to him as young Archibald," he adds.

"Archibald is not really his name, but it makes me feel warm and fuzzy inside when I refer to Mr X as young Archibald."

"Hence, he's called young Archibald," he adds.

The two men exchange glances, and Mr. X gives Colonel Smith a meaningful look. Major Watkins appears slightly annoyed, his displeasure stemming from the mere presence of this gentleman for reasons not entirely clear. The man rises from his chair, straightening up as he strides towards the desk.

Mr. X, a slim figure with black glasses, is in his late forties. He is smartly dressed in a suit, shirt, and tie. He looks like an intelligent man but has that look about him of deceit. Mr X resembles someone you would not trust; I don't know why, but it's his 'boat-race'. He looks like a snide and a fucking backstabber to put it bluntly. But saying that he also resembles a Geezer of significant importance though, in this arena of shadows. Mr X puts out his outstretched hand for Major Watkins to shake, who decides to salute instead while he stands. There is a moment of slight awkwardness between the two men as they go to correct themselves and then do not.

"Balderdash and poppycock to all this petty nonsense," Colonel Smith calls out sternly.

"Come on, chaps, let's play nice, as we are all signing off the same hymn sheet now," Colonel Smith adds.

"Let's sink some battleships, the German kind," he adds.

"Pull up a pew young Archibald," he adds.

"Let me tell you about operation Mirror, mirror on the wall."

"Who's the maddest of them all?" Colonel Smith chuckles.

"It's only operation Mirror, mirror."

"But I like the sound of the rest of it, though," he adds.

"It makes me feel warm and fuzzy inside, like young Archibald does when we've killed a few more Krauts in battle," he laughs.

"Damn and blast, these bloody Krauts," he adds.

"You're a cheeky chappie, I'm sure you and your chaps will deal with this," he adds.

Colonel Smith tries to lighten the mood with his brand of humour, as the atmosphere within the room has now become more tense. Slightly hesitant about the situation, Major Watkins pulls up a chair, as does Mr X, and they sit down. The light from the desk lamp floods the desktop, as the rest of the room is only lit by the eerie glow of the roaring open fire.

Colonel Smith opens the file and starts to explain what the plan is within this covert of operations against the Axis powers. It is some heavy stuff, military strategy coupled with secret intelligence, and hopefully some divine guidance? Tension fills the room as Major Watkins helps himself to another drink, guzzling down the contents of his tumbler as some form of Dutch courage due to what is passing through his ears. Major Watkins is amazed by the sheer balls of the plan, but is he negative towards elements of it? How blatant is it, how daring and how British? If this does not highlight the tenacity of the British, then nothing else will, Major Watkins thinks to himself. Mr X continues to interject snippets of information on how they are going to pull off this mission behind enemy lines. Major Watkins is the key to this operation, and his success will mean the difference between stopping that Madman or not. No pressure then; the entire outcome of the Second World War is being placed on the shoulders of our Major Watkins here.

The long and short of the plan is that Major Watkins will be dropped behind enemy lines in Nazi-occupied France as a team of eight men on a mission to kidnap Adolf Hitler and replace him with an impostor. In the meantime, if things go wrong, they need to cause as much arse ache to the German war machine as they can while they are treading fine French grass under foot. In other words, blow up, stab, kill and impale as many Nazis as one can while on a turkey shoot in Provence.

This is the long and short of it. Talk about having your cake and eating it. The crux of the whole mission is the team Major Watkins must recruit, train, and have battle-ready within weeks of this pantomime playing out. His team are military prisoners, serving time and awaiting execution in some cases.

These men Colonel Smith refers to as 'The Rum Bunch' are not just any soldiers of the King's army. No, no, no, far from it. As I just said, they are prisoners awaiting execution for murder, while others have long sentences for desertion and even theft. This group of ragtag soldiers who have lost their will to fight, let alone be dropped behind enemy lines, could be a tall order in anyone's book. They will have a simple choice: either option one, they fight, or option two, wait for the hangman's noose or rot away in military prison. If they do not accept option one, then option two is inevitable. This element of the cunning plan does not ruffle Major Watkin's feathers, but what does ruffle his feathers is the second element of this cunning plan. The element in which Adolf Hitler is kidnapped and exchanged for an impostor. An impostor who would steer the German hierarchy in a different direction regarding the war. Maybe save thousands of lives within the process of removing this unhinged little Geezer from his throne.

The throne, which I may add, is made of stolen Jewish gold. Major Watkin's mind is racing about what is being discussed here. It is one of those do I laugh or cry moments, but he is a big ugly Geezer, so he takes it on his hairy-chinny, chin, chin.

Colonel Smith reclines, leisurely lighting his pipe while exchanging glances with Major Watkins. As he extinguishes the match, he puffs away as a plume of smoke gracefully ascends. He then cedes the floor to Mr. X, who initiates a discussion about this audacious plan. The impostor in question is a skilled individual named James Hall. Originally a German-born man named Otto Keller who, interestingly, attended Oxford, he evolved into one of Mr. X's devoted associates. Hall is not just a number cruncher; he is a thespian, an actor who revels in treading the boards. His unwavering love for his homeland and the belief that he can save countless lives drive his commitment. His vision is to restore Germany to its former glory without resorting to bloodshed and devastation. Since joining forces with Mr. X, James has undergone rigorous training and even undergone surgery to bear a striking resemblance to the Führer. Mr X explains the processes he had undergone to make him mirror the madman, who was originally from Austria. The pain and suffering he had endured, so hopefully, a swift end could be brought to the war.

James had not seen his family for years, who still live in Germany and believe their beloved Otto is now dead. If James survives the war, he will have to undergo surgical procedures once again to give him his original identity back. As you do not want to look like the spitting image of Adolf Hitler, now do you? It is difficult to imagine his conviction and what emotions he must suppress to carry out such a daring plan. The heartache he must feel at the fact his family thinks he is dead. Mr X's boys laid a trail of breadcrumbs, highlighting his demise, which he takes immense pride in mentioning within the meeting. Mr X has an element of smugness about him. He is rather self-centred for Major Watkin's liking.

Since all the medical procedures, James must be kept out of sight; imagine someone being spotted in London who is the perfect likeness to Adolf Hitler, as I said earlier. That would go down like a lead version of the Hindenburg. That will certainly cause a stir within certain circles, let alone the public. He probably would be lynched up from the nearest lamppost.

So, James is still under wraps till the team's training is completed and Major Watkins feels they are battle-ready. This task alone sounds like an uphill struggle, taking the military prisoners' files into consideration. Colonel Smith interrupts Mr X mid-sentence and taps his pipe onto a pile of brown files that sit on his desk. He asks Major Watkins to look at the motley crew of military prisoners with whom he must work. He gives him an overview of these players, their skill sets, and what they have been charged with. Finally, they discuss their sentences, and a percentage of them are due to be executed by hanging within six weeks. This gives Major Watkins a small window to get these men on board with the idea of being dropped behind enemy lines to certain death or sitting within a cell till the hangman calls.

The way Colonel Smith wants to sell this cunning plan to the men is simple: they either all go along and sing off the same hymn sheet, or they will all die by the end of the next month. Only three of the prisoners have life sentences, which means they will still rot within a concrete shoebox if they choose not to participate. It is going to be an arduous task to sell this cunning plan to the six men who have been handpicked for the task at hand. The Major asks for Lieutenant Harvey to be drafted in for the job, as he knows this fella can certainly handle himself. They have previously served together, and Major Watkins knows he will need help in this tall order he is being palmed off with here.

Major Watkins requests the Lieutenant be brought in, or this will be a hard nut to crack. Colonel Smith looks at Mr X, who pauses for a moment before he nods in agreement. Colonel Smith assures Major Watkins this will be the case. So, by the looks of it, James Hall and Lieutenant Harvey are coming along either way. The Lieutenant is in his mid-forties and of average build with a shaved head. Being of a short height, he is an austere man with a rigid outlook on authority. He is a hardened soldier who will whip these boys into shape at the Major's request. He is a military man like the Major, with principles and morals.

The Colonel points out that any good Sergeant could probably do the job. He highlights, would the Lieutenant not feel overqualified for all of this? Major Watkins assures Colonel Smith he is the right man for the job and would be delighted if he could be drafted.

The Colonel pauses again and looks over at Mr X before looking at the Major again. He explains to the Major this will be the last time he will see either himself or Mr X again, hopefully till after the war. He asks Mr X to organise the Lieutenant to be here by tomorrow at the latest, to Mr X's slight surprise. He goes on to recommend that Major Watkins have the pleasure of meeting the men the day after tomorrow at 0700 hours. Colonel Smith concludes the meeting and explains that Mr X has arranged a rendezvous with an agent in France. This slightly takes aback Major Watkins, as Mr X is insistent that this occurs. Major Watkins explains he only collaborates with agents he previously knows, and this could upset the apple cart.

"Damn, the applecart, no set fire to it," Colonel Smith calls out.

"I'm a rebel, so let's be having it," he adds.

Major Watkins attempted to interject and explain his perspective, but Colonel Smith consistently interrupts him. The Colonel delves into the intricacies of the British military hierarchy, illustrating Watkins as an 'expendable pawn' who ought to understand his place. Colonel Smith employed the analogy of a Jack Russell dog nipping at ankles to drive home his point. This irritated Major Watkins, who felt belittled and spoken down to, especially in the presence of Mr. X, who lacked a military background. Watkins could not help but hold the opinion that without firsthand military experience, one could never fully grasp the challenges and sacrifices inherent in a soldier's life, including what it takes to advance in a military career.

Yes, he may have a few letters after his name, and yes, he may be a military strategist, but he has never served on the battlefield. Maybe he went to the same public school as the Home Secretary, which is how these things normally work. Major Watkins feels his wings are being clipped once again by the military machine he serves, as he is a proper rebel and can certainly act the part if need be. Mr X does not appreciate the Major's defiance and bolshie body language. Suddenly, the two men are comparing the size of their wedding tackle. Mr X kindly points out how disposable the Major is, to his annoyance, and the fact he could name numerous less decorated officers who could pull off this mission. This really takes liberties out of Major Watkins, who is not going to bend over for anyone, let alone some jumped-up pen pusher, he thinks to himself.

Major Lenny Watkins is an outspoken soldier who has been in hot water before due to his outbursts in the presence of Colonels and Brigadiers. He is headstrong and will push the agenda till he gets his way. Some would call him a deluded bulldog, but he is a loyal deluded bulldog to King and Country. Suddenly, Colonel Smith raises his voice and slams his clench fist onto the desk due to Major Watkin's protest. Suddenly, the two Military Police officers on guard duty burst into the room. They are holding their truncheons with vigour and look serious about doing some damage here.

Tension fills the air at what is going to happen next. Colonel Smith calmly reassures them that everything is under control, and they were discussing something. The two men reluctantly leave, starring at Major Watkins as they close the door.

He, in return, glares back at them, slightly flexing his chest to show his defiance. This ensures the Colonel has the right man for the job. Colonel Smith continues to calm the situation down and relights his pipe with a match. While smoking, he extinguished the match and places it in an ashtray. He explains to Major Watkins that emotions are running high, and he is fully aware of his last mission, where women and children were killed.

Mr X butts in, going on about 'collateral damage' within wartime, which infuriates Major Watkins once again. He turns and glares at Mr X, saying that Colonel Smith must get involved again. He barks at Mr X, to his surprise, as Mr X feels he is superior to this soldier who is seated next to him. Tension fills the rooms once again. What Mr X is not aware of is that Major Watkins's family were part of the 'collateral damage' he refers to.

A Lancaster bomber dropped its payload in error, which resulted in a bus of civilians being killed in Kent, where they had been evacuated from London. This event within Major Watkins's life has caused him far too much trauma and heartache. He suffers from flashbacks of this tragic event and is heavy-hearted about the whole affair. He blames the pen pushers like Mr X, who sits behind a desk and is not on the sharp end of any conflict. How can they comprehend the personal loss of any 'collateral damage'? How could the 'Bomb-Aimer' be so stupid? Maybe his bout of airsickness didn't help matters. He was too busy puking his guts up to see a bus full of civilians being evacuated.

The look of distress is clear to see, and it is slapped across Major Watkins's boat. The heartache he endured due to losing his wife and daughter because someone dropped a bomb in error. This could be why he has an issue with authority himself. The reason he is a heavy drinker and has that look of hurt, which he carries around with him. His love for his family has now changed to rage and anger. Major Watkins helps himself to another drink, which he throws down his throat. Colonel Smith brings the meeting to a close; he offers his support within the mission. Major Watkins stands, salutes the Colonel and glares at Mr X. Major Watkins turns and picks up his satchel before he leaves the room, closing the door behind him. The Colonel and Mr X look at one another in silence as the Colonel continues to smoke his pipe.

Two days later, at 0700 hours, Major Watkins and Lieutenant Harvey are standing in a military prison courtyard. Two Military Police officers accompany them as they stand, waiting for the prisoners to be brought out for inspection. The high stone walls enclose the space, with a watch tower that hangs over them. An armed guard stands watch over the whole courtyard, rifle in hand. Major Watkins looks up at the barbed wire that lines the huge stone walls in case one of these prisoners decides to try going over the top and making a run for it.

Suddenly, a heavy metal door slowly opened, making a screeching noise. One of the Military Police officers walks forward towards the doorway with his truncheon under his folded arm.

"Come on, quick march!" He screams.

"Left, right, left, right, left, right, left right."

"The Major is waiting, come on ladies," he adds.

The prisoners slowly meander towards Major Watkins and Lieutenant Harvey, each at their own pace. They form a ragtag group of men, appearing undisciplined with little respect for authority or any discernible conviction to fight. Major Watkins gazes at them, patiently awaiting their slow alignment for inspection. Despite additional orders barked by a Military Police officer, the commands fall on deaf ears, as these men clearly exhibit a lack of concern or compliance.

"Attention!" he screams.

A few of the men react immediately to this, but a few of them are here as they have no choice. One man in particular, looks like he will be trouble. He looks hell-bent on getting under someone's skin, especially an officer. This gentleman we talk of plays the fool in a certain way. He pulls faces at the Major, making eye contact with him.

In some attempt to gain some form of reaction from him. The Major just glares at the man. He is too cool to be drawn into whatever this man is trying to do. The Military Police officer salutes the Major and hands over to the Lieutenant. He steps backwards and stands to the side of the two officers.

"All present and correct, Major," Lieutenant Harvey adds.

"Thank you, Lieutenant," Major Watkins replies.

"At ease, gentlemen," the Major adds.

The prisoners slowly continue to amble into formation before Major Watkins and Lieutenant Harvey, each at their own pace. They constitute a disparate group of men, projecting an undisciplined demeanour with scant respect for authority. Major Watkins continues to survey them, patiently waiting for their sluggish formation for inspection. Right from the start, he scrutinises the troublemakers, leveraging his worldly experience and astute judgement of character. He turns and looks at Lieutenant Harvey before looking at the men who are standing before him. Suddenly, one of the men calls out.

"Who's this hot shot, Major, they've sent us?" he calls out.

"What have we done, girls, to deserve this?"

"Leave it out, Pauley," another soldier calls out.

"Why should I? We don't need this shit," Pauley replies.

"You wouldn't be nothing if he wasn't standing behind you," he adds.

"But he does," Lieutenant Harvey replies.

"Fuck you, Francis, you keep your Mick arse outta this," Pauley replies.

The rather stocky-built soldier, Francis, moves slightly forward towards Pauley, who is still within the Major's face. Tension fills the air at what is going to happen next. The guard within the tower readies his weapon and points it towards the courtyard.

The Major notices this from the corner of his eye. Another soldier holds onto Francis's wrist to stop him from attacking Pauley.

"Come on, Francis, I'll have your guts for garters," Pauley screams.

"Go on, Francis, do him," Another soldier calls out.

"Yeah, lamp him," he adds.

You can see within Pauley's eyes an element of hatred and madness. He turns and walks towards Francis, who is still standing in line with the rest of the soldiers. You can sense trouble. Is Pauley going to kick off here? A fisticuff, a proper tear-up of all tear-ups is imminent. Pauley is now within Francis's face, even though Francis towers over him due to his size and stature. This doesn't deter Pauley; he is after blood, by the looks of it.

"Come on, Francis, you big Irish fuck," Pauley screams.

"You want some," he adds.

The remaining men start to chant and encourage the two men to fight. Like some playground punch-up when we were kids.

"Fight, fight, fight," the men call out.

This situation can go down like the proverbial lead balloon at any time, becoming a debacle of all debacles. This is not the greeting Major Watkins was expecting, but he knows deep down blokes like Pauley only want to cause trouble. So, Major Watkins calmly walks up behind Pauley and presses an area near his neck. Pauley falls to the floor immediately, like a sack of spuds. Unconscious due to whatever the Major had just done to him. What the Major had just done was simply squeeze his pressure point, which relaxes the body. Hence Pauley passing the fuck out. As Pauley hit the cobbles, the Major just stepped back. This suddenly amazed the men, and a few of them started to talk among themselves about what they had just witnessed.

The Major addresses the remaining men as the two Military Police officers move forward and drag Pauley away. He explains the general situation and what he expects of them. He keeps the finer points of the cunning plan for later. Major Watkins quite clearly empathises with how long they all have before the hangman comes calling and the fact this is the only way they will cheat him. Certain details are left out for now, but the importance of the men getting the relevant training and bonding as a unit is the Major's priority. A few men call out, asking what they would be doing or where they would be going. Lieutenant Harvey interjects, "These details will follow within due course, but for now, listen to what the Major has to say."

Major Watkins explains the importance that they do not try to escape, as they firstly will be shot in the head, and secondly, the remaining men will be returned back to prison to serve out their remaining sentences. A few of the men look at each other on hearing this, especially with prisoners like Pauley. The Major continues that they will be removed from the prison and housed within a training facility, where they will only report to him and the Lieutenant. Most of the men start to talk among themselves, as a sense of relief is plain. They might not meet the hangman now. The Major drills it home; they are still fighting for King and country. The prisoners are excused, and the Major walks off with the Lieutenant. The men look on with mixed emotions about what has just been asked of them as they continue to talk among themselves.

Later that evening, Major Watkins occupies his barracks, seated at a desk. He meticulously pores over the files of the six men, contemplating the weight of the assigned task. As he indulges in a smoke, he shakes his head, grappling with the intricacies of the cunning plan he must execute. Flicking through file after file, he assesses the attributes of each man.

Franciscus Morris, also known as Francis, stands out, of stocky build and an amateur boxer hailing from the East End of London. In his early thirties, he exudes the essence of a genuine Geezer, as evidenced by his attempt to intervene during Pauley's earlier altercation. He looks fearless to the Major, hopefully someone he can count on in a time of need.

Francis has Irish heritage and is six feet plus with dark brown hair. He is only ninety-nine per cent Irish when his heritage is ever brought into question. Only the good part is what he says. He is British as the next Tommy if you ask me. His skill set is that he was a Royal Engineer and understood things that go bang. He got drunk after catching his fiancée in bed with some GI, crashed his car into another and seriously injured the occupants. Not before getting into a punch-up in some boozer with the offending GI's army pals, he accidentally killed one of them. The judge took minutes in charging him with malicious wounding while in charge of a motor vehicle and murder in the first degree. He sentenced him to death by hanging as the car was being driven by someone of importance.

Then, we have Arthur Jones, the man who stopped Francis from fighting with Pauley. From this action alone, Major Watkins can gauge he is, too, a good man. For him to stop Francis from fighting says something about him and his character. He is in his late twenties, of slim build with mousey brown hair and was a miner from Yorkshire before the war started. He looks like a committed man who is a grafter and not shy of taking any slack.

He got drunk one night and had a fight with a local, but it got out of hand. Before he knew it, a Geezer had cracked his noggin open on the concrete and bled to death. That was that he was charged with manslaughter and assault, death by hanging.

Next, we have Clive Hawkins he is in his mid-thirties and had lived in Germany before the war. His parents both worked at the Embassy in Berlin for years before the war broke out. He can speak fluent German and looks the part, too. He is of medium build with blonde hair and blue eyes, and is educated at Cambridge, where he earned a double first in chemistry. He is obviously an intelligent bloke who feels remorse for what he did. His skills lay within communication and electrics, which could be helpful too.

He fell asleep on guard duty; he did not notice the candle he was using to read with had caused a fire and destruction of a neighbouring ammunition dump. Three men were badly burnt in the fire; he was given twenty-five years of hard labour.

Then we have Jack Douglas, the Rottweiler of the pack. He is an ex-Military Police officer. He likes to be called JD; he is in his late forties, is heavily tattooed and is a bruiser of a man. He doesn't possess many good attributes; unfortunately, in prison, it's all about looking after number one. He has a short temper and can easily fly off the handle over the most trivial of things. After serving time, he joined the army to straighten himself out. With his prison tattoos and weathered exterior, he had seen many a punch-up in the prison yard, which often turned ugly. If Hawkins is the brains, then JD is certainly the brawn of the team. He was in the wrong place at the wrong time, as he was arrested with stolen guns. He protested his innocence, but his earlier record helped him gain a twenty-year prison sentence. This was due to the beating the soldiers took when the guns in question were stolen.

Next, we have Gary Willis, who is in his mid-twenties, a small man with brown hair and a slight limp. He was shot in training and carries this limp throughout his service. He is a funny Geezer, he plays the piano and is always fooling about, trying to make the boys laugh. He uses his skills to entertain and make people laugh to hide his own insecurities. Gary is a caring man and will do anything to help others in need. He was caught forging his papers to gain leave to see his family. They only gave him five years in prison for the error of his ways. Unfortunately, five years is far too long for someone like Gary to be banged up.

Lastly, we have Paul Brown, AKA Pauley, who has already made a good impression on Major Watkins. Pauley is in his late twenties, with brown hair and brown eyes. He is very judgemental and argumentative and is always looking for a punch-up. Being of a stocky build, he likes to use his size to intimidate others, like Gary. He is egocentric, uncaring and shows no remorse for what he did. Pauley is the loudest in the room and again hides certain insecurities since childhood.

Pauley has been hospitalised after hearing voices of dead women and children after he was part of an infantry unit which bombed a church hall in error. Killing everyone inside who was taking shelter from the Luftwaffe air raid. Due to the fact he was drunk at the time and his error with the coordinates, which led to this loss of life. The judge handed him a death sentence like he gave to those people within the church. So, there you have it; the line-up of undesirables, this motley crew of men who soon will be entrusted with pulling off this cunning plan in Nazi-occupied France. Bloody fingers and toes crossed.

As I said, Major Watkins sits within a classroom-like building, a simple wooden hut adorned with desks, chairs, and a blackboard at the front. The military prison, in an act of kindness, has permitted them to use a set of outbuildings within the prison grounds. Despite this generosity, the buildings remain under the watchful eye of a guard tower and Military Police, serving as a deterrent in case any of the men contemplate making a run for it. The first structure houses the officer's quarters, where Major Watkins and Lieutenant Harvey reside. The second, more rudimentary, serves as the living quarters for the enlisted men, and the last is the classroom.

Washing facilities and latrines are located within a small brick-built building to the rear of the compound. So, Major Watkins is seated in the classroom we talk of when he stops reading and places the files down as he pours himself a drink. He throws it down his throat and looks at the glass before he places it down. He looks slightly burdened for some reason. Maybe it is the fact he has just read through these prisoner's files. He rubs his eyes, and an element of concern is slapped across his boat. There is a knock at the door, and after a slight pause, Lieutenant Harvey walks into the room. He salutes the Major and is asked to take a seat. He asks the Major.

"Why the long face?" he asks.

The Major highlights his concern about the ability of these men to pull off such a cunning plan, especially behind enemy lines. The Lieutenant asks the Major where he learned to do that thing he did earlier to Pauley. He explained that his father was based overseas and was in China for several years. He had learnt breathing exercises and about the body's pressure points. He went on to talk about Chi, which is the energy released by the body. The Lieutenant listened anxiously to what the Major is telling him, so when Pauley got far too rowdy for his liking, he just manipulated his pressure point near his neck, which made him pass out.

The two men both take a drink. The Lieutenant talks about certain prisoners and how they have expressed remorse for what they have done. The Major feels some of the sentences are quite harsh after reading the prisoners' files and how they realise the error of their ways and would do anything to put things right again. This is true for only a percentage of the men, though, as men like Pauley want the world to burn. Lieutenant Harvey assures Major Watkins that they will have the men ready within the timescale Colonel Smith has given them. Major Watkins is slightly hesitant about what is being said but takes another drink and looks at the Lieutenant.

The Lieutenant asks to see the Major's pistol, as he caught a glimpse of the stock earlier. The Major removes it from the tan, leather holster and hands it over to Lieutenant Harvey. He feels the weight of this classic Smith & Wesson six-shooter. On closing one eye, he takes aim and checks it before he passes the six-shooter back as he turns the stock around at the last minute so the Major can take hold of it. He asks him regarding the picture of the pin-up girl on the stock.

Major Watkins looks at him and sighs, saying that was a friend from a different life. He pours himself another drink and throws it down his throat, with a certain look of heartache slapped across his boat. The Lieutenant thinks it must be an old flame or sweetheart from the Major's past.

The Major definitely carries a lead weight around his neck. Due to the loss of his wife and daughter, which still burdens him to this day, it is evident to see. The flashbacks he experiences, waking up within a pool of his own sweat most nights. The thought of using his own six-shooter on himself to put an end to all this torment and heartache he endures daily. The heavy drinking which subdues these dark thoughts of ending it all. He cannot get the image of both his lifeless wife and daughter laying on the cold marble slab at the morgue out of his mind. The identification process he had to be part of, to bury these souls he loved. The army, his second family, the only thing which has kept him sane throughout this journey of misery.

The Lieutenant knows him better than most, and what he has endured with the loss of his family. What he does know is the Major will always perform his duty to its fullest, whatever he is going through personally. Due to their friendship, he has stood by him throughout this dark time but also knows there is no time to wallow in self-pity now and he must grieve in his own time. As the mission before them needs the Major firing on all cylinders for it to be a success.

The Lieutenant abruptly enquires if he can speak candidly, and the Major simply nods in agreement. He addresses him as Lenny and expresses concern about how he is coping after the tragedy. The Major's agony is palpable as he pours himself another drink, creating a tense atmosphere and leaving everyone on edge to anticipate the Major's reaction. His body language speaks volumes. Downing his drink, he pours two more, apologising for not offering him one earlier and questioning whether his behaviour befits an officer. The Lieutenant interjects, clarifying that he did not mean it that way and expressing genuine concern for the Major's well-being. Major Watkins reassures him, emphasising that he is well and highlighting that the mission is the sole focus. A brief pause ensues as the two men exchange glances; the Lieutenant takes a sip of his alcoholic beverage.

Later that evening, the men sleep in their bunks. It is raining outside. What do I mean by rain? Proper rain, bloody huge grape-sized droplets of good old cold British rain. These little depth charges cascade onto the roof of the outbuilding the boys sleep in, making that rat-a-tat, tat noise. It is like some crazy Tommy gun spraying out some lead.

The Lieutenant walks into the room, leaving the door ajar. You can clearly hear the rain now as it is coming down hard. He stands there, dripping wet, as water drips to the floor from his military poncho. He stops and pans the rooms at the sleeping beauties that are within the land of nod. He produces a Bren light machine gun from underneath his poncho and slowly points the barrel towards the air. Garry moves slightly, changing sides within his bunk so the Lieutenant pauses momentarily. Once he is convinced, he has fallen asleep again, he cocks the gun and starts to shoot.

BANG! BANG! BANG! BANG! BANG! BANG. The gun sounds.

Suddenly, all hell breaks loose. The men all jump from their bunks like they've shit the bed or something. Like silly buggers, some grab whatever they can find to defend themselves while others take cover. The shell casings fall to the floor as the Lieutenant's gun of choice spits them out. He ejects the magazine and replaces it with another before; he chambers a round and continues his alarm call for the boys.

BANG! BANG! BANG! BANG! BANG! BANG!

Pauley falls to the side of the Lieutenant from his bunk; he manages to grab the Lieutenant's side arm. He points it at the Lieutenant even though he is fully aware of who he is about to fire at. To his surprise, the magazine is empty. The last thing the Major would want is for his right-hand man to become cold as clay by the hand of one of these recruits this early on within the process. As the men still scramble, taking refuge from this sudden display of power, others realise it is the Lieutenant and highlight their disappointment in his actions.

On realising the gun is empty, Pauley attempts to rechamber another round and realises the magazine is empty, to his disappointment. He tries to attack the Lieutenant, using the stock of the gun as a weapon, but the boys put a swift end to his plans. JD disarms Pauley and throws him to the floor with force. Pauley grabs a wooden stool and throws it towards JD in some attempt to strike him.

JD brushes it off with his arm so the stool crashes to the floor. The Lieutenant has stopped shooting by now, as the second magazine is empty. JD takes hold of Pauley and cracks him one on the chin, which knocks Pauley out cold. He falls to the floor, crashing against some wooden boxes. Suddenly, silence fills the room as the gun stops firing, and all the men hear is Pauley crashing against the wooden boxes.

Smoke emanates from the barrel of the Bren light machine gun, which looks red hot, making that noise cooling metal makes. The Lieutenant scans the room, which has now fallen into an eerie silence, besides the Bren gun cooling down. Bullet casings are scattered across the floor. The tension is only disrupted by the Major, who enters the room, treading underfoot the empty bullet casings which litter the floor. The noise only disrupts the silence before he starts to clap his hands while he looks directly at the men. The Major displays contempt for the men before him with tones of sarcasm.

"Attention!" The Lieutenant barks.

"What a fucking shambles!" the Major calls out.

"Well done, chaps; certainly showed the Lieutenant who is boss," he adds.

The men have already moved and are all lined up by now, besides Pauley, who remains on the floor. The Major looks over in his direction and shakes his head in disappointment.

"What's this, Lieutenant, a causality of war?" He asks.

Some of the men start to laugh, but the Lieutenant gives them a stern look. They stop and correct themselves while looking straight ahead. The Major walks over to where Pauley is lying and bends down next to him. He lifts Pauley's hand as he holds onto his wrist, which he lets go of, and Pauley's lifeless wrist falls towards the floor.

The Major stands back up and jokes about how Pauley is the pride of the British army and how he represents what the army is not. He continues to pull Pauley apart as an individual for his faults. What he is trying to do is use Pauley as an example of what not to be. He also knows this one bad apple could spoil the whole barrel. The Major knows the others will not let Pauley bring them down with himself, as they are all reliant on one another to get through this. The last thing any of these fella's want is the hangman's noose around their Gregory's.

Major Watkins points at Pauley as he addresses the other men, offering congratulations to some for their quick-witted responses and commendable handling of the drill they had just partaken in. His remarks, tinged with sarcasm, underscore the gravity of the situation; had the Lieutenant been less capable, they might all be in dire straits by now. The Major's worry stems from the realisation that the success of the entire mission rests on this group of individuals, who, in his view, display a level of selfishness that could jeopardise the collective effort. While this sentiment holds true for certain members, it is important to note that there are a few commendable individuals among this band of renegades.

The Major expresses the urgency of being ready before he once again walks over towards the door and opens it. It is still raining hard as the rain pounds the roof of the building, making that noise it does. On standing within the doorway, he looks over at the men.

"You've got Pauley to thank you for this," the Major calls out.

"Taking into consideration, he was going to shoot Lieutenant Harvey here," he adds.

"Why do you think the Lieutenant would let his sidearm be taken like that?" The Major adds.

The Major looks over at Pauley, still lying on the floor. He then tilts his head to gesture the men leave and make their way outside. The men look at one another, slightly confused, before the Lieutenant barks for them to march into the drill yard for manoeuvres. Most of the men are wearing only vests and shorts and are barefoot. The Lieutenant again barks orders for the men to march out of the building and into the yard. He follows them as he continues to shout at the men.

"Come on, you heard the Major," he screams.

"Outside, left, right, left, right, left, right," he adds.

"Come on, ladies, hurry up, let's be having you."

"It's not a Vicar's tea party, now is it," he adds.

The men reluctantly move to start with before marching outside into the pouring rain. They march into the centre of the yard and line up, side by side. The Lieutenant orders them to drop and give him fifty press-ups each. They all slowly move into position and start the drill, but the disenchantment is clear to see. The Major stands within the doorway, which floods light onto the yard area. He watches as the Lieutenant drills the boys into the early hours as the rain continues to fall.

Some of the men look at one another, and they look pretty cheesed off by Pauley's actions. The Major senses this and glances over at Lieutenant Harvey. As Pauley is still lying on the floor, this action alone will instil a group understanding that they cannot let one person bring them all down like this.

Over the next twenty-one days, the men are put through their paces. Firstly, at the firing range, they all take pot shots at the targets. Pauley, being the trained sniper of the bunch, stands within the watch tower. After the other night, due to his little stunt of pulling a gun on an officer, he now displays a black eye and bruising courtesy of Francis and JD. He has his set of targets, which he shoots at while the Major and Lieutenant watch over them all.

Pauley shoots a near-perfect round as the Major takes the binoculars and focuses on his handiwork for himself. He looks at the Lieutenant; they smile at one another in agreement. Pauley ejects the empty magazine and replaces it as he chambers a round. He starts to aim at the targets again but wanders off course, slightly now aiming at the Major's head, which is magnified by the rifle's telescopic sight.

"BANG!" he calls out.

"That's how easy it is, Mister," he adds.

As he lowers the rifle, he suddenly notices the Lieutenant is pointing a sniper's rifle in his direction, to his surprise. He starts to laugh loudly at this, falling backwards against the guardrail. He puts both his hands into the air while still laughing at what has just happened.

The men attack an obstacle course next, crawling through mud under the barbed wire while the Lieutenant shoots above their heads. Some climb ropes, while others are on cargo nets. Once the men finished the course, they are lined up for inspection. Just before being instructed to drop and give the Major fifty press-ups. Next the Lieutenant distributes a few wooden knives for combat training. The men playfully taunted Pauley, suggesting he would rather prefer a real knife and might have already stuck the Major. Pauley laughs it off but maintains a focused gaze on the Major while skilfully spinning one of the wooden knives on the palm of his hand. As he gestures towards the Major, the men engage in mock attacks, attempting to disarm each other. The Major and Lieutenant observe the training with keen interest.

Parachute training was important as they were being dropped into Nazi-occupied France. The men did not know this yet; all they knew was they had to fall from the skies without breaking an arm or leg, let alone their bloody Gregory's. Garry is scared of heights; he found climbing the rope tower a mission, so jumping out of an RAF aircraft was really challenging for him. They were reaching the end of the training period, and the men were coming on. They have bonded well as a fighting unit and, besides Pauley's little outbursts, are on track to finishing this boot camp of theirs.

The 'Rum Bunch' even excelled at the underwater training, where they had to set explosives. The lads had to work in pairs, holding their breath and swimming down to their surprise. Major Watkins did not want to risk anything to chance. What his thinking is, imagine they lose their underwater apparatus, or it becomes damaged.

If the boys can set the explosives without using the breathing aid, when using the apparatus, this should be a piece of Manor House cake while sipping a cup of the old Darjeeling. Major Watkins is pleased with their progression and feels it is time to take the training to the final stage. He has consulted with Mr X's office, so they are waiting for a guest speaker today. The men are not aware of this and are within the classroom. They have communication and weapons training as normal. The men have been split into two teams and practise what they have been asked. They all wear black hoods as they assemble a Sten submachine gun; this is to replicate doing it within the field in pitch darkness.

The Lieutenant watches over them, timing their progress; to the Major's surprise, they complete the task efficiently. One by one, the men place their completed weapons onto the table and remove the hood they are wearing. Lieutenant Harvey presses the stopwatch and holds it up to show the Major, with a grin on his boat. Major Watkins nods his head in agreement at the results. The Lieutenant and the Major both walk over to inspect the weapons. On picking up Pauley's, the Major is surprised, as he was one of the first to finish. On placing the gun back down on the table, he pats Pauley on the back for his achievement. It seems Pauley has adopted a different mindset compared to before. He suddenly shouts, "bring it" and nods his head with an element of smugness.

On finishing the inspection of the weapons, the Lieutenant walks back over towards the front of the classroom and the Major, by now, has walked over towards the rear of the room. The Lieutenant asks the men to put their weapons away as they have something they need to discuss. The men look at one another, slightly apprehensive at what is going to be said. The Major stands at the back of the classroom studying them before he walks forward and turns around a blackboard. The men all stop what they are doing and look towards him. He points at a map with a stick to where their objective is. France is the country he points to, more precisely, a place called Dieppe. He explains they will rendezvous here with their contact, dressed as simple French farmers. The Major assures the men they will still be wearing their British uniforms underneath, as they do not want to be shot as spies. Once they confront Jerry for the showdown, they will be dressed in their British uniforms, so Jerry knows who is here to kill them. Some of the men talk among themselves about what is being shown to them.

Their primary objective is to infiltrate an agent into France disguised as an airstrike. The carpet bombing will create the opportunity they need. Major Watkins explains that once their agent is in place, they must capture a key figure from the Nazi hierarchy, who will be discreetly transported back to Blighty via a slow boat. Some of the men appear slightly confused by the explanation. What the men fail to grasp is that the individual referred to as the agent is a man named James Hall.

He is a professional actor who has undergone numerous procedures to convincingly mimic Adolf Hitler. What Major Watkins knows is that he looks like him, he sounds like him, and he will certainly fool the men, let alone any Germans. Suddenly, there is a knock at the door, and it slowly opens. The men all turn around to see who it is.

Suddenly, two men walk into the room, pushing a wheelchair. A third man is seated within the wheelchair; he is wearing medical bandages that cover his face. The two men are dressed smartly and look like Mr X's merry men. They push the wheelchair towards the front of the classroom while holding a black leather satchel, which is passed to Major Watkins. He removes a brown file from it and flicks through the documents. The men watch on anxiously as they know something is going on here. One of the two men pulls up a chair, while the other walks back over and stands within the doorway, lighting up a cigarette as a guise he is smoking. As the man unbuttons his jacket, you can see a handgun under it. Pauley notices this and shoves Francis to look over too.

An element of tension fills the room as to what is about to be discussed and who could be this man within the wheelchair. The man in the wheelchair slowly moves his hands and starts to unravel his bandages, to the surprise of most of the men within the room, including Lieutenant Harvey. They all watch with bated breath at who this may be. The trepidation builds as each layer is removed till the man slowly reaches the end. The men move slightly forward in anticipation of who this may be. The sheer curiosity factor alone intrigues them as they sit there engrossed. One of the escorts, who is sitting on the chair, nods slightly at the other man as if to ready themselves for some form of reaction.

The man near the door places his hand within his jacket to reach for his handgun. The last layer is slowly removed, and the man slowly looks upwards. To the amazement of the men, who are gobsmacked on seeing who the man sat before them resembles.

Even Lieutenant Harvey is taken aback by their guest speaker, too. Suddenly, all hell breaks loose. Pauley and a few of the others jump forward to attack the man. They are not aware it is not the real Adolf Hitler. The two escorts jump into action, and even Major Watkins pulls his revolver in an attempt to calm the boys down. The two men and Major Watkins protect the masked man as they all tout their handguns, which hopefully keeps the men at bay and any incoming attack.

"What the fuck!" Pauley calls out.

"Yeah, Major, what's this?" Francis adds.

"Everyone calm the fuck down," Major replies.

"You heard the Major, back in your seats," Lieutenant Harvey adds.

The men all slowly take their seats as Pauley picks up his chair, which he throws to the side on seeing who the man is in some form of protest. The men are taken aback by what they see before their own eyes. The Lieutenant looks over at the Major, slightly surprised, too.

"Major, what is happening?" Lieutenant calls out.

"Nice to have some fucking answers," Pauley calls out.

"They are Nazi dogs," he adds.

"In line, soldier," Major Watkins screams.

"That's an officer you're addressing," he adds.

The Major slams his revolver onto the desk before him and glares at Pauley, creating a tense atmosphere reminiscent of a very British of Mexican standoffs. The room's tension is palpable and cuttable with the sharp side of a bayonet. Suddenly, James speaks in a soft British accent, his mood sombre. He introduces himself as James Hall, astonishing the men with his declaration of serving his King and country. He delves into the heartache he has endured due to his assigned duties, detailing the sacrifices and pain, both mental and physical.

Pauley has taken his seat by now, and the men are fixated on James. An element of empathy for James emerges among some of the 'Rum Bunch.' He stops speaking for a moment. On standing up from the wheelchair, he brushes his hair over with his hand, and there is a slight pause. He suddenly starts to speak in German loudly, aggressively like Adolf Hitler, waving his arms around and pounding his clenched fist onto the palm of his hand. The passion with which he communicates is flawless, as the Tommies are bewildered by the man-monster that stands before them.

A few of them shake their heads at what they are witnessing. He has certainly mastered the art of public speaking the Adolf way, the way he commands the audience with eye contact and gestures that grow his presence on stage. Garry falls backwards off his chair, in sheer astonishment at what he is witnessing.

Tension fills the air, and Pauley jumps to his feet in some attempt to attack this Nazi who stands before him again after everything that has been said. The Lieutenant must grab his sidearm and wave Pauley back to his seat with force. The Major remains quiet, letting this scenario play out, just observing what the boy's reactions are. James continues to talk in German, explaining something. As one of the men understands German, Clive starts to smile and then laugh. The others turn and stare at him, and he laughs louder as James or Adolf continues to speak in the eyes of the Tommies.

The rest of the men ask him what he is saying. He jokes that Adolf Hitler wants them to land in Nazi-occupied France, find the real Adolf Hitler and swap him for the little angry bloke who stands before them. Then quietly sail the real one back to Blighty while he derails the Nazi war machine from within. Suddenly, James stops talking and stares at the men, who still cannot believe their eyes.

The atmosphere within the room is still tense; what is going to happen next? Major Watkins explains roughly what is happening to the men, why he has decided to show them James and what is going to take place within France. He, of course, holds back on a few details; call it an ace up his sleeve. The Lieutenant waves Pauley back, who gets above his station like he often does. He starts ranting and raving that the Major is a Nazi lover, and a spy placed here by the Krauts. That is when the Major prompts James to speak in English once again.

His distinct British accent catches the men off guard again, as they look confused at what is happening, even though the Major has just explained the situation to them. As James continues to talk about himself, his family, his job and where he is from, the men slowly calm down. You can see the relief on their boats. It makes sense now why they have a Geezer dressed and looking like Adolf Hitler standing before them. The Major explains the secrecy of what they are witnessing but chose to tell them earlier than he originally wanted to due to the unrest within the group.

James's long pain-staking procedures we talk of, which have meant many months within a secret medical facility, away from his family. This is the level of commitment he has displayed so we can stop this unhinged-psychopath Geezer from conquering the world. James is a refined gent; he listens to classical music and drinks fine wines. He was chosen due to his academic skills and his uncanny looks, which made him the ideal choice for this cunning plan.

He underwent an evaluation to determine his compatibility with the stresses and strains he would endure throughout this process. Once they were satisfied that he was the right man—considering there were others, men like him, eager to put themselves forward to stop Adolf Hitler—James emerged as the top candidate for the job. There was something extra about him that set him apart, a quality Mr X believed made James Hall stand out among these gentlemen of valour. He underwent weapons, explosives, and combat training, similar to the foot soldiers, but his mission was something none of these soldiers could have ever dreamed of.

James had to become an expert in communications skills, from the radio to scaling telegraph poles to sabotage German phone lines. The greatest task which lay before him was to mimic Adolf Hitler in his speech, his mannerisms and general demeanour. How the madman would project his voice within speeches, and how his mannerisms transformed his presence into a mighty giant of the stage? He had this knack of increasing his body size and presence on stage with hand gestures and erratic movement of his arms. This was always followed by aggressive, high-pitched speaking, near shouting at his select audience, which was present to see this fearless new leader. This was an art form Adolf Hitler had down to a tee, something which James had to master, let alone pull off in front of hundreds of Nazis.

After James' little speech, he got a good handle on what was needed from him. One plan was to kidnap Adolf Hitler and wound James in public so that it would affect his vocal cords. This would mean no public speaking, which in turn reduces the chance of being caught out. The issue with this plan was that he would be hospitalised and would be temporarily relieved of public duty. This could mean no military decisions and a lack of input into the war effort against the Allies. Mr X and his team ran every scenario and outcome before the final decision was made to drop James into Nazi-occupied France and make the swap at a gala event in a Château in Dieppe.

The carpet bombing would function as a diversion, and within the chaos, the Tommies would work their brand of magic. The plan is for Major Watkins and his 'Rum Bunch' of Tommies to attempt to assassinate the Führer at this gala event we talk of. With the backdrop of the bombing campaign, the Führer would be whisked away to a waiting car before being driven off to safety. This is where the Tommies come into play, and they would ambush the car and swap James for the Führer. The Major feels James would have to take a slight knock to his noggin just to highlight he was in the car which crashed after the driver was shot dead. The remaining escort would be brown bread so that no one would talk. As long as the beloved Führer was fine, with a few scratches, hopefully, the Nazi hierarchy would swallow this hook, line and sinker. The Tommies had to kill as many Nazis as they could in the process, painfully, of course.

Maybe just maybe, things do not go to plan, and Jerry will think they are bungling idiots. Hopefully, the switch would occur among all this palaver and jobs a good'un. So, replace Adolf Hitler with a British spy; safely tuck the little madman away in some underground bunker or other for the rest of his days. Our man James spearheads a different military campaign or even surrenders to the Allied forces, and there you have it; we have just won the war. This sounds like a pukka plan, as pukka plans go. So, there you have it: Burno is your uncle and Foxy Fanny's your Fräulein.

After weeks of rigorous training, the 'Rum Bunch' of Tommies have now become a lean, mean fighting machine. The Major, along with his team, is seated within a Douglas C-47, a Gooney Bird, as the RAF liked to call them. They are flying over the English Channel on their way towards France. Silence fills the air besides the roar of the aircraft engines. They sit within near complete darkness; a few bulkhead lights throw an eerie glow onto the entire fuselage. Major Watkins is seated next to Lieutenant Harvey; they sit opposite James, who nervously fidgets. He is wearing a military camouflage jacket, but underneath this, he wears his Nazi uniform. It is a classic double-breasted grey blazer the Führer likes to be seen in, with a white shirt, black tie, and black trousers. Not forgetting the Golden Party lapel pin, as worn by Adolf Hitler.

Sources had already confirmed the Führer's attire for the evening, down to the last detail. Despite the apparent madness of the plan, there is a genuine chance it could succeed. As the two men observe their Adolf Hitler doppelgänger in sheer amazement at the uncanny resemblance to the real Führer, they fervently hope he remains undiscovered. The boys, clad in black leather trench coats, are prepared to unleash their worst, causing as much pain, and suffering as a human could endure if he was captured and then there is the SS to deal with too. I am referring to the Geezer, Heinrich Himmler and his super organised motley crew. How do you imagine they will react to the audacious act of the British kidnapping the Führer and replacing him with a British spy?

Mr. X and his team of brown raincoat-wearing agents have thoroughly briefed James on his mission and its significance for King and Country. The potential achievement is monumental; a metaphorical dagger thrust deep into the heart of Nazi Germany.

Each member of the 'Rum Bunch' prepares themselves for the landing in their own unique way. Some of them ready their equipment, making last-minute checks, while others stare into the darkness of the fuselage. The Lieutenant commented on the new uniforms and boots the MOD delivered to them yesterday. He admires his new boots, which were slightly different to the old army-issue boots he had worn in service. Gary produces a black and white photograph of his gal, admiring it before Pauley grabs it out of his hand. Pauley makes a few comments on what he would do with her before Gary tries to grab the photography back from him. Pauley, being the larger of the two men, pushes Gary backwards.

Gary does not take this kindly but cannot say much to Pauley. Francis intervenes and grabs the photograph from Pauley, who goes for his knife. Francis makes a tutting noise as Pauley soon realises there is a Sten submachine gun pointed at his bollocks. Francis shakes his head in disproval of what Pauley is thinking of doing. Pauley backs down, gently removing his hand off his knife, and smiles as he holds up his hands jovially. He attempts to turn the whole situation into some form of joke or other. The Major watches this from the other side of the fuselage. Pauley looks over at him and shouts.

"If the Major doesn't find himself on the receiving end of a German bullet, I'll oblige him," Pauley calls out.

"Private Brown, you watch your tone," Lieutenant Harvey calls out.

"Just messing," Pauley replies.

"You're out of line, soldier," Lieutenant Harvey replies.

"Fucking sort yourself out," he adds.

The Lieutenant glares at Pauley before shaking his head in disgust. The remaining men all sit in silence, as they are all too aware they could be dropping to their deaths. The intelligence regarding the German movement can change at any time. What if Jerry is waiting for them? Suddenly, the Major hears something over the headset he is wearing from the pilot. He removes the headset, hangs it up behind him, and nods at the Lieutenant. He shouts the command for the men to get ready; the drop will be T-minus ten minutes. The men get to their feet in readiness for what is coming next. JD pats Gary Willis on the back for reassurance. James, too, stands up; he still looks nervous as he straightens himself up.

The Lieutenant offers him a hand and checks his parachute in readiness for the jump. The two men exchange a long stare, and the Lieutenant gestures to James in an attempt to reassure him that everything will be well. Suddenly, the whole aircraft rocks abruptly, throwing the men sideways due to the German anti-aircraft guns which are targeting them.

BANG! BANG! BANG! BANG! BANG!

Is the sound as the shells which explode within inches of the aircraft. The Major steps into the cockpit to see how the pilots are getting on under this barrage of gunfire. One reassures him that he will get them within metres of the landing zone, but it all depends on how they fare under Fritz's onslaught. He mentions that the Lancaster bombers are returning to base after pounding the German forces, giving them the opportunity to fly straight in under all the chaos thereafter.

The pilot struggles to keep control as the flak exploded around the aircraft. Bright light floods the cockpit as this occurs, with the navigator calling out they will be over the landing zone within T-minus five minutes. The Major and the Pilot wish each other the best, and the Major returns to the fuselage. The men watch the Major as he places on his helmet and checks his parachute. An air of trepidation consumes them all as the explosions rock the aircraft.

BANG! BANG! BANG! BANG! BANG!

James locked eyes with the Major, who nodded reassuringly, making a silent promise that everything would be alright. In gratitude, James reciprocated with a smile, subtly conveying his appreciation for the Major's unwavering support.

Unexpectedly, a wave of nausea overwhelmed him, and he vomited onto the floor, a stark manifestation of the gravity of their impending mission. As he wiped his mouth, he surveyed the scene. The atmosphere was palpably sombre, and even the Tommies seemed on edge. Raw emotions were laid bare, and the air charged with anticipation for what awaited them upon landing. The weight of their undertaking became unmistakably clear, settling upon each member of the group in a sudden, collective realisation.

The fuselage indicator light turns red and after a few minutes' it changes to green. On arriving from the cockpit, the co-pilot opens the aircraft door. Suddenly cold air blows into the fuselage, adding to the realisation of what is about to take place. The men all shuffle forward and clip onto the line, some mumbling a quiet prayer while another Tommy kisses a cross around his neck before touching his chest to replicate the sign of the cross. The bright lights and flashes of the explosions going off with their distinct odour are all so evident once the door has been fully opened. Bullets whiz past, with the tracer leaving a trail of light as the sky looks like it is on fire.

The roar from the aircraft engines makes a deafening sound, but the explosions can still be heard and felt as the aircraft rocks abruptly, as flying shrapnel is present. This is it; the men can now sense the severity of their mission. Suddenly, they all realise they are virtually over the area where Jerry is, as the Lieutenant gives the order to jump. The Tommies start to bail the aircraft, and one by one, they jump. The white of their parachute's contrasts against the pitch black of the night sky, which in some areas glows due to the anti-aircraft shells going off. They all slowly float downwards towards the ground.

"Go, go, go, go!" Lieutenant Harvey calls out.

He guides the men out of the plane as they continue to jump. When it is James' turns, he stops momentarily with a worried look on his face. The Lieutenant must force him forward and reassures him that he will be right behind him when he exits the aircraft. After a short pause, he edges forward with his boot heels, hanging off the ledge of the doorway. He nervously moves forward, turns, and finally looks at the Major before jumping. The Lieutenant follows at once as he promised. This is then followed by the Major, who takes one last look around the aircraft before he jumps. The metal harness clips attached to parachute webbing wave around in the wind, banging against the fuselage, which is now empty of souls. The co-pilot closes the hatch, and the aircraft climbs into the clouds for cover as the heavens open. The whites of their parachutes can clearly be seen as they slowly fall towards the ground, under the cloak of darkness among the chaos of the ground attack.

Back to James's past, he is a man of simple taste; he is married with a baby daughter called Elizabeth. His significant other is called Jane, and he is an accountant by trade. James works for a small accountancy practice and loves chess, the outdoors, and acting. Yes, our would-be Adolf loves to tread the boards as he is a true luvvie at heart. Mr X and his boys signed up this young thespian straight from Oxford, this breeding ground of academic shadow people. What I mean by shadow people is they are the people who live within them for the art of spying for the King and the country for its betterment. Wars have been won and lost within this grey, murky world of shadows in which James has been nurtured. James was born, but he was Otto Keller from Mosel before he moved to Blighty as a child. His parents had been killed in a tragic car accident when he was still at boarding school in Blighty.

They were wealthy wine producers, a family tradition that he did not want to follow for some reason after this tragic event at first. From an early age, he was always academic and loved numbers and solving riddles. The allure of the family's wealth and thousands of acres of vineyards appealed to him when he was younger, but after the accident, this all changed for some reason.

His godparents felt it was only best for him to continue with his education before moving back to Germany to settle down and start a family. This was after that horrific day he was called into the headmaster's study and told both his parents had been killed in a car accident. This news devastated the young Otto, who missed growing up in Mosel's wine-producing area. With its rolling countryside and scenic views, he always wanted to return to his family estate when he was younger. His godparents oversaw the family business of wine production after this tragic event till the day when he may take over the helm. He attended the funerals in Germany and met with the remaining family before coming back to Blighty.

His parents had instructed family lawyers on what to do in an event like this. Otto's education was paramount, and it had to be finished. They had set aside funds for this, which covered his schooling and board. He joined Oxford University, where he grew as a member of the chess team and other societies like wine tasting and debating. This is where he was recruited and developed into the man he is today. Well, within reason, of course, considering that he has undergone numerous medical procedures to make him look like Adolf Hitler.

James feels that he can stop the bloodshed and the destruction of his beloved Germany, as this is at the heart of his conviction and drive. He wants Germany to be transformed back to its former glory before the Great War. Yes, he knows the National Socialist German Workers Party did bring economic change and had boosted the country after the Great War, but he also harbours his hatred of what the Nazis are doing to their fellow man. So, Otto Keller was killed off, and James Hall was born. James shortly fell in love with Jane, whom he met via acting classes. It was a short romance before the two of them were wed and little Elizabeth came along. She cemented their love for one another, but neither mother nor child was aware this life was a lie. James Hall's only other love was to bring down the Nazi regime and stop the war.

Due to the sensitive nature of the medical procedures, James found himself entangled in a web of fabricated stories, ultimately leading to a rendezvous with his mortality. The consequence was a vehicular mishap that left him severely burned. Aware that this revelation would shatter Jane, leaving their infant daughter to navigate life without her father, James faced the grim reality with a resolve fuelled by a sense of purpose.

As James bid farewell to the world, his funeral became an intimate affair attended by Jane, Elizabeth, work colleagues, and fellow members of the societies to which he belonged. Mr X had a few of his subordinates attend this sombre occasion too, just to keep a close eye on everyone present. The heavens wept on the day of his interment, and the congregation was drenched to the bone by a relentless downpour. In a modest church service, his employer eloquently shared a brief homage, illuminating the essence of James as a friend. The subsequent wake at their family home maintained a subdued atmosphere, offering solace to those grappling with the sudden void left in James's wake. Mr X's office also kept the Godparents at bay, with false information regarding Otto and his new life within Blighty after finishing at Oxford. With counterfeit letters from their beloved Otto, telling them of his new life and his wish to remain within the United Kingdom. The letters stated he wanted no further contact with his family in Germany any longer due to the war and he was happy where he was. This trail of breadcrumbs laid by Mr X's office, paved the way for James to now continue with this cunning plan and kill off Otto.

What Jane was not aware of was that James attended his own funeral, watching from the sidelines as he witnessed his wife breaking down and sobbing as they lowered the coffin into the ground. What a surreal feeling it must have been for the Geezer, watching his loved ones experience these emotions of grief and heartache. He knew what was at stake here, and he had to walk away from this life of his. Mr X had assured him that once the war was over, he could return home to this life he was about to leave behind with a heavy heart. He knew of the burden that Jane would have to raise Elizabeth without him till he could walk back into their lives as the saviour of humanity one day.

The deal he had struck with Mr X would mean he would hang up his brown raincoat and call it a day. Leave the arena of shadows for good, never to return to this dark, murky world again. Part of this arrangement would mean he and his family could return to Germany if they pleased, without any interference from Mr X's office. James would also be returned to his original facial features by undergoing the medical procedures which changed his life in the first place. The United Kingdom would financially reward James, and in the way of an honour for his services to the crown. James knew this day would be a long way away from where he stood but endeavoured to go through whatever it took to bring Adolf Hitler down.

Meanwhile, the Major and his team discreetly touched down in Nazi-occupied France, under all the chaos. Jerry sensed an impending disturbance, likely spotting the parachutes descending after the bombardment. The nocturnal landing aimed to elude Jerries watchful eye as they executed their mission. The approach lacked sophisticated military strategy, opting instead for a brute force method: to cause as much havoc for Jerry as possible, more like a royal pain in the arse. Their directive was clear: sabotage, dismantle, obliterate, shatter, incinerate, eliminate, and mutilate as many Nazis as they could get their hands on, but only after the crucial switch had occurred.

Their task was simple: once they had switched Adolf for Adolf, these boys are to let loose with their creative imagination on the Nazis. This will fuck up the Nazi war effort, while James, Aka Adolf, will steer Jerry into surrender. The rain is thrashing down as they land within a heavily forested area of France, their destination town of Dieppe. They have a rendezvous with their contact from the French resistance. The Führer is attending a ceremony at the Château de Dieppe, within the small town of Dieppe. This medieval castle is the location the Nazis had picked to celebrate Hitler's Youth within the area.

A group of these little bastards had located Jewish families being harboured by French farmers within the area from the Nazis and grassed them up. The young German soldier whom Private Singh had saved was called Hugo Kruger; he is not a fully-fledged soldier yet and is part of the Hitler Youth organisation due to his age. He visited the local area during his training of the Hitler Youth. Hugo had played a part in organising this event to be held here, but due to being injured, could not attend now.

The French contact had the final details, which they will discuss with Major Watkins regarding the best route forward and how they will pull off this cunning plan. Others prepare their weapons as the men gather their parachutes and hide them within the undergrowth. Francis and JD go for a scout as the Lieutenant rallies the men. They are to meet the contact and bring them back for a chinwag.

They all gather around to listen to the Major, who holds up a map within a transparent plastic wallet with markings on it. The rain pounds the men, and it makes a noise as it strikes the plastic wallet. Arthur calls out that the radio has been damaged within the drop as he inspects it. The Major asks if he can repair it, to which he replies he will try. That is when suddenly the Major notices that James is missing. He knows he jumped as he and the Lieutenant jumped after him.

Panic sets in as they know he is pivotal in this audacious, cunning plan. The Lieutenant orders the men to spread out and look for him, as he looks at the Major with a concerned look slapped across his boat. What if Jerry had already captured James? What if he is injured? Tension consumes the two men as the remaining soldiers continue to look for our would-be Adolf. After their aircraft was spotted, they cannot make too much noise as Kraut patrols will be about.

The men continue to look, as Pauley comes across a small barn-looking building. He slowly opens the door and enters. It is deserted, to his relief, as he looks through some empty containers on a shelf. He sees what looks like a bucket of milk, but he does not see a cow. However, he still picks up the bucket. He takes a drink and soon spits out the contents, as it is stale. On throwing the bucket to the floor, he kicks it over, and the stale milk splashes him.

"Fuck, that's proper nasty," Pauley calls out.

He grabs his water bottle and takes a drink, spitting some water once he has rinsed out his mouth. As he wipes his mouth with his sleeve, he turns to leave and notices two of the other Tommies have also entered the barn, which startles him. They joke at the refreshment he had found, and Pauley gives them a two-fingered gesture to show his disapproval of their witty banter. The three men leave the barn via the same door they entered by. The rain is still coming down hard outside. The three Tommies start to make their way back towards the landing zone when they hear something.

On producing their guns, they slowly make their way towards where the noise is coming from. Trepidation fills the air as two of the Tommies make their way towards the noise while the third approaches from the rear, like some pincer movement. They are ready in case it is a Jerry patrol, with fingers on triggers. To their horror, it is James; he is caught up within the trees. His parachute flaps in the wind as the rain pelts him. His lifeless body sways as he hangs from the trees. On first impressions, they think he has passed out. Maybe he has struck his head. Francis climbs and cuts him down as the others take hold of him. As Francis tries to revive him, he soon realises that he has broken his Gregory while trying to land, as there are no bullet wounds and there is redness around his neck area. JD examines him and can see the redness around his neck, where the parachute cords must have become entangled in the wind. James' parachute still waves around in the wind, flapping against other trees nearby, making that noise. By now, the Major and the remaining party have made their way over to where the dead man now lies. The disappointment is clear to see on the Major's face.

The one key factor of London and Mr X's cunning plan now lies on the ground, dead as a dodo. All that planning, the intelligence reports, the training these men had gone through for nothing. Pauley removes his helmet and throws it onto the floor. Enraged, the remaining soldiers do not look too chuffed at what has happened either. The Major knew bringing James in separately by safer means would have been ideal, but this is not an ideal situation they find themselves in.

Major Watkins knows he needs to turn this situation around and make the best out of what hand they have been dealt with at this eleventh- hour. He knows all bets are off. These boys are back on track to be swinging from the rafters due to the deal the military had done with them, which is now officially off. The fine print clearly stated that if the mission failed, their pardons would be flushed down the crapper. His concern is that if one of these boys realises this, he will have munity on his hands. This is the last thing he needs on a cold and wet evening like tonight in Nazi occupied France. So, he gives the Lieutenant a certain type of look, which the Lieutenant understands with a slight nod in return. The two men know they must now employ these men to become the proper 'Rum Bunch' and cause Jerry as much shit as they can. The thought does cross the Major's mind regarding taking the fresh cadaver called James with them and somehow swapping him for Adolf Hitler, but this is even a long shot for him.

Why not take it a step further, leave the lifeless body on full display, and perhaps even give it a dramatic exit, like a controlled explosion? This way, when Jerry stumbles upon the remnants of their beloved leader, our dear James, it might just be enough to make them reconsider and head back home. Deep down, Major Watkins knows that the other four deranged individuals surrounding the once-loved Führer will eagerly step into his shoes, continuing the madness where he left off. However, he quickly discards this unsettling thought as mere folly. Each of these four individuals is even more unhinged than the last, making the prospect of them taking charge far more daunting than Major Watkins initially imagines.

Suddenly, an air of defeat washes over the men. They look like they have lost the will to fight, seeing their cunning plan is now turning white as a sheet due to his demise. The Lieutenant tries to rally the men and asks them to carry out what they had trained for. Francis and JD offer to see to James by burying him with some form of dignity within the situation they find themselves in. The two men pick up James's lifeless body and carry him into the forest for burial. Gary and Clive remove their helmets as they walk past the group of Tommies as an element of respect. The Major just watches, in disbelief, as James is carried away. Silence fills the air as they are all speechless at the loss of James and the freedom he had promised. As the thought of this slowly sinks in.

The Major opens a brown envelope that is marked for stage two of the operation behind enemy lines. Reading it under torchlight with the rest of the men looking on, with a look of defeat slapped across their faces. He neatly folds back the letter and places it back into the envelope. He lights up a cigarette and starts to laugh out loudly, to the surprise of some of the men. Pauley starts to cause trouble like he does by asking what is so funny. Suddenly, there is an atmosphere within the group, which is what the Major finds so funny regarding the situation they find themselves in.

The Lieutenant slowly moves his hand over his sidearm in case he needs to use it. Garry asks the Major what the orders are. The Major suddenly pauses mid-laughter and stares at Clive. The look slices through the younger soldier, as this is not in the Major's character. Silence, besides the rain and wind blowing through the forest, fills the air. The Major glares at the men, one by one, before he throws his cigarette to the floor and stubs it out with his boot heel. He tells the men what the letter states but pauses and looks up at the men.

"Fuck up the Nazis," the Major calls out.

"Yes, that's it, fuck them up beyond comprehension."

"Who needs orders? Let's do some proper fucking damage," he adds.

"Let's do this for James Hall," he adds.

The men are slightly confused by his remarks at first. Pauley starts saying that the Major has already failed the mission, so they will all be getting hanged soon. This starts to cause a stir among the men; as Lieutenant Harvey is ready, as his hand hoovers over his sidearm. The Lieutenant tries to calm down the men, as suddenly attitudes change within the group to hostility, which now rears its ugly head. Francis and JD have returned to the group by now and are still holding digging spades after burying James. Pauley calls out that the orders are to fuck up Jerry. The men start repeating this among themselves, and the conversation takes a more jovial twist. The Major interjects with a wry comment about the necessity of thwarting the Nazis once again, treating it almost like a joke.

However, instead of dampening the mood, this remark adds fuel to the banter among the men regarding the nature of their new orders. To the palpable relief of the Lieutenant, who withdraws his hand, sensing that the threat of the men lynching him and the Major has dissipated? The atmosphere shifts as the Tommies burst into laughter, revelling in the prospect of undermining the Nazis at their own game. In response to the Major's unspoken tribute, the Lieutenant signals for the men to move out, and gradually, they comply. As they depart, the Major steals a glance towards the area where James rests, rendering a silent salute.

Suddenly, the mood changes among the men when they see this, and they stop their banter and look over at James' last resting place. The remaining men, too, salute in the direction of the newly dug grave as moments like this put everything into perspective. The Tommies make their way through the dense forest in the pitch black towards the town of Dieppe, where they are to meet their contact. Suddenly, the whole area is swarming with Krauts on the hunt for the soldiers who have just been dropped in by air. Major Watkins is fully aware it is dangerous to lead his men right into the viper's nest but also knows now things have gone horribly wrong, seeing the cheese has slid off the army-rationed cracker. This is the only option left to them now.

The morale of the men is not looking too good, considering they have just lost the most integral part of the jigsaw here. They continue to cut through the dense undergrowth; tension fills the air as they can hear the barking of dogs within the distance. They all know Jerry will soon be upon them, as most roads will also have checkpoints. They reach the edge of the town after some time and look exhausted. They spot an old barn-looking building with other smaller outbuildings surrounding it. There is an old tractor and what looks like abandoned farm machinery near one of the smaller outbuildings. The place looks empty, so JD and Francis slip in to have a butcher's before reappearing and calling out that it is disserted. An old fuel tanker sits near the entrance to the barn; it must be empty as the rain makes a pitter-patter noise as it pounds it like some tap dancer doing a number.

The men all make their way into the building and are just relieved to get out of the bloody rain and get some rest. Some of the Tommies remove their packs, while the others have a butcher's around the barn. The Major and the Lieutenant discuss the plan as they look at the map they are carrying. They both agree that JD and Francis are possibly the two best men to send out with the Lieutenant in tow to make this rendezvous with their contact. The rain pounds the roof of the barn, making that rat-a-tat, tat noise it does.

Arthur asks if he can make a small fire, which the Major agrees to, as he is not too good with the cold due to his bronchitis. He collects some old pieces of wood and an old rag he finds and lights a fire within an old bucket. He starts to warm his hands in front of it. Clive walks over towards the fire for some much-needed warmth, too. It floods the barn in an eerie glow of light as Gary watches this from his lookout point within the rafters of the barn.

The rain suddenly stops as silence fills the air once again. Pauley produces a hipflask from his pack, which he takes a long hard drink from before he throws it to Clive, who does the same. They slowly pass it around till it reaches the Major, who takes hold of it at first. He stares at the hipflask for a while; suddenly, a slight air of tension fills the room before he wipes the opening and takes a drink, too.

"To James Hall, a courageous man," he calls out.

Suddenly, the men straighten themselves up, and Clive salutes with all the men following for their fallen comrade in arms as a show of respect. There is a sombre mood within the barn before Gary calls out that Fritz is approaching. Clive puts out the fire, throwing the barn into darkness again, and the men arm up. Arthur climbs upwards to where Gary is to have a look. Two German soldiers on a motorcycle and sidecar are approaching as they follow the road, which snakes itself towards the barn.

Gary calls out what he sees, and the men ready themselves. Arthur climbs back down and quietly slips out of the barn from the rear while the others lock and load for some action. The motorcycle and sidecar pull up towards the front of the barn as the two German soldiers' dismount, talking among themselves. Clive listens in whispers that they are on a general scouting mission and does not mention anything about the Tommies. They appear disinterested in engaging in a firefight, casually surveying their surroundings as they approach the barn doors. The Major signals everyone to take cover within the cloak of darkness. Slowly, the door creaks open, and the two German soldiers enter, guns ready, using a torch to inspect the area. An air of tension permeates, and silence envelops the barn, broken only by the faint sounds of the two guests exploring. One of them calls out, lowering his MP-40 submachine gun to produce a packet of cigarettes. He extends the offer to the other man, who takes one from the packet.

The first soldier lights both cigarettes, and they begin to smoke. What they are not aware of is that mere feet away from them is a handful of British soldiers who are hiding within the cloak of darkness. While they are smoking, one notices the bucket, which is still giving off some smoke, and he slowly raises his gun as he makes his way over towards it. Clive is crouched to the side of him and slowly impales him with his knife; blood instantly trickles down his hand and arm. The soldier starts to choke on his own blood as Clive puts his hand over his mouth to silence this.

The other German soldier hears something but cannot see what is happening. He calls out before Pauley's arm wraps itself around his neck. He struggles frantically, desperately kicking; as his boot heels rub against the barn floor. He tries to grab at a wooden beam near to him but cannot grip onto it. Pauley tightens this noose as life slowly drains away from the German soldier in question, and his kicking and thrashing slows down and eventually stops.

Arthur returns and assures the Tommies no further Germans have arrived. Both dead men are searched for paperwork as the Major asks Pauley to push the motorcycle and sidecar behind the barn. He leaves the barn and slowly pushes it behind the building. He first slips in the mud, gets up, and slips again. Enraged, Pauley gets back to his feet. He is not the happiest of campers, considering he is now caked in mud. Mumbling and cursing, he pushes the motorcycle and sidecar until it is hidden from the main road. He breaks some large branches from a tree to cover it so it can no longer be seen from the roadside. As he turns around, he hears a round being chambered within a gun. He stops immediately as he knows any soldier worth their weight in army rations will kill him from this short distance. He lifts his hands up and slowly turns around to what he thinks is his soon exit from this earth. To his surprise, the person holding the shooter is a lady; she is no Nazi, he thinks to himself.

Pauley, being Pauley, goes for the gun, thinking this lady of the fairer sex may give it up without a struggle. To his unfortunate surprise, she moves and uses the butt to pistol-whip our have-a-go hero. He ends up in the brown stuff again, to his anger, as he looks up at this attractive, near angel-faced lady holding a Mas-38 submachine gun in his face, and she looks like she means business. He slams both his clenched fists into the ground, just to highlight his disproval with no reaction from the lady. She gestures with the gun barrel for him to get to his feet, which he does, and they walk towards the barn door. He stops just short, so as not to open the door at first.

She digs the barrel of the gun into the small of his back with force, just to highlight she is not playing silly buggers here. Pauley slowly opens the door to reveal the rest of the Tommies, who are all standing in the middle of the bran. A few of them go for their weapons, but our angel-faced killer here is far too quick. She suddenly produces a knife and holds it to Pauley's neck as well as pointing her gun at the remaining Tommies. Clive still slowly moves for his gun; she calls out that she will kill him in English but with a French accent. Blood trickles from where the point of the knife had broken his skin. So, Pauley calls out for everyone to remain calm as this lady means what she is saying. The remaining Tommies stand back, and once she is confident that none of these girls will be any more of a handful than this sweetheart she has found outside, she pushes Pauley forward. On landing on the floor, he grabs his neck and looks pretty hacked off. She moves back slightly and points the weapon higher, intending to let off some lead. The Major calmly lights himself a cigarette and blows out the flame on the lighter.

She asks if he is in charge, and he replies he is the highest-ranking officer present. Tension consumes all the men at what is going to happen next as she moves slightly forward and aggressively plunges the gun into his chest. The Major tries to reassure the lady they are British soldiers here to help the French to fight the Nazis. The lady moves forward, takes his cigarette from his mouth, and starts to smoke it. She takes a few long drags before she stubs out the red-lipstick-covered butt on the barn floor.

She asks why they are dressed as simple French farmers. What is the proof they are British soldiers? The Major slowly unbuttons his coat to reveal his British military uniform underneath. He produces his orders and holds them up. She grabs them, opens the letter and starts to read. She then tells the men that she is the contact they are looking for, and her name is Coco. She is one of the nuns at the church in the town, and they will help them as they work with the French resistance locally. She swings her gun around, puts the strap onto her shoulder, and puts her hand out for Pauley to take, who is still sitting on the floor where he landed earlier.

Pauley refuses to take her hand in some act of defiance and is teased by the rest of the lads. His anger turns to a sheepish grin as he soon realises, she was only protecting herself, and her hand is still outstretched. He eventually takes her hand, and Coco tries to help him up. In return, Pauley trips her over, and Coco, too, ends up heaped on the floor. She turns and glares at him initially but then discovers the humour in the situation. The other men respond with smiles and laughter, witnessing the unfolding scene. An unusual chemistry is palpable between them, evident to anyone observing. Meanwhile, Francis, JD, and Lieutenant Harvey enter the barn. The remaining soldiers swiftly grab their guns, startled by the unexpected entrance. They quickly realise it is the returning scouting party. The three newcomers are formally introduced to Coco as their contact. Lieutenant Harvey briefs Major Watkins on their observations: Jerry is seemingly everywhere. The Major instructs the men to be prepared to move within five minutes, acknowledging that the entire area will soon be swarming with Nazi scum.

The Lieutenant asks the men to check their equipment as Major Watkins talks to Coco about what has happened. He explains that 'Operation Mirror- Mirror' could not go ahead at this moment. They must either contact London and ask for new orders or continue with an ad-hoc campaign to cause the Nazis as much pain as they possibly can muster.

Coco agrees that the Major could have just the solution to it all. He tells her that their radio was damaged on landing, and they need to source a new one quickly. She assures him that a message could be sent via her network within the resistance, but he harbours concerns about this getting out, as there are too many yellow rat bastards about. What Coco was trying to say was German spies as walls had bloody big ears. That is when she remembered the power station had a high-frequency radio transmitter they could use.

First things first, they must get to the church and rest and get some food as the German patrols are all over the gaff. The party exit the barn and makes their way towards the town. Coco leads the way with the 'Rum Bunch' of Tommies following. As they enter the town, the streets are deserted. They make their way through the rubble and debris which adorns the streets after the heavy bombing.

As Coco takes the group through deserted buildings, they end up near the river. The noise of the flowing water interrupts the eerie silence as they continue to make their way towards the town. A dead cow floats within the water, bloated as its lifeless carcass bobs up and down near the bank. The smell is so awful and pungent that the Tommies cover their noses as they walk past. To their horror, they discover bloated lifeless bodies floating within the water, too, women and children who had been shot by the SS. Their skin all wrinkled and grey in colour, as well as that horrible smell.

Suddenly, Pauley vomits violently due to the awful smell. The other Tommies poke fun out of him.

"Go on, boy, you might cough up an ace of Spades," Francis calls out.

Coco looks at him and shakes her head, smiling at the men's reactions. Pauley, this big, stocky man, moaning like a little girl, is what Coco calls out in French. She gestures and curls her bicep muscle to highlight the macho man about whom she is talking. The Major and the Lieutenant both smile at one another on hearing this as they both understand what she is saying.

They enter the town, and on making their way through the deserted café building, they must climb through a small window into another deserted building. On entering another street, they notice an armoured vehicle with soldiers. Suddenly, Francis is ready with his gun, luckily Coco stops him. Firstly, the noise of gunshots ringing out would alert the local Nazis to their presence, and secondly, these soldiers, as mentioned earlier, are already brown bread.

Coco tells them the Nazis often leave their dead where they fall when they leave. She tells the men to follow her as they are nearly there as they make their way past another dead German soldier. He is quite young-looking. His dead body, with another, is slumped over their anti-aircraft gun mount where they fell. Garry makes the sign of a cross on his chest as he walks by and kisses his crucifix necklace.

Finally, the Tommies arrive at the church after they have carefully manoeuvred themselves around the cobbled streets of this small town of Dieppe, avoiding the local German forces, who are hunting them. They make their way towards the rear door. Coco knocks twice, stops, and then knocks once and then pauses again before she knocks twice again. This code must be what they are using. The door slowly opens, and an attractive young nun stands within the partly opened doorway. She smiles at Coco, who enters, and the Tommies follow. They make their way through the main church, towards a rear door, which is behind the pulpit. Clive and Arthur bow their heads, and Gary kneels on the floor before he quickly lights a candle. The group pauses for a minute as Francis and JD look around, still touting their guns. Coco reassures the men that there is no risk to them within these walls, and they should follow her.

She lights a candle, and they descend a spiral metal staircase that resembles some sort of cellar. Her candle illuminates the dusty sandstone walls, prompting the Lieutenant to exchange glances with the Major. These men habitually scrutinise situations from every conceivable angle. Arthur strikes a match to better survey their surroundings, bringing up the rear. As the party progresses deeper into the cellar, a musty smell of dampness becomes evident. Coco lights a lamp, casting an eerie glow across the space, while JD illuminates it further with two additional lamps. A table against one wall supports stacks of old wine crates, and older furniture which had been haphazardly piled besides a small window, providing limited light. Coco suggests the men take a break here; she'll arrange some food for them.

The Tommies start to remove their wet civilian clothing and move a few chairs aside so they can sit down. Coco assures them she will be back with some food; the Major asks if any of the men could offer her a hand, which she kindly refuses. She goes back up the staircase, and the men look around the room. Clive sees some old bottles of wine and decides to investigate if some still have any alcoholic contents within them. To his annoyance, they are empty; he checks a few more before giving up. The Major talks to the Lieutenant regarding starting their new plan. They will decide on this after dinner but not before they have spoken to Coco. JD sees piles of old suitcases up against another wall; he opens one to see what is inside. To his surprise, it is full of children's clothing and toys.

He picks up a small bear and looks at it before he throws it back into the suitcase and closes it. Suddenly, unexpectedly, Coco is standing next to JD, who is slightly startled by her presence.

She explained that there was a shortcut back to the main church. She also tells him there is a tunnel behind the stack of old suitcases, which leads under the graveyard and towards the forest. JD asks whose suitcases they are as Coco pauses for a minute and, with a heavy heart, tells him they belonged to Jewish families who were fleeing the Nazis. Priest Henri Baunard would take them in and hide them, but one day, the SS turned up and rounded them all up and took them to the death camps for extermination. They hung him from the tree outside the church for helping enemies of the Third Reich. He was a good man, with principles and helped any soul in need.

His drinking was his Achilles heel, but this did not hinder him from saving hundreds of Jewish lives with the help of his brother Claude and the French resistance. She explains the Hitler youth are prevalent within the area, and these children go around spying and then inform the Nazis where the Jewish families are hiding. The French farmers try to help, but the Nazis just shoot their cows and destroy their farms to teach them a lesson for helping the Jewish people.

Her face suddenly changes as she tells him this; you can see an element of grief and heartache. Maybe she has lost loved ones, Clive thinks to himself. Coco closes her eyes momentarily and then opens them, calling out that they need to follow her again, too, to their surprise. Coco feels under a wooden shelf, and suddenly, the whole bookcase opens to the Tommies' surprise. Slowly pushing it open, she walks through; bright light floods the cellar area. The Tommies cannot believe their eyes at first at all these secret compartments the old church has.

They all look at one another at first, in sheer amazement, gobsmacked. This is before JD plucks up the courage to follow Coco. She turns and reassures him she does not bite, not even if they are English. As the men walk through, what they see can only be described as utopia, especially when you are a male soldier who has not had the company of a good woman for months. The right rotten tart who sold her soul for a few Francs or Reichsmarks is not a good woman, if you catch my drift. What the 'Rum Bunch' witnessed next will never be forgotten by most of them.

Coco, as mentioned earlier, is a formidable member of a vixen death squad comprised of beauties with a mission to eliminate Nazis. While during the day, they don the attire of nuns, their transformation into lethal warriors occurs at night when they confront the Führer's forces. As the Tommies unwittingly intrude on the ladies midway between their serene nun personas and the ominous 'Fräuleins of Death', as dubbed by the Nazis, they are met with a scene of subtle sensuality. Fishnet tights are delicately rolled up, revealing glimpses of soft flesh as neatly painted toes disappear beneath the alluring embrace of black fishnet. The ritual continues with the donning of leather cat suits, the securing of tied-back hair, the zipping up of sleek garments, and the application of lipstick to lush, inviting lips. The chosen hue of lipstick, needless to say, is that unmistakable tinge of rouge.

This is before the numerous weapons of choice this bevy of beauties like to use are prepared. Bullets are loaded into magazines, magazines placed into pockets, crossbow bolts gathered, grenades tied up, shotgun shells loaded, and finally, magazine clips slapped in, and rounds chambered. The poor Tommies see these two acts, which are enough to make any red-blooded male hot under the collar. So, Coco introduces the Tommies to the girls before they can all eat. War can bring the best out in people, as they say; the 'Rum Bunch' certainly tried to shine on these girls at the dinner table as they dined on hot stew and even had red wine to drink. The Tommies make the most of this combination of attractive company, alcohol, and a hot sit-down meal. Coco sits with the Major as she wants to discuss how they are going to disrupt the Nazis to the best of their capabilities or fuck them up, like he put it earlier.

Chapter Three: The Bavarian Lion

Private Singh is flanked by two German soldiers; these German soldiers are not your normal Jew-hating Nazis. These two Geezers are dressed differently, to the normal Jackboot-wearing Kraut. They look special like they are some form of a special unit within the German army, which is of grave importance. Oh course, these two blonde-haired, blue-eyed boys of the Fatherland are from the SS due to their 'Totenkopf' or 'Death Head' insignia. SS stands for Schutzstaffel, the Führer's protection squadron, and private bodyguards which soon became the elite guards of the Nazi Reich. It all began from humble beginnings known as The Saal – Schutz, comprised of party volunteers. Till Heinrich Himmler joined in 1925, and this little gathering of Nazis soon developed into the SS, who are responsible for surveillance, security, and terror, which they performed by ridding the world of the Jewish community. They are considered as enemies of the State and other groups are classed as the undesirables. Sorry, look at me. I'm not here to give you a history lesson, but I do get sidetracked. Where were we?

Oh yeah, Private Singh is being marched along some corridor. He glances at the men who are escorting him; they have a steely look about them and stare straight ahead only. They walk down this huge corridor, with doors leading off it, to either side of it, which look like offices. The walls are painted black, with huge Nazi banners which hang from them, the bright red and white of the Nazi swastika logo so clear to see as it stands out against its backdrop.

Marble plinths line the length of the corridor, which have busts of the Führer sitting on them, which are cast in gold. What Private Singh cannot get his head around is hundreds of thousands of people are dying around the world, and here, the opulence and grandeur which is on display is excessive, to say the least.

They turn left and stop at the foot of a staircase where another two SS-soldiers are standing. They ask who this man is as they talk in German. Private Singh cannot understand what they are conversing about but gets the gist from their actions. One of the guards produces a brown envelope from a black leather briefcase he carries. On removing a letter from the envelope, he passes it to one of the soldiers, who starts to read it and looks at Private Singh as he nudges him slightly to reflect his feelings towards him for some reason. Probably due to the fact he is an enemy of the 'Third Reich', and his identity does not cut the mustard either way.

The second guard raises his voice, prompting the soldier to quickly straighten himself up. Returning the letter, he is instructed to frisk the Sikh soldier for weapons, which he does with unwavering determination. What really takes the Tea biscuit is that they have already checked him for weapons earlier. Deliberately, he roughs up Private Singh during the process, maintaining eye contact. The issuing guard disapproves, expressing his discontent with a tongue-lashing shout. After completion, they receive permission to proceed upstairs. Tension lingers as Private Singh refuses to tolerate any mistreatment from these Nazi guards, responding with a defiant attitude. A subtle standoff ensues as he initially refuses to budge, prompting the guard who performed the search to intervene assertively.

"Bewegen," the guard calls out.

"Easy now, you Nazi wanker," Private Singh calls out.

"Before you get a fucking slap," he adds.

"Schnell, schnell," the guard replies.

The guard raises his voice and grabs his rifle before being barked at by the original guard, who has been escorting the prisoner. Suddenly, everything escalades into a near punch-up. You know Private Singh is a proper Geezer and is not going take any old pony from these fucking Krauts. He would probably land a few punches before they bungle him to the ground and shove a rifle butt into his gut. Luckily for all involved, it does not escalate to this as tempers are controlled and boiling blood calmed the fuck down. One of the original guards kindly asks for Private Singh to continue with a hand gesture to his surprise.

There is a slight pause by Private Singh before they climb the huge grand staircase, which again is in ornate gold metalwork with black marble treads and risers. Private Singh is still carrying the shrapnel wound from earlier, so he takes it easy. Him, being the Geezer he is, would probably refer to it as a scratch, which he picked up. All I know is he's in some form of slight discomfort as he climbs the stairs, as his 'boat-race' paints a different picture. The guard continues to eyeball Private Singh as he climbs the stairs, mumbling something. So Private Singh decides to offer him a hand gesture back for what he said earlier.

The guard reacts to this, raising his voice and calling out something in German. Private Singh disregards the comments, as he feels a lot better that he has got that off his chest. As he continues to climb the staircase, light floods in from a huge window as they reach the top. The staircase curves to a grand-looking landing area where two more guards stand on duty. They click their boot heels and salute the guards escorting the prisoner.

The guard once again retrieves the black leather briefcase, deftly extracting a worn brown envelope. From within, he carefully withdraws a letter, passing it to a fellow guard who begins to peruse its contents. Private Singh scans the expansive corridors branching off the landing, each leading in distinct directions. A luxurious scene unfolds before him, featuring an ornate, hand-carved walnut and gold side table nestled against the wall. Commanding attention at the centre are two opulent gold table lamps with elegant black shades. Dominating the grandeur is a colossal set of meticulously crafted wooden doors standing adjacent to this lavish arrangement. Private Singh cannot help but surmise that this marks the culmination of their journey.

Once again, one of the guards frisk him, to his surprise. The guard questions his 'Kara', or steel bangle all Sikhs wear which is part of the five K's of the 'Khalsa'. Private Singh is not baptised but is a practising Sikh, so observes these elements of Sikhism. The guard starts to kick up a stink about the 'Kara', asking for it to be removed as it could be used as a weapon. The escorting guard tries to explain to this over-jealous young Nazi that he has already been through security checks twice, and there is no danger of him concealing any weapons on his person.

Private Singh moves forward slightly, holding onto his 'Kara', pulling it to highlight to the German soldier that it is not going to come off. Suddenly, the whole situation gets slightly heated once again. You know what these Krauts are like? Well, Private Singh is a hot head, too. Maybe it is, from all those years of having bigoted comments made about his identity.

The two escorting guards try to calm down this younger soldier, who is raising his voice by now. Once again, tempers start to get frayed, and the lack of translation does not help either.

"Oi cunt, it's not gonna come off," Private Singh calls out.

"Do you comprehend that, Fritz," he adds.

"Now fuck off," he adds.

"Scheiß auf dich, Tommy," the German guard replies.

"Yeah, yeah, flap your gums, you fool," he adds.

"Have they got a tuft of grass here, where you and moi can settle this the old-fashioned way" he adds.

"Come on boy, put your fucking dukes up" he screams.

The guard and Private Singh edge closer towards one another in some attempt to deal with this matter the old way. The guards on both sides try to pull them apart from this happening. Tension again fills the air at the outcome of this soon-to-be fisticuffs. Suddenly, one of the huge wooden doors opens, making a noise which huge wooden doors do. To everyone's surprise, Heinrich Himmler himself pops his head from around the door as they all stop dead in their tracks and silence replaces all that shouting which was taking place.

"Heil Hitler!" The guards call out.

"Heil Hitler," Himmler replies.

Immediately, all the German soldiers salute with a hand gesture, clicking their boot heels and straightening themselves up, standing to attention as he raises his hand in return. Private Singh, too, straightens himself up and looks towards Himmler, who is still halfway within the doorway. Himmler converses with the guards as he glares at Private Singh before one of them produces the letter from the leather briefcase again. He moves forward and passes Himmler the letter, which he takes hold of and folds up without reading. He discharges the guards and asks the original two escorting guards to bring the prisoner into the room.

Private Singh turns and glares at the young Nazi, who was playing silly buggers with him only moments ago. The soldier does not make eye contact with him because he is standing before Heinrich Himmler now. Suddenly, he is quite like a church mouse and displays no attitude anymore. Private Singh parts company with a young Nazi, with a few choice words in the King's English. The soldier remains silent and looks straight ahead. The original two guards nervously enter the room with their prisoner in tow, closing the door behind them. Himmler walks over towards a drinks trolley, pours himself a drink, and walks back towards the desk.

Another young German soldier enters the room and salutes Himmler. He greets him with a smile, and they converse in German. The young man sits at a side desk and prepares some paperwork. The room is colossal, with towering concrete pillars from floor to ceiling. There is a roaring open fire to the left of the room, with a hand-carved stone fireplace surrounding it. The side pillars look like dogs sitting up with a fierce look about them.

A fur rug sits on the floor, with two armchairs and a small side table between them. Besides a few wall lights, there is an eerie darkness in the space. The main light is coming from the open fire, which highlights the immediate area. Private Singh walks over towards the centre of the room, still flanked by the two German soldiers and they stop in front of the desk. He notices something tall covered by a white sheet, which sits to the side of the room. A wooden toolbox and other equipment sit on the floor next to this covered object. One of the guard's hands, Himmler Private Singh's personal correspondence and a wooden-looking weapon from the black leather briefcase.

The item is a set of wooden nunchucks, which Private Singh traded with some Chinaman in some boozer in London. Himmler has not seen anything like this previously and examines them closely. Private Singh feels he needs to mention what they are, as Himmler seems to think they are something else, which only the mind of a deranged man knows what. Once Private Singh has fully explained what the implement of death are, Himmler nods and places them down, even though he does not understand what is being said. Maybe he understands the King's English, Private Singh thinks to himself.

Suddenly Himmler picks up the nunchucks again and maintains a stoic silence, meticulously scrutinising them before fixating on the ruby-red stone embedded within one of its handles. Private Singh, initially displaying a hint of apprehension during Himmler's close examination, proceeds to elucidate the significance of this weapon of choice, which are his nunchucks. One of the guards says something in German and makes a gesture holding onto his own wrist.

Private Singh realises what is being said and holds his arm up, highlighting his 'Kara', as he emphasises its constant presence on his person, dictated by religious beliefs. Himmler, devoid of any discernible reaction, gazes at Singh as he narrates, offering no response. Private Singh concludes his explanation, prompting Himmler to delicately place the nunchucks on the desk. He looks at his photographs and after a thorough examination, Himmler strides away to replenish his drink, leaving an air of unspoken tension in the room.

He watches Private Singh in silence with his menacing looks as he stands next to the drinks trolley. He is a short man with dark hair that is shaved around the sides. He resembles a mole with beady little eyes and a boat you want to slap. Not just any old slap, but a proper man slap. You know, the slap which brings clarity to the proceedings when someone is fucking about.

Not on the same page as you, fanning about with the details or the information to hand. You must have been in a situation when someone is dragging their heels about something, and it takes the clotted cream out of your scone, and all you want to do is slap this individual into submission. Well, this is what Himmler needs: a proper bloody man slap. Private Singh glances over at a large dining table with chairs around it. Red velvet curtains hang from the ceiling to the floor; they really contrast against the crystal chandeliers that hang from the ceiling and the stone walls. They also camouflage a wooden door, which is behind them. The door resembles a château-style door, with its arched top and diagonal ribbed panels. The only reason Private Singh notices it as light cascades from underneath it, where could this lead to? He thinks to himself.

By now, Himmler walks back towards the desk and takes his seat as he continues looking at his prisoner throughout this. To the surprise of Private Singh, he asks the two guards to leave them. They are slightly surprised by this and look at one another before they leave, slightly reluctantly. Himmler watches them as they close the door behind them; one stops and looks over at them before he closes the huge wooden door behind him. Trepidation fills the air, as does the silence, only disturbed by the crackling and hissing noises of the open fire as the flames lick the wooden logs. The young soldier opens a desk drawer and removes some writing materials.

"Bruno," Himmler calls out.

Suddenly a large dog appears from the fireplace floor area. It must had been camouflaged by the fur rug. The dog looks like a bloodhound or other. It slowly walks past Private Singh, slightly docile in its manner and sits to the side of Himmler's chair. He starts to play with the dog by rubbing it under the chin and bringing the dog up close towards his own face. It is clear to see Bruno means a lot to him from the affection he is displaying here. They do say a dog is a man's best friend; what about a Nazi's? Himmler talks to Private Singh directly this time. He does not understand any German and looks at him. This is when the young man suddenly starts to speak, as he must be an interpreter. Why did he not intervene earlier within the conversation? Private Singh thinks to himself.

He asks Private Singh if he would like a drink, which he accepts and is told to help himself, after Himmler tells the young interpreter this. Private Singh, at first, reluctantly walks over towards the drinks trolley and pours himself a cognac, not just any old cognac but fine French champagne cognac. The Nazis, during the war, dined on the best food and drinks money could buy, purely due to the fact everything they wanted was liberated, looted, stolen, half-inched, call it what you want. So, the hierarchy enjoyed Beluga caviar, Dom Pérignon champagne, Belgian chocolate, and Italian coffee, to name a few of the delights or spoils of war in their case. Private Singh cannot believe he is chewing the fat and having a drink with Heinrich Himmler himself, and he feels he must pinch himself.

Private Singh offers Himmler another drink, and, as before, the young man translated the gesture. Himmler accepts the offer, so Singh walked over with the bottle of cognac to pour Himmler another drink. He called out to Private Singh, requesting that he leave the bottle and take a seat. This communication flowed through the young man involved in this three-way conversation. Himmler retrieved a gold cigarette case from his military tunic pocket and extended an offer to the prisoner. Politely, Private Singh declined, explaining to Himmler that Sikhs do not smoke due to their religious beliefs. The young man conveyed this information, and Himmler nodded in understanding before lighting a cigarette for himself.

He first blows the smoke in Private Singh's direction, then realises he does not appreciate this and soon changes his direction. Private Singh wonders to himself why he is sitting here with the head of the SS, these cocksuckers who hate anyone who is not a member of the National Socialist German Workers Party, let alone brown-skinned and wearing a turban. What is afoot here, he thinks to himself.

Himmler continues to smoke, just staring at Private Singh; it is like he is sizing him up. His gaze examines his prisoner, from his bushy beard to the neat folds of his turban. Then suddenly, he speaks up, and the young man starts to translate once again. To Private Singh's surprise, he apologises for blowing smoke in his direction. Himmler looks curious and speaks up again, making eye contact with Private Singh. Himmler suddenly stubs out the cigarette in the ashtray, as he continues to glare at him.

The young man asks on behalf of Himmler, why Sikhs do not smoke and why he wears a hat. Private Singh explains that it is a 'Dastar', but it is referred to as a turban within western culture and is not a hat. He must always cover his 'Kesh', or uncut hair hence he wears a 'Dastar'. This three-way conversation delves into Sikhism, its identity, and its core beliefs. He continues to explain that any form of tobacco or intoxicants cannot be inhaled or ingested due to being one of the main four transgressions within Sikhism. The other three being cutting or shaving of hair, consuming 'Kutha' Halal or Kosher slaughtered animal products and adultery. The issue is we are in the middle of a bloody world war, so one must overcome the challenges faced in observing one's religion.

Hence, once the war is over, he would like to become baptised on arriving in the Punjab, observing the way of the 'Khalsa'. Giving up alcohol and becoming a vegetarian, praying in the early hours, and living his life as a humble man. He would practice 'Sewa' which is selfless service to others without the five thieves of Sikhism. Which are lust, wrath, greed, attachment, and ego. Private Singh knows he should not be discussing religion taking into consideration he is having an alcoholic beverage, but it is the situation he finds himself in. Throughout the conversation, Himmler and Private Singh make eye contact, sometimes looking at the young man for answers as they converse.

Himmler learns forward and pours Private Singh another drink, and this three-way conversation continues, but in the back of Private Singh's mind, he thinks, what the hell is happening here? He knows he is a prisoner of war, and the SS are famed for torturing and then killing most of their prisoners. So why is he sitting here, playing house with Heinrich Himmler? He suddenly thinks, what if his drink is laced with something? Panic consumes him slightly, but then it dawns on him that Himmler is drinking from the same bottle, too. There is a sudden knock at the door, and another person walks into the room, and it is a Fräulein. She wears a white blouse tucked into a grey skirt, with nylon tights and black shoes, with her brunette hair in the Gretchen frisur hairstyle. She walks over and whispers something into Himmler's shell-like.

She looks at Private Singh, staring at him in amazement before she turns and leaves. She glances back at Private Singh, who turns and has another butcher's at her. He is surprised she is wearing nylon-seamed tights with a black line running up her pins, the giveaway seeing we are in the middle of a bloody world war. He soon remembers that Nazis love the finer things in life, especially when they have been on the take. Himmler opens a file on his desk and starts to read through it, flicking the pages at speed, the reflection of the documents visible within the reflection of his glasses. He looks up at Private Singh as he scans through the file and stops for another drink. Private Singh sits up in his chair slightly, as he can sense something is coming. Himmler closes the file and removes his glasses, which he wipes with a white handkerchief from his pocket. On placing the glasses back on his face, he lights up another cigarette and looks at him. There is a slight pause before he speaks.

The young man starts to speak after he has finished talking again. Himmler is now asking Private Singh regarding the landings on the day he was captured and if he would divulge further information regarding the Allied plans to him in return, he would be comfortable throughout the remaining part of the war. Private Singh speaks up, making eye contact with Himmler and refuses to give up any information which may put Allied lives at risk, which, to his surprise, Himmler understands. Soon after this is translated, he nods as he replies, and the translation is he would do the same to save German lives. He picks up another file with black and white aerial photographs of the French coastal defences. He points at the images; his voice slightly rises as he highlights something.

The young man quickly translates what is being said again. Himmler continues to talk about how German held territories like France will be fought over till the last German soldier is standing if the Allies try to land on French soil. His temperament changes as his voice escalates, and he continues to point, bending the photographs. He states it will not be as easy as Sicily, as he makes eye contact with Private Singh. The young man continues to translate in his gentle, softly spoken voice, which is the total opposite of portraying Himmler's true feelings on the subject. Passions are running high as the little man's voice continues to screech.

Himmler takes another sip of his drink and picks up the cigarette which has been slowly burning within the ashtray. On inhaling deeply and blowing out the smoke, he looks like it has settled him down slightly as he stares at Private Singh throughout this. Tension fills the air again, and suddenly, the telephone rings on his desk. This cuts the silence, the ringing noise ever so piecing. Himmler answers the telephone and listens; he does not speak again besides saying good morning. Private Singh even knows what this is from fighting against Jerry. Himmler places the handset down, which rocks within the cradle due to the force with which he placed it down with. His mood soon changes again; he becomes calmer, and he continues to smoke. There is a short silence before he starts to talk again. The young man translates the conversation after every sentence is spoken. Himmler mentions the young German soldier Private Singh had helped. He saved his life, and even though he knew he would be captured, he still chose to help the boy. Himmler's steely exterior seems to have relaxed slightly as he starts to talk about the young man.

Hugo Kruger is the name of this young German he had helped. How he is doing now and whose Godson he is and how he saved his life. This means so much to him and the Führer. That is when the penny drops. Private Singh soon realises what this is all about. Why was he helped and tended to within the military hospital and then brought here? Instead of being rounded up with the rest of the prisoners of war and shipped off to some POW camp or even shot like the SS are famed for. Himmler continues to talk about the young soldier and his family and how the boy will one day become a military leader thanks to him, as he saved his life.

Private Singh expressed gratitude towards Himmler for displaying compassion despite being on opposing sides of the conflict. However, as Private Singh contemplates this acknowledgement, a wave of resentment surges through him. He cannot help but find irony in the situation, considering that the same man extending gratitude oversees the mass slaughter of thousands. A sudden surge of anger envelops Private Singh, triggered by the apparent condescension in Himmler's words. The idea of swiftly ending Himmler's life crosses his mind. The silver letter opener resting on the desk becomes an ominous yet tempting tool in his imagination, poised to pierce Himmler's neck and release a macabre cascade of crimson or the red stuff. In other words, drip-drying the Geezer and letting the red stuff leak out. As if sensing the intensity of Private Singh's gaze, Himmler locks eyes with him, acknowledging the shared awareness of the lethal object which sits on the desk so innocently before them.

The atmosphere thickens with anticipation, both men silently sizing each other up, contemplating the imminent consequences. Will Private Singh succumb to the visceral urge to eliminate one of the Führer's high-ranking henchmen? Or will Himmler unleash the guards, sealing Private Singh's fate with probable torture and execution in the Führer's name? An uneasy silence prevails as Himmler pauses in his discourse, realising that Private Singh has not responded to the recent string of sentences. The room holds its breath in a tense stillness, leaving the outcome suspended in the air.

Suddenly, the small door towards the rear of the room underneath the curtains opens, with someone quietly walking through it. The person walks up towards the desk from where Private Singh is sitting. Suddenly, Himmler stood and saluted, putting his open palm upwards at the wrist and clicking his boot heels.

"Mein Führer," Himmler calls out.

"Heil Hitler," the young man calls out.

Suddenly, the young man jumps to his feet and salutes, lofting his outstretched arm into the air with vigour. Private Singh turns to see Adolf Hitler himself, the Führer, to his surprise. The fact that Himmler is saluting someone and is saying, "Mein Führer", should have been the giveaway to Private Singh.

The young man is overwhelmed by the fact he is in the same room as the Führer, let alone breathing the same air as him. He looks star-struck, to say the least. Private Singh, too, stands to reflect an element of respect for the man.

"Hells fucking bells," Private Singh calls out under his breath.

"It's the main man, Adolf fucking Hitler," he adds.

He is firstly surprised to see Adolf Hitler in the flesh but looks equally surprised at the fact that he looks slightly dishevelled, like someone who has seen better days. What he notices is Hitler looks aged and weak, like some washed-out alcoholic. This is the stark reality compared to the propaganda films Goebbels is churning out where the Führer looks like a giant on that stage, powerful, vibrant, and ready to conquer the world. He is wearing a grey pinstripe double-breasted suit jacket, a white shirt with a black tie, and black trousers. Not forgetting his Golden National Socialist German Workers Party lapel pin.

In hushed tones, he gracefully lowers himself into Himmler's chair, gesturing subtly for Private Singh to join him. Himmler, in response, swiftly fetches an extra chair and takes his seat alongside them. The Führer directs his gaze towards the prisoner before him, his eyes betraying a vacancy—a soul seemingly absent. To Private Singh, he appears to be burdened, maybe due to the nefarious activities he was involved in. Hitler taps his finger rhythmically on the file resting on the desk. His head inclined in reflective silence. Dark strands of hair obscure part of his countenance as he fixates on the contents of the dossier. A heavy, quiet blankets the room, punctuated only by the crackling of the open fire. Himmler inquiries about the Führer's preferences, to which he requests tea. With a nod, Himmler reaches for the telephone and arranges for the requested beverage.

The Führer lifts his gaze slowly, scrutinising Private Singh as if deciphering a warrior from a distant realm. He asks how Hugo Kruger is, the young man he saved, and Himmler answers that he is recovering in the hospital in Berlin now. The Führer asks Himmler to send his regards as he has not had the opportunity to see him since it happened. To Private Singh's surprise, the Führer thanks him for saving Hugo's life. This is translated by the young man, who still looks gobsmacked that he is having a four-way conversation with the Führer.

The Führer asks questions about Private Singh's identity, similar to what Himmler had just asked him earlier. The young interpreter answers the questions asked by the Führer, which, to the annoyance of Private Singh, were already translated earlier on. Maybe they are trying to catch him out, he thinks to himself. Then, Adolf Hitler asks why he did not attempt to kill any of them, taking into consideration the letter opener, which is sitting on the edge of the desk. The young man asks him. Private Singh pauses for a moment and then addresses the Führer directly, with the young man translating what he is saying. What Private Singh was not aware of was that the young interpreter had a small handgun pointed at him since he sat down. Maybe this was why the letter opener sat on the desk within his reach, a test to see what transpired. If he lunged forward in some form of attempt to kill the Führer, he would have been mowed down in a hail of bullets anyway.

Private Singh pauses momentarily before he expresses his hatred of the British due to the fact they invaded India which had a significant impact on the country. It was the East India Trading company who first arrived on its shores before the British government took over and the British Raj of India began. How they forced the Indians into poverty, famine and enslaved them. How the British killed at will like the 'Jallianwala Bagh massacre of 1919', when a peaceful gathering during the annual 'Vaisakhi' fair to protest against the 'Rowlatt Act' and the arrest of certain pro-Indian independence activists turned into a bloodbath. Why were defenceless men, women and children mowed down by callous gunfire without any warning. India was the Jewel in the Crown of the British Empire, due to its natural resources, strong military presence, and economic opportunities like the export of goods which were sold for a profit. This helped fund the Industrial Revolution in the United Kingdom. Suddenly his mood changes, he faulters and stops mid-sentence. After a short pause he musters up the strength and goes on about how Sikh soldiers were the backbone of the British army but were only thought of as 'cannon fodder' by the hierarchy.

They were the first wave of attack in many iconic theatres of war, like Somme, Gallipoli, and now fighting in Burma against the Japanese. How the British officers and fellow soldiers verbally and physically abused the Indian soldiers throughout training and the battlefield. He told the Führer how they were labelled as Sepoys, the term highlighting a foreign soldier severing under the crown. His voice becomes high-pitched, and the rage is apparent to see.

The Führer and Himmler listened quietly as Private Singh poured out his heart to the last two men on earth, he thought he would be having a chinwag with. He speaks with conviction, tearful at one stage due to the death of his brothers in arms fighting for the British. How he was sick of the British, how they felt they were superior to others, and how this small Island decided to rule a percentage of the world. He knows deep down this is something similar to what the Führer is doing now, but he is heavy-hearted and needs someone to express his views to lighten the load. Private Singh takes another drink of cognac and pours another rather large one that he throws down his throat.

Before he delicately wipes away his tears with a handkerchief retrieved from his pocket, a hush descends upon the room. The Führer breaks the silence, locking eyes with him. He commends the soldier, acknowledging his bravery, moral compass, and principled actions that saved his Godson Hugo's life. The young interpreter conveys these sentiments in a gentle yet confident tone as Hitler resumes speaking. Expressing a desire to spend more time together, Hitler extends a job offer, proposing that the prisoner become his driver. Curiosity lingers as the Führer questions the discovery of a chess piece among the Sikh's possessions. Private Singh responds, explaining that the king chess piece he carries symbolises a Sikh soldier. The turban, a Sikh's crown, signifies a commitment to defend against any adversary. With conviction, Private Singh shares insights about Sikhs as warriors, members of a young religion only four hundred and seventy-odd years old yet rooted in peace.

He emphasises the teachings of humility, truthful living, selfless service, and the importance of equality for mankind.

Additionally, he reveals his passion for chess, portraying it as a valuable skill applicable on the battlefield. The room absorbs these words, bridging the gap between cultures and ideologies.

Himmler and the Führer continue to listen as the young man translates what is being said here. For some reason, it strikes accord with the Führer, who takes a liking to this man who is sitting opposite him. A man who could have easily tried to assassinate him but chose to display peace and humility. The Führer, too, has a love for chess, which Private Singh was unaware of, which he tells him about. He produces Private Singh's chess piece and places it on the desk, which he leans forward and takes hold of. His face lights up as he admires his chess piece. The Führer turns to Himmler, and they talk, but the young man does not translate what is being said this time. Private Singh obviously realises this and thinks it is something they do not want him to understand. The two men converse in German before the Führer again turns towards Private Singh.

Suddenly, the Fräulein from earlier enters with a tea tray and walks over towards the side desk. She places the tray down, pours a cup of tea, and walks over towards the Führer with it. She verbally salutes him and carefully places the cup on the desk. They converse in German before she smiles and leaves the room. The Führer picks up his fine bone China cup and saucer. Taking a sip of tea from the cup, he places it down. He calls out something in German, which the interpreter repeats in English. The Führer is interested in the tea supply from India and China. Which Private Singh is slightly taken aback by, as they are in the middle of a bloody world war and the Führer is interested in cornering the world's tea market.

The Führer takes another sip of tea and places the cup down again. He looks up at Private Singh and starts to talk again, with the young man translating. The Führer highlights his interest in meeting with him again to play chess and chat about India and Sikhism. He expresses his interest and how he would like to learn about this alternative religion. Himmler, by now, is standing behind where the Führer is seated, like some form of protector here to save the old fella from this threat which sits opposite him. He looks intrigued by the appearance of the prisoner before him and cannot stop just staring at him. It is like he is sizing him up, studying him in a way.

The Führer has a menacing stare about him; his dark eyes look lifeless without a soul. What do you expect after all that murdering of innocent human beings which is taking place? It has to affect the soul somehow. The silence fills the air and soon becomes uncomfortable as the two men look at one another. This is only broken by the ringing of the telephone; Himmler moves from behind the Führer and answers it. He places the telephone handset back, learns in towards the Führer, and whispers something into his ear. Adolf Hitler continues to look at Private Singh throughout this conversation, not breaking eye contact, which makes it slightly uncomfortable for him. Private Singh thinks something is up. Why are they talking and looking at him? Trepidation consumes him as he knows of Adolf Hitler's mood swings and volatile temperament.

So, within a heartbeat, he could be arrested by the boys in black, hanged, drawn, and quartered. Yeah, alright, we all know that Jerry does not do this, but their reputation does precede them when it comes to disposing of people in gruesome ways; that's where the SS come in. We have all heard the stories around the campfire, noshing down our army rations about the SS and what the Gestapo do to their prisoners. He is slightly apprehensive at this new so-called offer of friendship by the deranged little Geezer across the desk to him. Maybe he is trying to help Private Singh, who feels the same after fighting for the British after they invaded India. While this train of thought is still rattling around his noggin, suddenly, a portly-looking man, with a receding hairline and glasses enters the room, who looks like some form of medical physician or other.

It is only Theodor Morell who is carrying a sleek black leather bag reminiscent of a doctor's satchel. The Führer rises from his seat, flanked by Himmler and this studious companion. Private Singh observes, noting a pallor in the Führer's demeanour, perhaps a manifestation of stress or illness. The weight of governing a nation, waging war on two fronts, and engaging in genocide undoubtedly takes its toll, a formidable challenge even for the most resilient of leaders. The Nazi figure, seemingly weathered by time, prompts Private Singh to reflect on the circulating rumours. Could it be true that Adolf Hitler relies on substances to endure the demands of his role?

The German army was renowned for its drug use. How can a soldier fight day and night without a break and keep on going? Pertin was used regularly by the Nazis, which was discovered by us when German soldiers were captured and searched. This was often discovered on them. I'm sure some Tommies must have had a go at this wonder drug; it's only human nature. We commonly used amphetamines and barbiturates, too, but only certain officers got their grubby little mitts on cocaine. Not like the Führer, he loved being injected with marching powder. How do you think he fought a war on two fronts? It probably kept the old motor running.

Where were we before interrupting our train of thought? Oh yeah. Private Singh stands up, too, as Adolf Hitler turns and looks at him again as he reaches the door, waiting for the guard to open it. The young interpreter jumps to his feet and salutes, clicking his boot heels with vigour, as he places a small handgun down on the desk before him to Private Singh's surprise.

"Heil Hitler!" he calls out.

The huge wooden doors open, and the two original guards walk back into the room. They, too, salute their Führer with vigour. Adolf Hitler looks over at them all without any form of reaction. Private Singh decides to nod his head towards the Führer to show some form of respect towards him. The Führer mumbles something, and Himmler asks him what he said.

"Bayerischer Löwe," he calls out.

The young man translates and calls out "Bavarian Lion".

The Führer stops and glares at Private Singh momentarily before he leaves the room. Himmler is slightly baffled by the Führer's comments and looks over. This is before the Führer and Theodor Morell both leave. The two guards walk over and stand on either side of their prisoner, who is still standing at the desk. He is slightly uneasy on his feet due to his wounded leg but held onto the desk to steady himself. On returning into the room, Himmler walked towards the drinks trolley and poured another drink. He sits back down behind the desk and lights up another cigarette.

He stares at Private Singh without saying anything for a while before he stubs out his cigarette after only a few drags. He starts to speak once again as the young man translates. Himmler tells them of the Führer's plan to meet with Private Singh in Berlin in one week, during which Hugo Kruger will be present. This is the young German soldier he saved from a sure death, thanks to his humanity, as the Führer had put it earlier. The Führer wants Hugo to thank him personally for saving his life. He also would like to know about Hugo's recovery process. Private Singh is taken aback by what he is being told regarding the meeting with the Führer in Berlin. Private Singh was under the apprehension that he was in Berlin as the doctor had told him. When he asked where he was today, he was surprised to find out he was in Munich. Maybe the Führer had business here, he thought to himself.

Private Singh arrived in Berlin a week later to have this so-called meeting with the Führer. He had returned to the French countryside, where he was originally captured. He now had cast iron travel documents, all thanks to Himmler's office. He wanted to thank the doctor who saved his life; hence he asked to travel back here. He was naturally given a chaperone who drove and translated for him. Often, Private Singh would go for midnight walks when his chaperone rested his eyes after far too much schnapps. They played chess together and drank late into the evenings to pass the time. His wound had nearly healed by now, to his relief. Part of him does not know what to make of this, but he harbours a concern that something is afoot here. Maybe, on the other hand, the Führer is just intrigued by him.

The distinctive appearance of a Sikh male, adorned with a turban and full beard, seems to have caught his attention. So, a week later, now in Berlin, he is directed to wait in a cosy café connected to the military hospital where Hugo is undergoing treatment. Positioned at a table, flanked by two guards, the café boasts black and white tiled floors and pristine white walls. The traditional dark wood furniture, including a high counter, contributes to the café's classic charm. A gleaming chrome coffee machine featuring a golden eagle on the front of it commanded attention on the countertop. Artwork with an aesthetic reminiscent of German propaganda posters lined the walls.

While Private Singh cannot decipher the text, the imagery speaks volumes. There is one particularly vivid scene: a soaring eagle poised to confront a hat-wearing rat with the 'Star of David' around its neck, concealed beneath the floorboards. The symbolism appears clear: the eagle, a representation of the resilient German people, contrasts sharply with the elusive rat, likely symbolising the Jews, hiding in a dark and evasive sewer. The stark visual metaphor captures the essence of what is being said here. Do you know what I mean, Harry?

Two young ladies are on service, and one walks towards his table with a cup of coffee. She places it down on the table and walks away. Private Singh thanks her, smiling before he picks up one sugar cube, dropping it into the cup, and stirs it with a small silver teaspoon. He knocks the spoon against the side of the cup and places the spoon down on the saucer before he takes a sip. It is an espresso coffee in a small cup.

He has never experienced anything like this before and finds it slightly odd to have something this small. After taking a second small sip, he places the cup down onto the saucer but the intense flavour hits him as does the aroma. Private Singh is a tea drinker, not any old tea mind but a cup of cha, that Indian art form of boiling water, adding loose leaf tea, then milk and other spices to boil on the shove for a good twenty minutes before you serve it. Yeah, many non-Indians who drink this hot beverage of choice normally complain that the milk tastes like it is burnt.

This is how traditionally tea is drunk within India and how the entire population of Indian soldiers who serve under the Union Jack like it.

Suddenly, an officer walked into the café, and the two guards saluted him. They both click their boot heels and salute him with their raised arms. He, in return, salutes them by raising his hand with an open palm.

"Heil Hitler!" They call out.

"Heil Hitler," he replies.

He asks Private Singh to follow him, and the four of them leave. Private Singh smiles once again at the young lady who brought over his expresso coffee earlier as she stands drying crockery behind the counter, but she just stares at him. They follow the German officer outside into a cobbled courtyard area, where an assortment of military vehicles are parked up. Medical vehicles come and go, ferrying injured soldiers. Private Singh watches as medical staff carry new patients from these vehicles into the hospital. Some can walk while others are being helped or carried out on stretchers.

These Krauts look well and truly defeated; the look on their boats is the true giveaway. They look like they have had enough of the fighting, a right gutful at that. They enter the hospital via a side corridor, but the medical emergency room's hustle and bustle is evident. Some patients groan in pain, as others are screaming due to their injuries. One German soldier washes the blood-covered floor, brushing water over it. He stops as the officer and the three men following walk over his hard graft. He stops and salutes the officer without conviction. Again, he looks like a beaten man.

Private Singh knows if this could be screened back in London, it would boost morale, seeing the Krauts beaten like this. He knows there are as many of these field hospitals like this one, which are full to the rafters with injured and dying Allied troops too. Nurses rush around their patients, trying to frantically save as many lives as possible. Private Singh looks solemn as he watches the injured soldiers being treated. What we can do to one another in the name of war is shocking. He thinks to himself.

They finally reach a small service lift, where the two escorting guards are asked to remain outside. The officer and Private Singh both enter the small space, and the officer pulls across the metal safety rail before pressing a button. The lift starts to move downwards with a jarring movement. Private Singh looks at the German officer. Within seconds of pressing the button, it stops with a jolt. The officer pushes back the metal safety rail and gestures for Private Singh exit the lift. To Singh's surprise, they are within a basement under the hospital by the looks of it. It does not resemble a basement, though; it has an Art Deco, mid-century feel to it. Walnut panels line the walls, with rich carpet and wall lights in that distant style. Green plants sit on the other side of the corridor, resembling a hotel lobby over it being in wartime and a basement underneath a military hospital. The stark reality of war, the death and destruction, feels a million miles away compared to these opulent surroundings Private Singh finds himself in.

The officer leads the way towards the only door at the end of this corridor. Two armed guards stand either side of the doorway with a steely look about them. They both salute the officer before them. The officer knocks and pauses momentarily before he opens the door. Adolf Hitler and Heinrich Himmler sit on armchairs around a mirrored and gold coffee table. They are both dressed in grey tricot military tunics, with matching trousers. The armchairs they sit on have walnut-detailed arms which wrap around from the front to the back with luxurious embroidered fabric. A chess board sits on a glass table to the side of the Führer, ready for a game to be played. This brings a smile to Private Singh's boat. A third man sits with them; his back is turned towards the door.

As the officer introduces Private Singh, the third man turns around within his seat. It is Hugo Kruger, the young man he saved. Hugo is dressed in a black Hitler youth uniform as his insignias are different from the normal military uniforms Private Singh has seen. He is still wearing his British military uniform, to Hugo's surprise. He jumps to his feet and, to Private Singh's amazement, embraces him tightly and thanks him. Hugo is near tearful as emotions become highly charged within the room.

Private Singh nods at him in acceptance of his appreciation of what he did. Even though Private Singh cannot understand what the young German is saying, his body language and mannerisms give it away. But hang on a minute, Private Singh is sure; he spoke broken English to him when they conversed on their first meeting. The meeting where this rooting totting Geezer was, waving a small shooter about, threatening a group of young Jewish kids. So, Private Singh goes along with this charade or whatever this game Hugo is playing here. Maybe the Führer is not aware that he speaks the King's lingo. Also, Singh noticed he has no visible head wounds as he was definitely a casualty of war, when they last met. Something is afoot here he thinks to himself.

"Look at you, boy, you're looking pukka now," Private Singh calls out.

"The belle of the ball," he adds.

"Danke, Tommy," Hugo replies.

"Danke," he adds.

"You can thank me later when we have a proper chinwag," Private Singh replies.

Private Singh admires Hugo, acknowledging that he owes his current well being to him, realising he might not had made it if it were not for Hugo. As they all take their seats, a delightful surprise awaits Private Singh: a cream tea is brought out. A display stand adorned with scones, clotted cream, jam, and an assortment of sandwiches follows, an unexpected departure from typical German fare.

Private Singh contemplates the cultural awareness of the German high society, noting their appreciation for fine French bubbles and Russian caviar. The German officer who accompanied Private Singh begins translating the conversation. After exchanging pleasantries, Adolf Hitler introduces Hugo Kruger as a prospective officer of the Waffen-SS. How Hugo will play his part within the Thousand Year Reich. Amidst the enjoyment of the cream tea, Private Singh relishes the fresh ham, a rare treat for him after eating army rations.

However, the Führer abstains from eating, focusing intently with lifeless eyes as the others indulge in the spread before them. The Führer suddenly starts to talk about Hugo's military achievements so far and what a good prospect he is for being an officer within the Wehrmacht, let alone the Waffen-SS. That is when Himmler charges his cup in a toast to the young man. The Führer continues talking about Hugo and his childhood and how they often went out together, meeting up at the Cologne Cathedral. He boasts that he helped Hugo paint the Cathedral on canvas and how good the brush strokes were. Hugo becomes slightly embarrassed by some of the comments the Führer expresses. Himmler interjects with his own story of when Hugo once ate apple strudel till, he was sick.

Then he goes on to set Hugo a small challenge before he was injured in France to prove he could join the ranks of the SS. Then it dawned on Private Singh, and this is what Hugo was doing with a truckload of Jewish prisoners, which he presumed were all to be executed as per the orders from Himmler himself. The officer translates the conversation taking place; the mood is very jovial, with smiles and a lot of back-slapping for Hugo. Himmler comments on how he knows Hugo's family well. After his father was killed towards the end of the Great War, Himmler felt it was his duty to look out for the family and his Godson. Himmler places his hand on Hugo's and taps it a few times jokingly. Suddenly, Hugo looks slightly uncomfortable with this and moves his hand away slowly.

The Führer is too busy drinking his tea to notice, but Private Singh does. Maybe there is something in their past that Hugo is not comfortable with. Private Singh's mind starts to race at what it could be. What if Hugo is Himmler's lovechild, he thinks to himself? That's it, Hugo's father had gone off to fight the British, and Himmler could have been getting his size eights under the table. Himmler does talk about the family and was often there when Hugo was a child. Maybe he had spent time with the family after he had found out that Hugo was his. He is a chip off the old block, taking into consideration he had murdered a truckful of Jews or had a hand in it.

Suddenly, Private Singh's blood starts to boil, thinking about what Himmler had requested this young boy to do. Hugo was still a young boy himself who had been sent to do a man's job. Himmler then turns his attention towards Private Singh and mentions that he had already been communicating with a man from his shores. Himmler explains that this person was willing to fight for the German army and was of Indian origin, too. He continues about how certain prisoner-of-war camps are full of Sikhs and other ethnic soldiers who fought for the British and were now ready to fight under the Nazi swastika. They were willing to pledge their allegiance to the Führer, Adolf Hitler. Himmler continues to talk about how he and the Führer are contemplating launching a new division of these soldiers to fight in upcoming campaigns. Private Singh is flabbergasted by the news, as he wants to revolt against the British and push them out of India but had not thought of joining forces with the Nazis. He wonders who this man could be that Himmler is talking of.

The Führer abruptly requests that Hugo leave, deeming the information unsuitable for his young ears. Hugo bids his farewell, shaking Private Singh's hand once more, before exiting the room. The German officer translates the ongoing conversation between the men. With Hugo's exclusion, Private Singh perceives the significance of this new strategy for the Nazi war machine. Could this be an opportunity to solidify ties with the Nazis and establish a new partnership? Private Singh contemplates the potential of leveraging the discussions between the other Indian gentleman and Himmler to his advantage. Perhaps he could exploit this information not only to join forces with the Germans against the British but, more crucially, to oust them from India with Nazi support.

They would pay for what they had done, pay for all the death and destruction of his motherland. For the atrocities, the British had carried out all the killings, the rapes and the theft of precious diamonds, emeralds, gold and land under the guise of 'The Raj'. How Indian people were enslaved within their own country by the foreign invaders. This made him even more determined to unite with the Germans and overthrow the British out of India. Eventually India would elect its own parliament to run the country. Germany naturally would help build its military forces and the Führer would have his supply of tea and other natural resources. You know the old chestnut of you, scratch my back and all that, cobblers. Seeing the SS recruited non-Germans from 'inferior races' as part of their ideology. The Waffen-SS often swelled its ranks with volunteers and conscripts from Europe and beyond.

So, the new Indian Division of fighting men would be an extension of this. The more he thought about it, the more sense it made. After just listening to the two men for nearly an hour now, he decides that this platform could offer him the chance to launch an attack on the British. He starts to talk about the Allied plans he was engaged in and how they were going to attack. As the officer translates the conversation, this piques the interest of the Nazis present, who, like English pisshead officers of the East India Company having a dirty Ruby in some Indian palace before the British Raj. You know the sort, only wanting butter chicken, quaffing down beers and only wanting more, bloody poppadoms. They salivate around the chops due to this offering of information served up by Private Singh without the mango chutney.

He tells the Nazis present all he knows and how he participated within the operation when he was dropped into France. To the amazement of Hitler and Himmler, he sang like a lark. They lapped up what was on offer, Himmler reassuring him this new Indian division would be pushed through quickly. The Führer was slightly more hesitant to begin with, but once Private Singh spilled his guts, he soon came around, too. The meeting was simple for Hugo to thank this soldier from other shores for saving his life, but now it had become the inception of something different.

Himmler assured Private Singh they will meet again and discuss this matter further. The Führer, on the other hand, wants to play chess and, through an interpreter, wants to find out more about this man who is sitting before him. To the Führer's surprise, Private Singh tells the men that chess originated in India in the sixteenth century. It was called Chaturanga or Catur, featuring similar pieces to the modern-day game they play today. This golden nugget of information impresses the Führer further as he sits staring at Private Singh throughout the conversation.

Private Singh is advised that the chess board had been brought in, especially for him. Unfortunately, the Führer will be leaving soon, and they will have to lock horns on another occasion. Suddenly, the Führer asks if Private Singh would drive him around on visits to German-occupied territories. He jumps at the chance, especially if this could lead to a division of Indian soldiers who could fight the British and pay them back for what they had done. The officer translating concludes the meeting by advising Private Singh that the Führer would like him to be ready for duty by the weekend, which he agrees to. Private Singh stands as the three men get up to leave the room; they walk towards the door. Private Singh only disturbs the silence by suddenly calling out.

"Down with the British." Private Singh calls out.

"Heil Hitler!" he adds.

The three men are surprised by this sudden outburst, especially the Führer himself, as he understands the verbal salute to him. He turns and nods his head in appreciation. The officer and Himmler reply and physically salute, even though Private Singh does not.

"Heil Hitler," they reply.

It seemed like he wanted to gain their reaction. After a short pause, they all leave the room, and Private Singh sits back down. He picks up a strawberry and takes a bite, as he had not consumed much fresh fruit since the war started. This bright red juicy strawberry was calling his name, so he took another bite. He had been looking at this bad boy throughout the meeting. You know, when you see something, and you just need to get your laughing gear around it. As he bites into the strawberry, sweet juice cascades from it, only furthering his enjoyment.

Only Himmler and the officer return to Private Singh's surprise, as he is still eating. Himmler asks if he would mind waiting for a minute as he wants to discuss something with him. Himmler asks Private Singh what he thinks of Hugo, now the Führer is not present. He tells him that he looks like a good young man who will go far within the German army. This pleases Himmler, who smiles and lights up a cigarette for himself.

As he smokes it, he looks over at Private Singh before moving his chair slightly forward, closer towards him. He wants to tell Private Singh that Hugo Kruger is a special young man, and saving his life meant a lot to him personally. He is very thankful that he had come along that day and showed him mercy, which resulted in him saving his life. If it was not for him, he could have died from his wounds. The wounds Private Singh could not see any evidence of. His mind starts to race at what the Nazis are up to Suddenly, Private Singh's earlier thoughts come rushing back to him regarding Himmler relationship with Hugo's mother. There must be a reason for this conversation to be taking place. Himmler shifts the discussion to Hugo's childhood, recounting day trips to other cities and moments spent at the coast before the war. The memories he reflects upon appear fond, to say the least. Himmler, not typically displaying emotion, reveals a different facet of himself when delving into Hugo's past. He then transitions to Hugo's mother, Lena, detailing their meeting many years ago, just before she encountered Hugo's father.

Himmler talks about how he had danced the night away with Lena before she met Oswald, his father at, some party event or other. He revisited the night of the gala dinner, which was held in Munich, where the SS were the guests of honour, and they were young and danced the night away. Himmler mentions Lena's flawless beauty, pale complexion, and the necklace he gave her, which highlighted her blue eyes. The flowing ball gown she wore, in black, moved a certain way when they danced. How they danced the Waltz, the Tango and other classical dance steps that night.

They danced in the empty ballroom into the early hours, even without any music playing. He fondly remembers her carrying her shoes in her hands, not before he swept her off her feet and carried her to her bedroom. This is where they sat sipping champagne, talking about life, love, and the future of Germany till sunrise. The officer translates what is being said but looks slightly uncomfortable as this story is very personal.

Himmler goes on to say that he had never felt so connected to someone in his life as he did with Lena Kruger. He mentions she met and fell in love with Oswald, and he went off to war. They never saw each other for years till Oswald's death after he returned home after the Great War ended. With his funeral being held in Berlin. This was the first time he had seen her since that night in Munich. It brought everything flooding back to him how they had felt for one another.

Himmler stares into the yonder with an expression on his boat. He pauses for a while. He suddenly clears his voice and pauses when he talks of her death in an air raid. The officer acting as an interpreter finds it slightly uncomfortable further as Himmler pours his heart out, but he continues. Private Singh feels certain things are being lost in translation here, as Himmler's emotions are on fire as he explains what happened. What Private Singh cannot comprehend is why Himmler is pouring his heart out to him, considering they have only met a few times. Maybe it was due to the fact that he had saved young Hugo's life. The translation does not have the same element of passion to it. Himmler continues of Lena's death and how the house collapsed, and she died, buried under the rubble; this was thanks to the RAF, of course. Suddenly, his tone changes again to the brash exterior without any emotion on show like normal. This is the Himmler the world saw, but for a moment, when he was talking earlier, there was a different being on display.

He stubs out his cigarette, which had been slowly burning in the ashtray, while he conversed with Private Singh. Suddenly, he stands up and briskly straightens his uniform. He asks Private Singh if he had heard of a group of ladies who were killing German soldiers, who were dressed as nuns. This is translated for Private Singh, who nods his head and advises him that he had just landed in France. Himmler just glares at him before he informs Private Singh that they will reconvene to discuss the other matter in greater detail soon. Private Singh rises as well, nodding at Himmler, who turns and abruptly exits the room, leaving Singh surprised.

Following the weekend, Private Singh is standing next to a Mercedes salon car, not just any old car but Adolf Hitler's personal mode of transport. He is now dressed in a suit and looks extremely smart in his appearance. He wears a black single-breasted suit, white shirt, black tie and his newly polished military boots. They even provided him with a black turban to match his outfit. He wonders where they must have got it from, and then it dawned on him that it must had belonged to another Sikh soldier, who had probably met with his demise.

The turban had been dyed, highlighting to him the effort they had made for him. For some reason, Private Singh refuses to wear a German uniform till the Führer himself can launch this division of Sikh soldiers to fight under the Nazi swastika. Maybe, just maybe, he does not want to be shot by the British as a spy, nor any trigger-happy Kraut who has not been conversed in who he is. The car is gleaming, all polished chrome, and it smells of new leather when it is freshly buffed. He adjusts himself slightly as he waits for the party to arrive. German soldiers give him looks, as most of them have not seen a turban-wearing Sikh, let alone one who is friends with the Führer.

The Nazi swastika banners flap within the breeze as they hang from the front of the building, the bright red so vibrant against the old stonework. He looks around at the soldiers who are lined up for military parade. These Nazis look immaculate, with nothing out of place, all pressed and dressed. Suddenly, he hears talking, and the Führer and his party of high-ranking officers appear at the top of the stairs. The chatter is jovial; he cannot make out what they are saying, but it seems pleasant, though. He uses body language as a tool to partially understand what is being said. Joseph Goebbels points at something and then puts his hands up to catch something like a film director does. You know what I mean when they form a square with their fingers to replicate a film frame.

With him being this newly found saviour of the German film industry, he churns out many propaganda flicks to his heart's content. As they make their way down the stairs, Private Singh is slightly nervous about meeting the famous five in one sitting. Their reputation proceeds them but saying that he is already chummy with Adolf Hitler and Heinrich Himmler, who are probably the worst of the bunch, so the others should be like a piece of Stolen fruit cake, he thinks to himself.

As they reach the car, out of respect, he nods his head at the party as the Führer introduces him. Goebbels stares at him, Herman Göring lifts his Reich Marschall's baton, and Martin Bormann nods, too. The men are all dressed in ceremonial military uniforms, each with its own insignias and matching visor caps. The men all converse in German while looking at Private Singh; he knows they are talking about him. The one thing he's noticed about the German people is they are quite direct. He found people often stared at him due to his identity and did not hide the fact that he looked different to them. But they did not say anything like the British often did, with their one-liners of verbal abuse.

Himmler requests that the other three men sit in the second car, and suddenly, Goebbels speaks up, requesting to be seated in the first car. Again, Private Singh picks this up from how they are talking, and the hand gestures being conducted. Goebbels asks Himmler to take a seat in the second vehicle. Himmler pauses and looks at him before smiling; you can see the disgruntlement slapped across his chops. Private Singh wonders why all five Rockstars are together in one place and how easy it could be for the RAF to drop a bomb on them. Firstly, these events are meticulously planned months in advance and the locations are kept secret till the last minute and all the guests are screened by Himmler's - SS. So, no information could be leaked, so Private Singh disregards his thoughts of bombs dropping due to this.

There is a slight tension between the two men for some reason. Private Singh quickly opens the rear door, and the Führer and Goebbels both take a seat. The remaining three men are seated within the second car, with Himmler staring at Goebbels as he enters the first vehicle. Himmler glares at him, with an air of resentment. Once everyone is seated, Private Singh starts the engine and selects the gear. It is all on the wrong side compared to Blighty, but he soon gets the hang of it. They start to drive as the German soldiers salute their Führer, who has stood up by now and is doing his public relations thing, smiling, and waving. Private Singh notices Goebbels staring at him via the rear-view mirror as they continue to drive.

The vehicle carrying the cinematographer and his crew positions itself to the side, just ahead enough to capture all the unfolding events on film. Goebbels strategically exploits these occurrences to enhance the party's popularity and underscore the ongoing war effort. This propaganda is wielded to boost morale among the ranks and garner continued support for Führer's actions, particularly during a period marked by numerous assassination attempts on his life. Goebbels is attired in a brown double-breasted suit jacket, complemented by a white shirt and black tie, while the Führer dons a detailed grey uniform. What truly captures Private Singh's attention is Goebbels' slicked-back dark hair and his unwavering, menacing stare that remains fixed in his direction. Goebbels showcased traits of an improper and facinorous man to Private Singh.

They make their way down the main street into a plaza area, where members of the public have gathered to welcome their Führer. Both cars drive around a large stone water fountain and stop before a raised stage area, which looks like it has been constructed for some form of ceremony or other. As the vehicles stop, a few Gestapo-looking Geezers make an appearance as they mingle among the crowds of people, as do SS-officers. We presume it is for the safety of the Führer and his party.

Private Singh exits the vehicle and walks towards the rear, opening the Führer's door. Who leaves the vehicle, followed by Goebbels, who stops again and stares at Private Singh. This makes him feel rather uncomfortable. They both make their way towards the crowds, like the other three men from the second car. A small girl approaches the Führer and gives him a bouquet; he places his hand on her head. Camera flashes go off as the event is being recorded for propaganda. A few people within the crowd notice Private Singh and look over. One small boy points at him, with the man accompanying him suddenly pulling his arm downwards. He, too, looks over at this being from another shore, which stands before them all.

A few more photographs are taken, and hands shook, before the party make their way onto the stage. They all take their places, with the Führer taking centre stage; he starts to make a passionate speech. Private Singh watches as he stands by the car, how the Führer's body language changes when he is faced with an audience. Two huge Nazi swastika banners hang from high up, with a golden swastika disk with an eagle perched on top of it. The Nazi swastika, with its red, black and white, which is a symbol of death and destruction, is a far cry from the angelic Hindu symbol of peace, which it seems to be based on. This is the backdrop to the Führer's stage as he makes his speech, which is being recorded again.

Then, a group of German soldiers are ushered onto the stage, and they line up to the side. Some look nervous, while others look overwhelmed by the whole event. Private Singh continues to watch when a German soldier with an Alsatian dog appears. The dog sniffs around the car tyres and Private Singh's shiny military boots.

The dog senses something, but his handler is more interested in the man who stands before him, and he pulls the dog back. The German soldier mumbles something under his breath as his facial expression changes when he clapped eyes on Private Singh. The dog starts to bark again but is pulled away by the soldier. This is only interrupted by the crowd's clapping noise as the Führer finishes his speech. The German soldiers are called forward one by one, saluting the Führer and given an Iron Cross medal, each for bravery. A photographer takes pictures as this takes place till everyone has received their medals. The noise of the crowd clapping and cheering crescendos as the Führer presents the last medal.

After the applause settles, the party makes their way off the stage and into another grand-looking building. The crowd slowly disburses, and the soldiers are ordered to leave as they all march and get into a military truck. Two of the Gestapo men stand smoking and stare over towards the direction of Private Singh. He senses they are talking about him, and for some reason, the German people cannot hide the fact he looks different compared to them. They seem to stand and stare, like what Goebbels had been doing since he clapped eyes on him. This is different from what he has experienced within Blighty; most English people will make a comment between themselves and snigger in jest. At least the German people stare without the bigoted commentary he has become accustomed to within Blighty.

Sikhs do not make bigoted and opinionated comments about the English now, do they? A German soldier walks over towards Private Singh; he offers him a cigarette but speaks English in a thick accent. Private Singh is firstly surprised that he can speak the King's English but kindly refuses his offer of the cigarette. They start to converse about what is happening today.

"Hello, fella," Private Singh calls out.

"Englischer, neger?" the German soldier asks.

"No, son, I'm not a negro; I'm a Sikh."

"I'm a Sikh, Indian," he adds.

"Oh," The German soldier replies.

After a brief pause, the German soldier nods. The tense atmosphere dissipates as he informs Private Singh that the group is heading for lunch, and he will be stationed here for several hours. Suddenly, without any warning, he reveals a shrapnel-damaged torso by lifting his shirt; the German soldier explains that he was on the front but got injured. He shares a sentiment common among many German people: being weary of the war and yearning to return home to their families. Nervously glancing around, he takes note of the Gestapo leather-clad individuals present before expressing his feelings.

He asks Private Singh about his turban and where he is from, but the million Reichsmark question is, how is he driving the Führer about? Private Singh explains how he saved the life of a young German soldier who is the Godson of the Führer, who wanted to meet him, and that is how he is now standing here chatting to him. The German soldier tells of how the conditions are on the Eastern Front, how men are going stir-crazy fighting the cold, lack of provisions and the Russians with a sombre look slapped across his chops.

He goes on to explain the party is now sitting in this grand hall, having a slap-up meal with all the trimmings, while the German soldiers have little to no food and are expected to fight on throughout any condition they face. He quickly flicks his cigarette to the floor and straightens up as two SS-officers walk by. He salutes them, and one raises his hand in return. The first one glares at Private Singh, while the other says something in German, before they both have a good old butcher's at him.

The German soldier tells Private Singh that the British soldiers are hated by the German people for what has happened. Private Singh asks what he means by this. The German soldier tells him that a unit of British soldiers have been dropped into France; they are going around killing German soldiers. Private Singh tells him this is war, and you expect there to be deaths once the fighting starts. The German soldier looks around, slightly nervously, before he continues to talk. He tells Private Singh these men are not just killing German soldiers. They are beating, torturing, and even placing explosives into certain bodily parts, which even the purest of German pilsners cannot even reach.

These loveable rouges then stood by and admired their handiwork. The German soldier in question here exploded for fun; this is their way of killing them softy, he presumed. His voice suddenly becomes higher pitched, with elements of agitation, as he lights himself another cigarette. His hand trembles, making this difficult, as he steadies it with the other hand while making eye contact with Private Singh.

"Blitzkrieg Tommies," he calls out.

"Verdammte FuBsoldaten des Teufels," he adds.

"Who are they?" Private Singh asks.

"Devil's soldiers," he replies.

He explains they are devils, like the 'Fräuleins of Death', which have been sent here to kill them all. They are here to punish the German army for their sins. He continues to smoke nervously, and his hand continues to shake as he speaks.

Private Singh can see the torment this is causing him as he continues. He goes on to tell Private Singh that there is talk of the Führer drafting a new division of SS-soldiers to hunt these Tommies down. Himmler will personally oversee these SS-soldiers from around The Fatherland, they will be the best within their divisions. They will be grouped together, so the best German skills can hunt and kill these English dogs. These SS-soldiers will be trained within a secret facility in Berlin somewhere; they will have the latest weapons and technology available. Private Singh asks what he means by this. He moves closer towards him and speaks in a softer voice.

The Führer is testing new drugs and scientific methods on these soldiers, which will make them better fighters. They will be stronger, faster in recovery after injury and more deadly than any German soldier before them.

"Hitler's Sturmtruppen," he calls out.

He adamantly insists that the Tommies will be killed but then abruptly changes his stance. Shaking his head, he declares they will not succeed in eliminating these 'Blitzkrieg Tommies', claiming them to be the devil's spawn.

The German soldiers are gripped by tales of the Tommies' atrocities and incessantly discuss them, fearful of facing the wrong side of their blade, bullets, or even a cricket bat. When Private Singh enquiries about the Tommies' last known location, the response is uncertain. The informant elaborates that they are elusive, skilled in explosives and hand-to-hand combat, and towering in stature like giants. Private Singh reflects that, whatever these Tommies are, they've certainly unnerved Jerry

Chapter Four: Slayings of Sainte – Geneviève – des – Bois

Meanwhile, somewhere in Nazi-occupied France the Tommies continued to conduct many silent but deadly attacks, like the changing of road signs, which caused a logistical nightmare for the transportation needs of the German army. Cutting of phone lines on a regular basis, which again caused Jerry issues. Their most daring of raids was the blowing up of the fuel reverses, which the Tiger and Panzer divisions were so reliant on. The rumour was, Rommel was proper displeased by this. They entered by overpowering a tank crew who had stopped for a piss break at the side of the road. It is funny what someone with no backbone will do to save their own hide. Clive, JD and Francis, dressed like German soldiers, pretended that one of them was injured and causally walked over to this tank crew we talk of.

The Krauts put their guard down as they were all outside the tank having a smoke and a schnitzel. Clive busted a couple of lines of German lingo as they approached, asking for help. It was a simple affair of shooting a few of the blokes, including the Captain of the Tiger in question here, as he was not playing ball. As soon as his brains were splattered all over the remaining crew, who knelt in the dirt with a shooter squarely pointed at their noggins, they suddenly were all aboard with this very British of masquerades.

So, they disposed of the now-dead Captain and his second-in-command, down some riverbank or other. They all bungled into the Tiger tank and slowly made their way down the road towards the fuel depot. Now, who in their right mind is going to question a Tiger tank that is making its way towards the fuel depot to refuel? That is right, no one, so they made their way through the numerous checkpoints by Clive sticking his head out of the top dressed in the dead Captain's jacket and visor cap who worked his magic with the old German lingo. The others were cramped like sardines in this tin can with a huge gun stuck to the front of it.

In defence of the Nazis, their war machine was undeniably formidable compared to our outdated vehicles. The Tiger tanks in particular, outclassed our rust-prone counterparts. Their sheer size and superior firepower surpassed that of the Allies' smaller Sherman and M3 medium tanks. However, every giant has its Achilles' heel, and for these German tanks, it was their rear end. A well-placed barrage from a Sherman or M3 into this vulnerable area could halt the mighty beast in its tracks. The challenge lay in manoeuvring into such a position without risking the loss of one's turret. Back to the boys, undeterred, they pressed on towards the fuel depot, slowly advancing up the muddy dirt road towards the main entrance.

Surely, once again, they were stopped at the main gate and asked for their papers, which the dead Captain kindly gave up earlier. The guard, for some reason, picked up the telephone and was about to call someone when Clive thought enough was enough. He produced a shooter with a silencer and placed a few holes into this overzealous Kraut, who had decided to use the blower and call someone for a chinwag. With his lifeless body falling to the floor after the red stuff had leaked out of his noggin, Francis, and JD both jumped out and moved the dead body out of sight. The Tiger continued towards the main fuel reverse, which was piled sky-high with metal drums of fuel.

They were simple fuel drums on which the tanks ran, so a lighted match, stick of dynamite or even a bullet would ignite them? The Tommies, being the Tommies, had to do this within traditional 'Rum Bunch' fashion, so they used the Tiger to fire anti-tank shells into these metal drums of fuel we talk of, and we all know what happened next.

BANG! BANG! BANG, as they fired the shells.

BOOM, BOOM, BOOM, as the fuel drums ignited.

The whole place went up like some grease factory during the Blitz. Francis and JD ensured any Krauts trying to fraught this very British of masquerades were met with a hail of bullets. Somebody did sound the alarm, which sounded like a dying chicken having its neck wrung. Francis dropped a few grenades into a canteen via the chimney stack as German soldiers were chilling, enjoying a chicken schnitzel.

JD decided to use the 50-calibre mounted on a Panzer, which was parked up next to them, cutting buildings and Nazis who thought they were hard enough to withstand a 50 Cal down to size. Between the three of them and the tank crew who were helping, they made a dog's dinner of the gaff. They made a mess; it only took a matter of minutes for the three Tommies, with help from their newly found German chums, to fuck up these Nazis.

Drums of fuel exploded and shot into the air, catching fire as did buildings and military vehicles. Some Nazis were burnt alive as the building they were in exploded, catching fire. They were glowing due to the fact a phosphorus anti-tank shell had just exploded next to them. Often, the Tommies would not shoot them. They would prefer to let them burn. This was carnage and mayhem the 'Rum Bunch' way; this was Major Watkins's plan, after all. His boys had only done him proud here, as he knew the Führer would be reading about this over his knackwurst sausage and eggs in the morning. The news about the 'Blitzkrieg Tommies' was doing the rounds within the Nazi ranks for sure. The Tommies relished the notoriety that came with the job.

The three remaining members of the tank crew also underwent a Tommy makeover afterwards. Despite their unfortunate involvement in the casualties, they contributed to eliminating a portion of their own comrades. Unfortunately, circumstances dictated their actions. After the intense scenes of killing, shooting, explosions, and the grim reality of burning Nazis alive, it was now time for these Nazis to face their fate. JD proposed a solution, opting to secure a hand grenade to each of the three soldiers' heads using gaffer tape.

Like the proverb of the three wise monkeys, the first one had it taped over his mouth, the second to the side of his head, and the third over his eyes. All three soldiers' arms were aloft as they begged and pleaded for their lives in German. JD, being an artist of sorts within his own mind showcased his vision of snuffing out these poor Krauts. The three men were pissing and shitting themselves as they knew either way, they were brown bread soon as. They were all begging for their lives, as Clive responded to them; this was the same way the Jewish people begged them for their lives to be spared. Suddenly, one of them tried to run, but JD put a round into his back. He fell to the floor, and the other two started to panic, holding onto JD's leg. So, he managed to drag them off himself. Clive called out that they must stand still, and they will drive off once they had gone, they wait a while and then they can remove the grenades.

As the three Tommies jumped into the German version of a jeep, the Kübelwagen, JD pulled both the pins, out via the wire he had attached to them as they drove off. The two German soldiers did not even have enough time to react, let alone remove the offending grenades.

BOOM! BOOM!

Body parts were thrown into the air, brains, balls, and blood decorated the ground on which these two poor fuckers had once stood. Clive just shook his head in disapproval of what JD had just done, taking into consideration the Allies were not monsters like the Nazis were. The Tommies also blew up an ammunition's reverse, too. They just rolled up and blew up the gaff. Pauley did take one in the arm, though, and luckily it just grazed him. He got stuck on some barbed wire while scaling the officer's accommodation. Jerry started taking potshots at him, when they noticed him tangled within the barbed wire. Deep down, Pauley knew this was it. So, he jumped onto a delivery vehicle's roof before falling to the cobbles. His ego took most of the brunt as the Tommies ripped the piss out of him for hours about this.

All the 'Rum Bunch' participated in this daring raid as they made their way from the forest, which led to the barracks where the ammunition was housed. Gary and Arthur came from the sewer system as a backup measure to the rest of the team approaching from the forest. JD and Francis had set explosives at the foot of the trees, so when they exploded, they came crashing down onto the military barracks below. Again, it was a crude plan for the Tommies, like some East End gangster doing a smash and grab in some jewellers on Bond Street, but they did not care. It was simple but effective if things went to plan, so the Tommies did just that. The explosives went off; the trees came crashing down through the roof of the barracks while Jerry slept.

A fuel truck parked near other military vehicles was an added bonus, which they blew up, too. This only exploded, with the other vehicles catching fire and exploding, too. The Tommies used plastic explosives with a simple time pencil, which you crashed, and acid would be released. This ate through, releasing a pin to the detonator and boom. Goodbye, farewell, ta-ta, au revoir and Auf Wiedersehen to a few more cocksucking Nazis.

What happened within the officer's quarters really defined what the Nazis thought of the 'Blitzkrieg Tommies'. It became known as the 'Slaying of Sainte-Geneviève-des-Bois'. This story spread like wildfire throughout the Nazi ranks. To put it bluntly, like shit through a Pheasant on a day's shoot on some posh estate in the glorious English countryside, like Kenwood House. You know those lazy afternoons, wearing a tweed hacking jacket, shorts trousers, sipping cold Bollinger, with your trusted 10-bore under and over shooter, slung over your shoulder. Which is ready and willing. Long story short, they blew up the whole gaff but kidnapped a handful of Waffen-SS-officers who wished they were in bed, a kip, counting images of Nazi pin-up girl, Fräulein Faust. Now, there was a beauty; many a Kraut played pocket billiards too, while in the trenches. She was their Marilyn Monroe or Bettie Page. Seeing a scantily clad, busty babe with blonde pigtails holding an anti-tank rocket like the Panzerfaust between her legs was enough to get any red-blooded Kraut hot under the tunic collar. I'm sure a few Tommies would have switched sides to have a tumble with her. Look at me getting carried away again with all this small talk about this hot Nazi chick with pigtails.

Where were we?

Oh yeah, these poor fuckers were purely treated the way they were due to the fact the Waffen-SS were a bunch of nasty cunts themselves and did things which would make your fucking toes curl. They did not take prisoners; they rounded you up and executed you if they felt generous. So, the Tommies had already heard via the resistance grapevine that the SS were putting a unit of soldiers together to purely hunt them down and kill them like dogs in the street. So, they decided they would send these Nazi fuckers a message in return, the 'Rum Bunch' way.

This is how the message went: Pauley and JD were the worst of the Tommies when it came to killing Nazi folk. They had the meanest of streaks, let's say, the 'Slaying of Sainte Geneviève-des-Bois'. Was their most defining work yet? What they did to those poor Nazi fuckers was eye-opening, to say the least. This tall tale started with JD seeing an underage Jewish-looking girl, soon to be molested by the six Waffen-SS-officers in question here, within the officer's quarters. If they were sound asleep like the rest of the foot soldiers, they probably would have died in their sleep and not endured what they did. So here goes, Pauley could see this jovial banter, these men were partaking in with this young girl, had a more sinister side to it as they were getting too touchy-feely for his liking. So, he took it upon himself to bind and gag these men and, threw them into the back of a German Sd.Kfz. 251 half-track armoured personnel carrier and ferried them away to a certain death. After most raids, the Tommies fled into the rural countryside, as they had help from the French resistance and the 'Fräuleins of Death'. The Tommies' eventually got to know the area for themselves, but a member of the French resistance was always helpful at checkpoints due to the French lingo.

Back to the story and how these two Tommies sent a message to Adolf Hitler and the Nazis. They found themselves in a deserted hotel, a macabre setting where they had transported their soon-to-be victims of the Waffen-SS to their final resting place. With the half-track now hidden from the road, the boys go to work. Each Nazi occupied a room with its own unique decor, as the duo had stumbled upon this seedy abandoned hotel. A hot bath and kip within a pukka bed was rare as rocking horse shit when you were in the field. Unfortunately, the hotel, proved to be deserted, to their disappointment, as every fighting man deserves a respite now and then, with the company of a good woman.

You are probably thinking, why do I mention this when you are thousands of miles away from loved ones and home, any female company is appreciated. Like the smell of a lady, her mannerisms, and her subtle gestures, like playing with her hair and flirting. It is the same as having a home-cooked meal and a few beers, very rare. Back to these Waffen-SS cocksuckers, so picture it: one Nazi tied up like a stuffed pig in each bedroom, awaiting the inevitable release from any lingering grasp of life.

The first bedroom had a bed centre stage, with its heavy-looking brass bed frame, frilly pink curtains, and a dressing table. Assorted items, like perfume, a hairbrush, and a hand mirror, sat on the dressing table. The inhabitant had left in a hurry, by the looks of it. A lady's nightclothes were still hanging over a screen near the window.

So, JD went first, he removed the officer's military tunic, folded it up neatly, and carefully placed it down before he removed his boots and trousers. He had the biggest of the men, some fat fucker who had certainly eaten all the sauerkraut and pork schnitzel. So, this rather large, pork chop looking Waffen-SS officer, in his white vest and shorts, is squirming like a good'un as he knows this little piggy is going to get drip-dried very soon. Halal, which is the new kosher, if he is lucky if our boy will do the drip drying properly. Drip-drying any protagonist or villain in this scenario can be a trifle ropey, to say the least; it is a bloody art form within itself, let alone busting out the need to pray mid-cut as some do.

JD used the soldier's own ceremonial dagger on the Geezer to cut away a few pounds of flesh, well, in his case, a love handle or two. Blood splattered the white bed linen as the knife went in and was turned. The Geezer screamed in agonising pain, but the noise was subdued due to the gag he was wearing. JD then used the knife to cut a swastika into his fat gut before impaling him in the side of the neck with the same knife. Once the fat fucker had stopped breathing, JD calmly walked over and used the water jug to wash his hands. He dried them on a white pillowcase as he glanced over at the dead man, admiring his handiwork.

He cocked his neck to the side to admire his fine knife work for a moment, grinning in appreciation of what he had created. This is when it dawned on him, he was supposed to ask the now-dead Nazi some questions. What a prize plum he can be, he thinks to himself.

Pauley was in bedroom number two of this establishment of indulgence, which was similar in layout and décor to bedroom number one. His attended victim was a tall, gangly Waffen-SS officer. He was tied to a chair and once again gagged for good measure. Pauley, being Pauley, removed the gag so the others could hear this Geezer screaming, which may have swayed them into giving up any information which they may have regarding the Tommies.

The issue with this game of cat and mouse is that a man, while being tortured, will tell you if he wears women's underwear and parades around the bedroom in them just to make the pain stop. These Waffen-SS-officers did not particularly look like they were anyone special or would have any information of use to aid the Tommies. This would not deter the boy from having a good old go at it, though.

What got Pauley's blood boiling was the fact that they were kiddy-fiddling with an underaged-looking Jewish girl. Even Pauley had limits and kids were a big fat no, no in his book. So, Pauley slapped the Geezer around the face a few times to soften him up, followed by a few gut shots. The brass knuckle duster he had slipped on did its magic. He also asked the fella if he could speak English, and he nodded in agreement. So, he asked the man if he knew of any Allied manoeuvres within the area, which he first refused to answer. So, Pauley went to work, afflicting more pain as humanly possible. Pauley gave him a few more jabs before a righthand like some professional boxer. The Nazi coughed up blood as the punches to his face did soften him up. Pauley asked him again, and he still refused to answer.

Anticipation filled the room at what Pauley was going to do next, as this Nazi was not listening to him. So, he removed his knife and waved it around the man's face, pointing it directly at his eyeball, and then he placed it under his eye socket. He asked the Nazi, once again, what he knew, but he just spat blood onto Pauley in some act of defiance. This enraged our boy, who decided the Nazi was not listening to him, so he straddled him. Pauley sat across his lap before he forcefully removed his ear, gashing at it with his knife. The Nazi screamed the gaff down, screeching like a little girl. He franticly tried to release himself from the chair, shaking and cursing. Pauley remained seated, straddling him, and waved his ear around like some trophy. He held it up towards his mouth and talked into it, and blood dripped downwards onto his hand and down his wrist. The Nazi squirmed in pain, stomping his feet due to the agonising pain being inflicted on him. He asked if the Nazi could hear him now before he asked if he knew of anything once again. The Nazi suddenly stopped his moaning and squirming. He just glared at Pauley in defiance as the blood poured from his wound. Pauley got off the man's lap and stood over him in a menacing fashion.

"English dog." The Waffen-SS Officer calls out.

"This English dog, you refer to Fritz, is gonna fuck you up now," Pauley replies.

"You go to hell," the Waffen-SS officer adds.

"You best pray, you Nazi cocksucker, cos I'm gonna tear you a new one," he adds.

"A proper new shitter, so go on, son, show me some more hatred, but make it your best mind."

"Cos, as I said previously, I'm gonna tear you a new one."

"A little German Cuckoo tells me, you Nazis love it up the shitter," he added.

"Well, do you," he screams.

The Geezer spat on Pauley's face again, provoking an immediate reaction from Pauley, who harboured no tolerance for such disrespect. Seizing the German soldier, Pauley pulled him closer, defiantly wiping the spittle from his face onto his military tunic lapel. Pauley, already grappling with anger management issues, found himself further incensed. In a fit of rage, he repeated the process, ruthlessly severing the Geezer's second ear, which he disdainfully glanced at before tossing it to the floor. With bloodied hands, Pauley wiped them on the soon-to-be-dead Nazi before decisively slicing the man's throat, allowing the crimson stream to flow. As Pauley cleaned his knife, he caught his reflection in the dressing table mirror. Absently, he picked up a bottle of fine French perfume, taking in its scent with a detached demeanour. This brings a smile to his face; he hears JD's footsteps as he walks down the hallway towards the next victim. Pauley glares at the dead Nazi as he admires his labour of love.

Next, JD grasped the ceramic doorknob but paused for some reason. On entering the room, he closed the door behind himself. Again, this bedroom was similar to the first two. This one had a wooden wardrobe against the wall, with what looked like hat boxes sitting on top. A female manikin stood on display near the window, wearing a fine dress. JD walked over towards the manikin and smelt the dress; he inhaled deeply as he rubbed the dress onto his face. He stopped momentarily and glared at the dress before walking towards the wardrobe and opening the door.

On looking inside the wardrobe, it was empty, to his disappointment, so he picked up one of the hat boxes and opened it. He discovered a lady's hat within the box. He picked it up and studied it as he walked back towards his next victim. This Geezer was a fairly young-looking Waffen-SS officer who was tied to a chair. His stare of defiance was the only giveaway as he struggled to free himself.

"Seig Heil," the Waffen-SS Officer calls out.

"Heil Hitler!" he adds.

"Well, fuck me, Geezer, that sounds like hostility. We don't like hostility, do we, JD," JD replied.

"There is only one way: the aforementioned thoughts rattling around your noggin can be removed."

"With your demise, my old Fritz," he added.

JD glared at him, circling the Nazi like a 'Great White', sensing blood in the water, but beneath his tough exterior, JD had a sensitive side. Even though his weathered exterior, coupled with bulging muscles and prison tattoos gave off a certain aura. His reputation did proceed him, like the sudden bouts of violence and his short temper. They called him 'The Beast of Wandsworth' in jail due to the vicious assaults on his fellow inmates which often resulted in him being confined to solitary confinement. Due to these savage attacks, he eventually got transferred to some other hellhole. Sorry, back to JD and his next victim.

Demonstrating this unexpected tenderness, he placed the lady's hat on the young officer's head. The Nazi, now even more agitated, struggled to rid himself of the offending fashion accessory. JD, displaying a subtle touch, adjusted the hat as he observed the young man. After a moment of silence, JD inquired if the young officer possessed any information concerning the Allied soldiers. Met with stoic silence and a steely gaze, the Nazi attempted to resist by aiming a kick with his boot at JD. Seizing the opportunity, JD retaliated with a powerful punch to the man's face, causing blood to gush from his nose. Instantly, the young officer's eyes darkened, likely a consequence of his newly broken nose. Clutching his face in pain, the Geezer winced, tears welling in his eyes, revealing a vulnerability beneath the tough exterior.

JD grabbed his hooter, which he pulled violently to gain a reaction+. The young Nazi screamed in agony as JD released the body part in question here. He wiped the blood off his hand onto the young man's uniform. JD walked towards the window, his footsteps making a noise on the wooden floorboards. As he walked over towards the window, he pulled the curtains aside slightly to have a butcher's outside. The young Nazi moaned in pain, calling out something in German. JD rested against the window ledge and lit a cigarette as he watched the young Nazi, who squirmed in pain. He continued to smoke and studied his victim before he threw the cigarette butt onto the floor and squashed it underfoot. As he walked back over towards the young man, he moved forward and removed the hat the young Nazi was wearing. Not before JD placed the hat onto his own head and brushed the Geezer's hair back off his face as if he cared for his wellbeing.

Then, JD paused and asked him how many Allied soldiers he had killed to be awarded this Iron Cross he wore with such pride. The soldier just stared at him with a look of contempt as blood continued to pour from his hooter. JD suddenly tried to remove the Iron Cross medal from around his neck; the soldier struggled in some attempt to prevent this from happening. So, JD gave him a few low blows, which calmed the young Nazi down instantly, and he stopped resisting.

JD studied the medal up close before he spat on it and polished it, to the horror of the Nazi. He suddenly started to speak German, and from the tone, he was not saying anything pleasant, which annoyed JD further. So, he removed the man's scarf and tied it over his mouth as the man struggled. JD calmly, while whistling, removed the man's black leather boots and his socks to reveal his feet. He walked over towards the wardrobe and opened it, looking around, but it was empty, which he already knew from before, but he took another look anyway.

Then he opened the chest of drawers and hunted around for something while he was still whistling. He found a few bottles of perfume and other lady's makeup within it. He pulled the lid off a lipstick and twisted the base to highlight the lipstick within. He glared at the lipstick and brought it up close to his own face before he placed it in his trouser pocket. On continuing his search, he suddenly stopped in his tracks and stopped whistling. The Geezer tried to catch a glimpse of what he had found, but JD's back obscured his vision. Suddenly, JD paused before turning around and glaring at him. He was holding a large metal decretive tin, which he shook as he held up close towards his ear.

The Nazi looked slightly confused at what he was doing, as suddenly JD's mannerisms had changed to being very jovial. He continued with this till he reached the man and shook the tin near his ear. He flinched slightly at first, as he was not aware of what this man was doing. JD opened the tin and removed a handful of white talcum powder, which he sprinkled through his fingers while making eye contact with the young officer. He suddenly blew some onto his face, to his surprise, which made the Nazi cough. He placed the lid back and continued to rub copious amounts of talcum powder onto the man's cheeks and forehead.

"Whose true Aryan race now, white as the driven snow," JD calls out.

"I'll call you snow-white, sweetheart," he adds.

The young officer tried in vain for this not to take place; by moving his face but JD held it within his large hand which prevented this. He then removed the lipstick from his pocket and carefully opened it, before he applied it to the man's lips. He again squirmed and tried to avoid this, but a few gut shots from JD calmed him down into submission. JD just stared at the man, and without any warning he smashed the metal tin into the young Germans feet, one toe at a time.

BANG! BANG! BANG! BANG! BANG!

The scene unfolded with the unsettling noise of metal crushing as he persistently wielded the metal tin as a weapon. The young man's screams echoed in pain as his pinkies endured a brutal assault. The Nazi, now sobbing, released tears that streaked down his face, leaving trails within the white talcum powder on his cheeks. JD momentarily halted, surprising onlookers by cradling the man's face in his hands, revealing an unexpected display of emotion. He brought the young Waffen-SS officer's face slowly towards his own, cradling it with love as he stared into his eyes.

Suddenly, JD kissed the man with force as he still cradled his head in his hands with the Nazi struggling to move as the red lipstick smudged over his face. However, this fleeting moment abruptly shifted as he relentlessly struck the man, resembling a crazed monster on the side of the head.

The blows rained down as blood splattered the white bedding nearby and the walls with a tinge of the colour rouge. JD did not stop till he could not lift his arms anymore. This frenzied attack of his continued till he fell to the floor exhausted. Suddenly, a pool of blood slowly seeped towards him on the wooden floor next to where his head lay. The doorknob slowly turned, and the door opened. Pauley was standing within the doorway, looking intrigued by what had been happening in here. He could see that JD had made a right old mess here and felt that JD did not need any more emotional stress in dealing with any further Krauts who needed dealing with. So, he threw JD a packet of cigarettes and assured him just to chill while he would put out the remaining rubbish. The emotionless and disconnected JD just glared into the blue yonder, so Pauley left the room and went to work.

Waffen-SS cocksucker number four was just simply strangled, with Pauley's bare hands, after being asked if he knew anything about the Allied plans, which he knew nothing of, or so he said. Due to the limited working space of this charming hotel, or tart's boudoir they find themselves in. Waffen-SS cocksucker number five and six had to share a bedroom. They even had to share a bed, where they were both hog-tied up next to each other. So, Pauley asked the older of the two Nazis first if he knew of anything. You know the saying age before beauty and all that, bollocks. He respectfully refused to tell him anything, so Pauley inserted his thumbs into the Geezer's eye sockets till the red stuff trickled out of them. The demise of this Nazi had to be as gruesome as possible, so the other one would hopefully talk, considering he was splattered by his blood.

As he died in this gruesome way, his bed buddy, a younger officer, decided he would sing like a Lark. All Pauley had to do, in the first place, was what he just did. This young Nazi did not care too much about Adolf Hitler and his brown shirt brigade. Why did the boys not just question him first? They would have saved themselves some elbow grease here. So, this young officer called Ludwig Koch, who spoke English, told Pauley two things: firstly, they had a price on their heads, which every German soldier was up for collecting, and a specialist SS unit was being formed to hunt them. This was no normal SS unit, but the elite soldiers handpicked by Heinrich Himmler himself, tasked with hunting them down and publicly killing them. He did not know the finer points of this plot to kill them, but this was enough for Pauley. He also mentioned they were in training in Germany somewhere or other.

"Blitzkrieg Tommies," Ludwig called out.

"Blitzkrieg Tommies," he repeats in a distressed voice.

"Yeah, what about these Tommies?" Pauley asked.

"You better spill your fucking guts, boy."

"Cos we the Tommy-Einsatzgruppen, you fuckers," he adds.

He told Pauley this is what the German soldiers called them. The second useful piece of intelligence he gave up was that the Führer had a new Allied friend. The Führer and Himmler seemed to have a soft spot for him. This man was also seen at meetings with other high-ranking officers, namely Himmler. Pauley took all the information on board, as this could be the key to their success. Pauley let the Waffen-SS officer live but explained if he went back unharmed, they would know he talked, so he asked Pauley to shoot him. Not so he would die, but something which meant he would spend time within a military hospital, hopefully for the remainder of the war.

Pauley asked to see his papers, which Ludwig pointed out were in his military tunic pocket. Pauley removed them and assured him he now knew where Ludwig lived and that he may visit him after the war if he did not keep his mouth shut regarding what had happened here.

So, Pauley cut the rope, binding Ludwig's hands to his relief. As he rubbed his wrists, he glanced over at the dead Waffen-SS officer next to him on the bed. Pauley removed a Luger which he had confiscated earlier, upholding his side of the agreement, and shot Ludwig in the foot, who screamed like a little girl after being shot. He released him so he could spread the word of the 'Blitzkrieg Tommies' further within the German ranks and not say anything about tonight, though.

Pauley threw Ludwig a pillowcase, which he wrapped around his foot. As Ludwig hobbled away from the bedroom, Pauley followed his trail of fresh blood along the hallway floor towards the bedroom where he had left JD. Ludwig scrambled down the wooden staircase towards the front door. He remained nervous and fearful of what this man could do as Pauley stood and watched him leave. Ludwig kept on looking back at Pauley as he made his escape.

On opening the door, JD was still lying on the floor with dried blood covering his hands and face. He was smoking as he stared at the ceiling of the room, lifeless with no emotion on display. He suddenly threw the burning cigarette to the side of him.

Pauley called out, which fell on deaf ears, so he clicked his fingers in his face to gain his attention. Pauley even shook him violently, which he finally reacted to. It was like JD was within his own world; he was not too responsive and looked like a man possessed. He looked mesmerised, maybe due to the fact of what he had just afflicted on another human being.

Pauley attempted to convey Ludwig's urgent message to JD, emphasising the need to evacuate swiftly. However, JD remained unresponsive. Frustrated, Pauley resorted to slapping him repeatedly, desperate for any reaction. JD, seemingly detached from his usual self, offered no response. This unusual behaviour concerned Pauley, who shook him vigorously in an attempt to elicit some acknowledgement. Despite their familiarity with each other's quirks from spending considerable time together, JD remained unresponsive. In an effort to break through, Pauley lit two cigarettes, placing one in his mouth and extending the other to JD. After a brief pause, JD slowly rose to his feet.

The two men made their way down the wooden staircase towards the front door. Pauley picked up a lamp and smashed it onto the floor, which started a fire. He knew in the back of his mind Jerry had conducted some nasty fucked-up shit throughout the war, but what they had just done was not far from war crimes too. Hopefully, the fire would conceal any wrongdoings, as the gaff should burn down to the ground. As far as Ludwig was concerned, he was fully aware that Pauley had seen his papers and knew where he was from, hopefully making him forget what he had witnessed here. The two Tommies left the building, with Pauley turning around once to have another look as the fire took hold. They both stood outside in the pitch dark and watched the fire take hold of the building. The flames licked the timberwork, and the glass windows smashed as the fire continued to burn. Within the pitch darkness in which Ludwig frantically escaped, the flames highlighted Pauley and JD's faces as tears streamed down JD's face as he glared at the fire.

After this, most of the other stuff the Tommies did was small fry, like the cutting of phone lines and changing of road signs, simple tasks which just annoyed the hell out of the Nazis. What was getting under the skin of these Jerry cocksuckers was this rabble of men they referred to as 'Blitzkrieg Tommies' had now become a thorn within the side of Adolf Hitler and his hierarchy. Their simple acts of heroism against the Nazi war machine had caused delays, loss of advantage to the Allied forces and loss of Nazi lives, too, as they became victims of the 'Blitzkrieg Tommies'.

The Tommies' tactics and how they concluded business meant these losses of German lives were far from normal. "I have been shot in battle, and now I am dead is one thing". These losses of Nazi lives we talk of are imaginative with the use of skill and brute force if needed, like the 'Slayings at Sainte Geneviève-des-Bois', for example.

Shooting a Nazi was not enough for this right 'Rum Bunch' of Geezers; they had to go that extra country mile. What I mean is ultra-violence, the use of tools within this newly found art form of killing Nazis in entertaining ways. Simply just killing them would not be good enough; it would not be cricket, so new ways had to be introduced in the demise of these Jerry wankers.

Firstly, we had the good old grenade, which could easily be gaffer taped to a Nazis nutsack or inserted into his rectum. Pull the pin, and happy days, boom, dead Nazi. Then there was the use of dull objects, which caused deep impact, known as blunt force trauma to the victim in question here, like bashing of the skull, broken bones, and internal bleeding, to name a few outcomes. JD had an old Irish thumbing stick, which certainly fitted the bill as an implement of death within this category or the cricket bat Arthur had brought along. Cricket, that old English pastime of leather onto willow while quaffing sandwiches and a cuppa on a lazy Sunday afternoon, had a new addition. Killing Nazis the 'Rum Bunch' way.

This was followed by traditional fisticuffs, slightly different to a normal altercation of sorts. No Queensbury rules applied here, as the Nazi involved in this punch-up will not be fighting back. A favourite of the Tommies was watching a handful of Krauts running across a minefield, having a wager to see if you could win an iron cross or other medals of choice.

This imaginative list of ways for a Nazi to die is endless; add a Nazi who wants to exit this earth for his Nazi beliefs, add a Tommy who wants to send this cocksucker straight to hell and there you go, bingo. You must add a small sprinkling of violence, pain, suffering and there you have it: hey presto, piece of cake, jobs a good'un, and voila. This onslaught the Nazis experienced at the hand of the 'Rum Bunch' had spread like wildfire throughout the German ranks. The campfire stories of the 'Blitzkrieg Tommies' made them out to be immortal giants who cannot be harmed by human hands. It was like they were devils sent here to punish the Nazis for their sins. Like the old German fairy tales of old, this really put the frighteners up the Krauts. To the extent some soldiers refused to face them and opted for a bullet instead or prison. These fuckers even guillotined their deserters.

On the other hand, certain Waffen-SS and SS-soldiers were volunteering to hunt down the Tommies and bring their heads on a silver platter for their Führer. Himmler had assembled a division of SS-soldiers after the Führer had demanded something be done about these British pests. While they trained in Berlin, the Tommies did their best to cause hell for the Nazis. This new division will surely offer the Führer peace of mind that his boys are not being subjected to these horrors anymore.

The Tommies loved a challenge and wanted these SS-soldiers to come forward to meet their maker, too. The rumours did the rounds, regarding the new drugs which were being experimented on these Aryan sons. Hitlers' doctors and mad scientists had to create the ultimate fighting machine. The Tommies revelled in the opportunity to have a proper ruckus with these odious characters.

Meanwhile, Private Singh had been summoned by Joseph Goebbels for a meeting in Paris. He knows it is not for a romantic meal and a stroll holding hands around the city of love. Why would Goebbels want to see him now, as the last time they met, the Geezer could not stop staring at him? It must be important they had sent a car for him, which collected him from the train station. He has just returned from Berlin from his duties of driving the Führer.

Private Singh sits in a rooftop café wine bar, glancing around the room as he waits. He strategically chose a seat just before the open windows, allowing him a vantage point as the RAF diligently dropped bombs on the Germans below. With Goebbels and his party exposed, they might as well be painting a target on the roof. The ambience of the place is more akin to a lavish ballroom than a simple café wine bar, muses Private Singh. The parquet oak dance floor, prominently positioned at the venue's centre, is a dead giveaway. What he is certain of is the opulence of the establishment's décor, adorned with massive crystal chandeliers suspended from ornate ceiling roses.

The bar itself is a spectacle, featuring a mirrored backdrop and a black-and-gold marble top, perfectly complementing the display of champagne bottles and glassware. The backlit presentation only serves to accentuate the grandeur of the entire bar area.

A waiter stood to the side of the bar, wearing a white dinner jacket with white gloves as the barman polished glasses. The waiter had already been over and seated Private Singh, with the best view of the house, overlooking the Eiffel Tower. The table set up, too, is second to none, with its fine silver cutlery and glassware. Private Singh picks up one of the flowers from the table display and smells it. This is a far cry from the smell of death and decay he has become accustomed to throughout the conflict. He has been asked to dress formally for the meeting, so he is wearing a charcoal grey double-breasted suit with a white shirt and black tie. He is still wearing his military-issue boots, though; he has given them a good old spit and polish for the occasion. Private Singh wonders what Goebbels wants with him, considering that he kept staring at him throughout their first meeting in Berlin.

Maybe, just maybe, he fancies him. He chuckles to himself and soon realises that Goebbels may be that way inclined. His chuckle soon dissipates as this thought sinks in. The whole venue has been emptied for this meeting, Private Singh presumes as not a single soul stirred beside him, the waiter, the barman and the maître d. Suddenly, he hears a motorcade pull up, with doors slamming and the general commotion when someone important arrives.

The noise of the soldiers Jackboots as they jump out of the trucks and the orders being barked at them are clear in any language. So, he straightens himself up slightly before the party we talk of arrives. Within minutes, the gold doors are flung open, two SS-guards appear and stand on century duty at the entrance. Goebbels then appears, making his way towards the table, accompanied by the maître d' and another young SS-soldier who must be the interpreter in tow. Private Singh stands up as the maître d' pulls out a chair for Goebbels to sit down on.

"Heil Hitler!" Goebbels calls out.

He makes a limp hand gesture, and Private Singh nods in response. Goebbels takes a seat, accompanied by Private Singh and a young SS-soldier who acts as an interpreter. Goebbels requests champagne, specifically the best from the house cellars. The Nazis, known for their indulgence, spared no expense in enjoying the finest foods and drinks throughout the war. A waiter approaches with a bottle of vintage Dom Pérignon, presenting it to Goebbels for his approval, to which Goebbels simply nods. The waiter pours two glasses, starting with Goebbels. He lifts the champagne flute and takes a sip, expressing his approval once more before the waiter tops up his glass. Turning to Private Singh, the waiter pours another generous glass of fine French bubbles.

Goebbels raises his champagne flute and looks at Private Singh before a slight pause. Then he calls out, "Long live the thousand-year Reich and may he continue to produce his masterpieces of cinema brilliance" in German, which is then translated by the young soldier. Private Singh, too, raises his glass and smiles in agreement with what has just been said.

Goebbels tells him the food here is amazing, the duck is to die for, and he should try it. He removes a gold cigarette case from his black double-breasted blazer, which he wears with pinstripe grey trousers, a white shirt, and a grey tie. Private Singh opted to dress smartly in his grey suit, taking into consideration the invite stated formal dress. The waiter quickly offers him a light as soon as he sees the cigarette case. He takes a drag from the cigarette and picks at a tiny bit of tobacco which has fallen onto the pure white tablecloth. He sprinkles it onto the floor and resumes talking. He goes on about how Germany will be victorious in the war, how Adolf Hitler will rule the world, blah, blah, blah, which is translated for his guest.

But what he is curious about is the Sikh man who sits opposite him. His identity, what it stands for and how he has found himself fighting for the British. Goebbels asks Private Singh if he knows of his work, to which he responds that they have seen certain films back in London, especially pre-war. Goebbels is not a modest man; he blows his own German Oboe about his achievements and what his vision is for the future of German cinema.

He explains he is a master orator and propagandist who presents the National Socialist German Workers Party in a favourable image globally. Private Singh goes with the flow and just nods, agreeing with what is being said here. Goebbels goes on about the Jews of Hollywood and how they had strangled creative representation within the film industry blah, blah, blah, blah.

Private Singh knows deep down there is an interior motive to him being here in the presence of this cinematic maestro. He asks the interpreter to inform Goebbels of this. The waiter pours some more champagne for both men. Goebbels picks up his cigarette from the ashtray, which had been slowly burning while he has been self-engrossed in his own accomplishments. He suddenly requests the waiter to leave them and produces a letter from his inner jacket pocket. He places a pair of reading glasses on, straightens out the letter, and clears his voice, very theatrical in his mannerisms.

He starts to read that the Führer Adolf Hitler would like him to make a presentation about a forthcoming event. This event will be held at the Berghof for a select number of party members only. This event is to celebrate the new forming of the Indian division, to be known as the 'Bavarian Lions,' further to his meeting with the Führer, Adolf Hitler, and Heinrich Himmler. They want to showcase to the world that fighters from other shores are ready to lay down their lives for the Führer, Adolf Hitler. He wanted to promote this to gain further followers so, eventually, India could gain independence from the United Kingdom of Great Britain. He explains this film will encourage Indian soldiers who are prisoners of the Third Reich and soldiers who are still fighting under the British flag to assume arms against their invaders, who are not their masters anymore.

Goebbels speaks with passion, yet his demeanour is notably calmer than the Führer's. His eyes, however, exude a subtle menace as he maintains eye contact with Private Singh throughout their conversation. Despite the language barrier, Goebbels communicates as if his guest comprehends every word, even though he is well aware that Private Singh doesn't speak a word of German. The interpreter efficiently translates in a hushed and softer tone, in stark contrast to Goebbels' theatrical delivery. Private Singh nods in agreement as Goebbels speaks, smiling at key points while glancing up from the document he is reading. Raising his glass, Private Singh, and Goebbels salute each other, the fine crystal champagne flutes producing a delicious toasting sound.

Private Singh beams with happiness as he takes this opportunity to thank Goebbels for this platform and the Führer for believing in him. He tells Goebbels how the British treat Indians within their own country by invading and raping the country of its natural resources. He continues but knows in the back of his mind the Nazis are doing much worse but needs Allies to defeat the British and remove them from his shores.

Suddenly, Goebbels is speechless as he listens to Private Singh talk, and he can see the passion. He tells him of his love of cinema, too, and how he would like to be a turban-wearing Sikh actor on the film stage globally. He also explains why his turban and beard should not detract from any acting or writing talent he has. He mentions he would like to be involved within the film industry, but his identity creates obstacles, a proper spanner in the bloody works. Often being judged on first impressions and all that, and how wrong they are. He explains to Goebbels that his first name is Param, and when he was younger, his parents would take him to the cinema. He would cover over the "ount", from Paramount, by holding up his hand and closing one eye. This meant his name, Param, would be up in lights. Having his name up on the silver screen is something he has always desired from an early age.

Maybe Goebbels can help him dip his toe into this pond of the film industry. Why can't he have his shot at the tittle, have a punt, watch his nag romp home, while sitting in the Royal Enclosure, dressed to the nines? Treading the boards or walking the red carpet, sipping cold bubbles at some celebrity knees-up, have his mugshot taken by the paparazzi and be embraced into the warm bosom of the film industry globally.

As he knows deep down, he is a natural-born filmmaker at heart but needs someone to take a punt on him. Why can't he live out his dream of being involved within the film industry in Europe and even Hollywood? Sorry, look at me getting on my soapbox again about Private Singh's dream. All he is trying to convey is, let him have a shot, punching above his weight, intriguing and captivating audiences globally with his characters of distinction, delivering razor-sharp words. Look at me getting carried away again, where were we?

Oh yeah, Private Singh asks Goebbels if he would contemplate offering him an acting role in one of his projects, maybe the one about a Sikh soldier fighting against the British. Maybe this could be one of his best masterpieces, 'The Bavarian Lion'. Private Singh goes on to blow smoke up Goebbels arse regarding how he has achieved so much with his film's blah, blah, blah. Suddenly, Goebbels starts to clap; he is nearly tearful after Private Singh stops talking. After a while, he stops his fake clapping, picks up a white napkin, and wipes away his tears, even though there are none. He is a true performer, too, right, an Oscar-rated star of the propaganda screen, to say the least. On placing the napkin down, he takes another sip of champagne and calms himself down.

He expresses the passion he has just witnessed, the conviction on display, and the fact that he would love to offer Private Singh an acting role in one of his films. Suddenly, Goebbels checks his watch and calls out that he has another engagement soon and must be leaving. He reassured Private Singh that his office would be in contact regarding the premiere, which they are planning. They both agree this will be a spear within the hearts of the Allies, that the Führer is behind the Indian soldiers and that he fully appreciates their sacrifices and endeavours within this conflict. Goebbels moves his chair backwards slightly, and the maître d' quickly walks over to help.

"Heil Hitler!" Goebbels calls out.

Private Singh stands up too and nods his head slightly as Goebbels lifts his hand to gesture the Nazi salute. Goebbels stops and asks Private Singh why he does not correctly salute the Führer. This suddenly changes the atmosphere within the room to an air of tension.

Private Singh remains silent for a while before, he explains that once the Sikh division is up and running, he and his men will salute the Führer as their true leader. Till then, he feels it is not appropriate to do so and out of respect for the Führer and other high-ranking members of the party like Goebbels himself, he shows an element of respect by bowing his head, even though he verbally saluted the Führer in one of their previous meetings. He goes on to explain why he does not salute the Nazi way when meeting higher-ranking German officers, as this is disrespectful in his eyes. Goebbels calls over his two SS-guards; suddenly, the situation becomes slightly tense. What is going to happen next, Private Singh thinks to himself? Why is he calling them over to join them?

Goebbels just stares at him before he asks the two guards to escort him from the building to Private Singh's relief. Goebbels picks up his gold cigarette case from the table, places it within his inner jacket pocket, turns around, and leaves, followed by the two guards and the young interpreter. Private Singh waits till they leave the room and falls backwards into his seat; relief is awash across his boat. He removes the bottle of Dom Pérignon from the ice bucket and pours himself a large glass, which he quaffs down before he pours another. It is like he has nearly been found out, considering his reaction, or maybe it is just nerves.

Days later, Private Singh is driving Himmler and another high-ranking officer around again. Due to the fact he does not speak German, his duties are limited, like driving to and from meetings. Cleaning and preparing the car for these outings. Then there was the Führer, who liked to have chats and play chess. Private Singh is housed with the other general household staff and has his own room. His room is quite small, with a single bed, a small bedside table and a wardrobe. The walls are adorned with a few family pictures, of loved ones. Inside the wardrobe, his British uniform hangs crisply pressed, alongside the limited assortment of suits provided for him.

Engaging in a ritual, he frequently dedicates time to meticulously polishing his army-issue boots, executing small circular movements with the black boot polish as if it serves as a form of stress relief. Holding up the boots for a close inspection, he often finds a reason to smile, placing both boots back with precision at the bottom of the wardrobe. Subjected to sporadic room checks, usually during the early hours, his room door is abruptly thrusted open, and two German soldiers routinely invade his space, conducting thorough searches for reasons unknown. Sometimes he is already awake, thinking of loved ones and his homeland.

His room is torn apart within these searches, his clothing searched, and everything left in a pile on the floor. Private Singh can never understand why they do this; he has been a prisoner of the Third Reich now for weeks and is trusted by the Führer and Heinrich Himmler himself.

So why do these searches take place? He thinks to himself. Maybe the Gestapo have a hand in this, due to his closeness with these two men; perhaps insiders within their trusted circle did not like him. He knows that Martin Bormann was present at one meeting. He sensed an element of distrust and enquiry into who he was. Maybe this is why his nunchucks have not been given back to him since he arrived here. He is trying to obtain some support and launch this Indian division backed by the Germans so he can fight the British, which is the conclusion he so desperately desires.

After being summoned by telegram, Private Singh was called to a meeting with Adolf Hitler and Heinrich Himmler, who are in France for some reason. The following day, he is driven down the French countryside, which looks similar to the British countryside to him. He even sees a few cows within a field as the car approaches what looks like a Château. As they drive up the main driveway, trees line either side before reaching a central paved area with dwarf trees. The vehicle stops, and a butler opens the rear door for him to exit. Private Singh notices two German troop carries reversed up towards the main doors of this grand Château we talk of. On leaving the car, he follows the butler down a hallway. He notices artwork is being removed from the walls and packed into wooden crates. One of the German soldiers closes the door as he looks in while walking past the room. What is taking place here? More looting he thinks to himself.

As they continue to walk, he notices further artwork has been removed off the walls within the hallway, too, due to the faded marks left where the paintings once had been hanging. Private Singh stops outside another room and bears witness to artwork being piled onto a patio area through open French doors. It is being manhandled and thrown onto the floor; this ever-increasing pile of fine oil paintings, maybe by the masters, are about to be destroyed by the looks of it.

The butler gestures with his hand that they should continue and points towards a set of doors, already open, towards the garden area. White net curtains wave within the slight breeze as Private Singh makes his way through the doors and down the concrete patio staircase. He can see the Führer and Himmler seated at a table, talking among themselves. On century duty, two guards flank the doorway at the foot of the stairs. Private Singh continues to walk down the stairs and is approached by two men. Suddenly, out of the blue, a man wearing a black leather trench coat stops him abruptly and starts to search him. Private Singh is surprised, as this is the first time this has taken place for a while now, within one of their meetings. He thinks the Germans are getting more paranoid for some reason. The man, who looks like he is from the Gestapo, moves aside and walks over towards the table. The two men continue to talk in German and, at first, ignore that he is standing there. A record is playing, some classical number by Richard Wagner. Even commoners like me have some interests as I said previously. That is when Himmler calls out, and within minutes, an interpreter arrives. It is a young man who salutes and clicks his boot heels.

"Heil Hitler," he calls out.

"Heil Hitler," Himmler replies.

Himmler lifts his hand, where the Führer looks up from what he is reading. Private Singh salutes the two men with a military salute by lifting his hand to the side of his head with a bent elbow, even though he does not normally do this for some reason. The Führer is wearing a grey pinstripe suit with a white shirt and grey tie, compared to Himmler, who is dressed in his military uniform. Private Singh is dressed smartly in a navy double-breasted blazer with gold buttons, a white shirt and grey trousers. He takes the opportunity to thank Himmler for adding new garments to his wardrobe.

The Führer appears somewhat unsettled, reading on without any discernible reaction. Himmler calls out, and the butler returns to pour tea for Private Singh. It is a proper silver service, complete with all the bells and whistles. As Private Singh helps himself to sugar and stirs, he knocks the silver teaspoon against the cup's edge a few times before placing it down. Taking a sip of tea, he carefully places the cup back onto the saucer. To his surprise, the butler brings over a cake stand adorned with an assortment of sandwiches, cakes, and scones. This marks the second time he has been introduced to these quintessentially British delights; he reflects. They're generously adorned with lashings of clotted cream and jam, a departure from the usual German fare, isn't it? How much cabbage, sausage and 'Kommissrot', dark rye bread can one person consume.

Himmler makes a hand gesture towards Private Singh to help himself to the goodies on offer. So, he takes a sandwich; to his surprise, it is cheese and pickle on white bread. He has not tasted anything like this for a while, as he wolfs it down. 'It's pukka grub' as they would say in the East End of London. Himmler watches him, smiling at the fact he looks like he is enjoying the food. Private Singh notices Himmler watching him eat and slows his eating down. He picks up a napkin and wipes his mouth before placing it back on the table. For some reason, he feels he has slightly embarrassed himself.

"Wunderbar," Private Singh calls out.

Even the Führer stops reading and looks over at him. Himmler lights up a cigarette and starts to smoke, smiling. He looks over at Private Singh as he removes his glasses, which he cleans. Himmler tells him that he has had another meeting with this other Indian chap. The one with an analogous way of thinking to him regarding making the British pay for what they have done. Ultimately, removing the British from India would be the ideal goal, and the Führer is happy to make this happen. Private Singh is overwhelmed with joy by the news and smiles. This smile we talk of is a proper smile, which is ear to ear as he cannot hide his happiness. Himmler congratulates Private Singh for his future success against the British, with the Führer nodding at him. He does not have the heart to tell Himmler that Goebbels has already informed him of the new Indian division in Paris. Private Singh does not understand this breakdown in communication within the German hierarchy.

It is like Goebbels wanted to get one over on Himmler regarding who informed him first. Himmler continues that the new division of men trained by the German forces and first deployed across Europe against the Allied troops before they are ready to march into India. Even though Goebbels had told him, he still could not believe his ears, so he listened and called out that they must celebrate this news. The slight air of tension is replaced with happiness. Himmler asks for champagne, and the butler arrives with a silver ice bucket and a bottle of Cristal champagne. Certain high-ranking German officers preferred the clear bottle, with the flat bottom so no explosives could be hidden within the dimple and masked by the dark green glass of the bottle. The butler pours three glasses and returns the bottle to the ice bucket. I believe the Führer does not drink alcohol, so why the three glasses? Saying that, if you are in service, would you want to miss him out. Maybe it was just for looks, so he is still taking part in the celebrations.

Beads of condensation trickle down the sides of the bottle as it rests within the ice bucket, wrapped in a white cloth napkin. Himmler raises his glass to salute as does Private Singh, the Führer just watches the two men as they charge their glasses. The Führer looks at Private Singh without saying anything. For some reason, he looks slightly off to him. Himmler continues regarding the new Indian division of men, about how he can instruct the removal of all the Indian prisoners of war from the camps for them to be brought over to Private Singh. He looks pretty excited about the plans; he talks regarding their new uniforms and divisional insignia. Private Singh asks questions, which Himmler answers via the interpreter.

Where they will be based, and which German officers will aid them with training. Private Singh glances over at the Führer, who still looks like his mind is preoccupied. That is when the Führer speaks up in a faint voice; he explains that an attempt was made on his life. He survived, as Private Singh could see, but the vipers within were nearly victorious in their plot to remove him from power and take his life. This is why extra security measures are now being implemented. Now the penny drops for Private Singh, who realises that his room was tossed last night and why he has undergone numerous searches on his journey here today to meet the two men. Private Singh sympathises with the Führer and assures him that God is on his side.

Himmler interjects, emphasising the heightened security measures around the Führer and his personal commitment to eliminating anyone deemed a threat to the Third Reich and the Führer. The atmosphere grows tense with the unexpected aggression Himmler displays. He forcefully slams his clenched fist onto the tabletop, defiant against potential assailants disguised in German uniforms. Sensing the shift in mood, the Führer invites Private Singh to accompany him for a walk, hinting at another matter he wishes to discuss.

The three men proceed towards the garden area of the grounds, with the interpreter following closely so he is still able to translate what is being said. In a hushed conversation, the Führer reveals that party members were involved within a plot against him and expresses concern for the safety of his associates.

"Scheiße, Scheiße, Scheiße," Himmler calls out.

"Blitzkrieg Tommies," he adds.

"Wer glauben sie, dass sie meine Jungs töten?" Hitler adds.

Suddenly, the Führer waves his frail clenched fist into the air and with aggression as he says, "Who do these men think they are for killing his boys?" His demeanour changes instantly, from a solitary man sitting contemplating his thoughts to an eruption of aggressiveness and ultraviolence. He goes on to explain how this group of men were responsible for the slayings of six Waffen-SS-officers at 'Sainte-Geneviève-des-Bois', even though they tried to conceal this. He displays a mixed bag of emotions as he speaks, slowly calming himself down after his fit of sudden rage.

Ludwig Koch, the sole survivor, had been picked up and spilt the curried beans regarding what had happened after everything Pauley had said to him. He asked Private Singh if he knew of this, to which he replied he was not aware of this. So, the Führer talked him through what these soldiers did to his boys, the gruesome acts of depravity which were afflicted against these Waffen-SS-officers and other German soldiers alike.

Private Singh can tell this is a testing time for the Führer as he suddenly looks weak on his feet and grabs at Himmler's arm, which steadies him. They all stop as the Führer removes a white handkerchief and wipes his brow before they start to walk once again. He continues to tell this tall tale of these honourable German soldiers being treated like dogs by these manic marauders. His voice slightly wavers due to the heartache he seems to feel. The young man continues to translate the conversation in his soft voice.

They stop once again as they reach a flower bed of white roses. The Führer smells one up close and smiles. He turns towards Private Singh and advises him that the British soldiers known as the 'Blitzkrieg Tommies' have been apprehended in a failed plot. The SS is currently holding them; Himmler himself will personally be conducting the interviews with this select group of prisoners and implementing his own brand of integration skills. Private Singh does not have any views on these soldiers; besides, he dislikes what the British are doing in India. The Führer seems to be trying to gain a reaction from him as he studies his face after telling him the news. Surely, the Führer knows where his loyalty lies. This suddenly infuriates Private Singh, who calls out that he would like to speak to these Tommies under the guise he is another British soldier who has been captured. See what information they will give up; if he can persuade them, he is a Sepoy in an analogous situation to theirs.

Private Singh tries to reason with Himmler that if he can gain him information regarding their plans, which may help Germany win the war. Suddenly, the Führer and Himmler start to warm towards the idea. What if they had their own spy within the British army? The Führer stops walking and looks at Private Singh, and apprehension washes over him at what the Führer will say next. Himmler walks over towards the Führer and speaks into his ear; they converse in German and glance over at Private Singh on a few occasions.

The interpreter remains silent, as they must have told him not to translate this part of their conversation. Himmler looks over at Private Singh, who is waiting anxiously to see what the two men think of his idea. Suspense fills the air as they talk. What will the Führer's answer be? The Führer speaks again and advises that yes, they will try this plan, and he will be placed in a cell with the British soldiers. Private Singh thanks both the men and is excited at the prospect of getting some payback, how small it may be, against the British.

Himmler interjects, mid-sentence, to explain that he will oversee every step of this plan. He emphasises that Private Singh must be physically beaten to display contusions and lacerations from prior interrogations in order to manipulate these British soldiers known as the 'Blitzkrieg Tommies' effectively. If they can persuade them that torture awaits if they do not cooperate, especially with the leverage of Singh's apparent suffering, Himmler believes extracting information might prove more challenging than anticipated. He recognises that if these men are prepared to sacrifice their lives, extracting valuable intelligence may be more difficult than initially perceived. He wants the 'Blitzkrieg Tommies' to meet with the most gruesome of deaths after the information has been extracted but still harbours a concern regarding Singh's plan.

Himmler glares at Private Singh, as his eyes are fixated on him as he talked, which unsettled him slightly. The four men cautiously approach the Führer's parked car, destined for another meeting. This time, his vehicle is only flanked by an armoured vehicle and two motorcycles. German soldiers are loading onto a troop carrier, positioned to follow the convoy in case of an attack. The Führer has significantly bolstered his security in the aftermath of recent events, largely credited to Himmler's efforts.

As the Führer walks over towards his awaiting car, the driver opens the rear door, and the Führer enters the car. He advises Private Singh he has a gift for him within the boot of the car and would like him to have a butcher's at it. So Private Singh and Himmler both walk around to the vehicle's rear, and Himmler prompts the guard to open the boot lid. On opening it, the guard stands to the side as both men peer into the now-open boot space. Himmler steps forward and removes the white sheet which drapes the object within.

He reveals what is underneath; the two men are gobsmacked. They are both astonished by the framed oil painting which sits before them. As they examine this work of oil paint on canvas, they remain silent, but Private Singh is quite taken aback by what he is looking at. Himmler's facial expression, too, tells its own story. He is overwhelmed by the gift and how much the Führer is prepared to give this man he barely knows. After a short pause, Himmler instructs the guard to cover the painting before he closes the boot lid. He places his grey visor cap back on his head and glares at Private Singh.

Suddenly, the Führer calls the interpreter and Private Singh forward. He tells him this gift is in appreciation for his selfless act of saving young Hugo Kruger. Why this was of grave importance as Hugo in his eyes is the saviour of the Third Reich and will be an integral part within the new SS unit. If something would have happened to him this would have impacted the project in Berlin. On hearing this Private Singh's mind starts to race, regarding the Führer's last comment.

What does he mean by this, he thinks to himself. The Führer continues, this is only possible due to the empathy and compassion, displayed by him hence the gift is a way of expressing his gratitude. He continues regarding the gift, which is worth an abundance of money, and he will keep it safe for him. Private Singh thanks the Führer for such a beautiful gift and congratulates him on his exquisite taste. The Führer nods his head in appreciation as this is translated. Himmler still stands to the side of the rear of the vehicle, which the Führer notices and quietly mentions Joseph Goebbels wants another meeting with him regarding the new Indian division Himmler is forming. He wants to showcase this globally and highlight to the world the 'Bayerischen Löwen' or the 'Bavarian Lions', who will fight under the Nazi swastika. This will be held at the Berghof, and only selected party members will be in attendance. The Führer adds that the world will bear witness to the might of the German war machine. Private Singh, thinks this must be the secret military programme, which Hugo is somehow got his little fat fingers in?

Private Singh is genuinely excited by the news, which Goebbels informed him regarding during the meeting in Paris. He does not fully comprehend what games are being played here but knows something is not right between the hierarchies of the party. Is someone within the inner circle trying to kill the Führer and take over? What if there is a coup about to take place to overthrow Adolf Hitler? Private Singh needs to know why certain bits of information are being drip-fed to him from different party members within different meetings. Maybe it is a test of his loyalty to the Führer, he thinks to himself. Maybe he should come clean and tell the Führer everything, further to his meeting in Paris.

The Führer asks Private Singh when they will meet to play chess as he is looking forward to this, as long as he doesn't introduce the 'Zugzwang' theory. He tells Private Singh they could drink tea and talk about Sikhism as he intrigues him. The Führer stares at Private Singh like he is examining him from top to toe. He smiles and nods slightly as he places his hand on his arm.

Private Singh cannot understand why the Führer is so interested in him. Goebbels, too, found Private Singh intriguing and was interested in gaining further knowledge about him. Himmler steps forward towards the two men and interjects into the conversation. He explains that gathering information from the British soldiers is far more valuable at this stage than putting on a picture show for the world to see. Private Singh senses an element of jealousy or power struggle here between Himmler and Goebbels. With this said, the Führer assures Private Singh that he will get what he wants, but he needs to show his loyalty to the Third Reich as the young interpreter continues to translate this four-way conversation.

"Heil Hitler!" Himmler calls out.

He salutes and raises his arm fully, with conviction. The Führer glances over at Private Singh, who pauses at first and then salutes the Führer in the Nazi way.

"Heil Hitler," Private Singh calls out.

Himmler nods at Private Singh with an element of pride in how he has just saluted the Führer, who shows the gratification of his leadership. Private Singh's arm is lofted high with his open hand, with pointed fingers. His conviction is evident to see in his ever-increasing loyalty to the Third Reich and its Führer Adolf Hitler.

Chapter Five: A pukka Nazi gathering

A few days later, Private Singh is pushed into a large prison cell where the so-called 'Rum Bunch' or 'Blitzkrieg Tommies' are being held, what they are called all depends on the colour of the uniform you wear. He falls to the floor due to the force he is pushed with. The cell has stone walls, rusting metal light fittings, and the stone floor is covered with some straw. A small window floods in some light, only highlighting the old-school dungeon they are in. What looks like old wooden church pews have been cut down and fitted within the space, which function as beds for its guests.

Private Singh has already been given a good seeing to, as prearranged with Himmler, hence his cuts and bruises. Some Kraut must have enjoyed himself, laying into this Geezer from other shores. Once Private Singh had been softened up a little to make this masquerade more believable, he was shown to the Tommie's cell. He is pushed forcefully into the cell, landing on the floor, as I said. Private Singh slowly gets to his feet and dusts himself down.

"Easy now," Private Singh calls out.

"You, Nazi cunt, before I'm forced to give you a proper slap,"

"Cos, you're playing silly buggers,"

"So, just cut out the dog and pony show, as it will save us all fucking about ere," he adds.

"Who do you think, you Krauts are,"

"Come on boy, let's be having you," he adds.

"Well come on then,"

"No more horseplay, just couple a Geezers having a ruckus,"

"Come on boy," he adds.

"Come on then," he screams.

Private Singh just glares at the German solider, his nostrils are flaring, and he has rage within his eyes. His last comment was a high-pitched scream directed at the guard. He is bouncing on the stop, like some professional boxer, limbering up ready for a punch-up. The two German soldiers look at one another, maybe they are aware of the plan and wonder what he is doing. They hesitate for a short while, as the verbal abuse continues to be hurled within their direction. The guard near the cell door says something in German and shakes his head, it resembles a look of, enough is enough.

Suddenly the guard within the cell thrusts a rifle butt into Private Singh's chest just to highlight his disapproval of his actions. Private Singh ends up heaped up on the floor in silence, only holding onto his midriff in discomfort, this time. The second guard slowly closes the heavy-looking metal door as the first guard leaves the cell. On bolting the door closed, the guard looks through the opening within the cell door and watches Private Singh momentarily before he slides it closed.

The Tommies hear their footsteps disappearing into the distance before they act. Some of the Tommies move forward to see who it is, Jerry has brought in. Private Singh picks himself up off the floor and dusts down his uniform as he holds onto the torn epaulette, which hangs off his shoulder. Suddenly, he grabs at his midriff due to the pain he is experiencing. Although he has a busted wing, Clive comes over to help him up. To their surprise, this Sikh soldier is wearing a British uniform. Clive asks him if he is okay; Private Singh answers he would be sipping a cold beer in the East End of London with the company of good women if he was. He asks what happened as he looks at his arm; Clive tells him that one went straight through. This breaks the ice slightly between the men as the rest of the Tommies, who look on.

Private Singh immediately salutes Major Watkins as soon as he sees him, as the Major sits in a dark corner of the cell. The Major and the Lieutenant both walk over to join the two men and salute in return. The Major asks Private Singh who he is and what unit he is from. Private Singh knows they will not suspect anything if he sticks to his own story.

"Sir," Private Singh calls out.

"At ease, Private," Major Watkins calls out.

"So, what's your story then?" The Major asks.

Private Singh must convince this rabble of renegades that he is singing off the same hymn sheet as them. It is not as if he is telling any porkies now, just leaving out the bit that he, the Führer and Himmler are all bosom buddies. He tells them about the air drops and how they drifted off course. How a few of them had been making their way through French countryside but were pinned down by a Nazi patrol, which shot and killed the others. He was arrested and beaten for information, which he did not give up as he knew nothing. Who would tell a Sepoy within the British army anything useful, he explains to the men.

The Tommies gather around him as he elaborates on the events that unfolded. He enquiries about their homes, wondering how London endures amidst the relentless air raids. Intrigued, some of the Tommies, who have never encountered a turban-wearing Sikh soldier, focus on this unique figure addressing them. Meanwhile, the Lieutenant exchanges a glance with the Major, observing Private Singh recount his narrative. Perhaps the Lieutenant is discerning something beneath the surface?

The Major asks him other questions that only a British soldier, who had been dropped into France, would be aware of. Private Singh answers them with ease as a percentage of what he is saying is true. Some of the Tommies are slightly standoffish, like Pauley and JD. Pauley makes a crack about his hat, not being a standard issue.

"Nice hat, mate, not gonna stop much lead," Pauley calls out.

Most of the Tommies laugh at this comment, to Private Singh's exasperation. He glares at Pauley with rage, as he has had a gutful of snide comments like this most of his life.

"Firstly, fella, it's not a hat, it's a turban," Private Singh replies.

"Secondly, if you've got the minerals to march into battle only wearing a cloth turban, lead entering your noggin shouldn't be an issue, should it, my son?"

"So, I suggest you get yourself an education, fella,"

"Maybe read a few books, and then maybe you'll understand,"

"If not, fuck off, you bigoted English cunt," he adds.

"Before I have your guts for a frilly blue garter," he adds.

Private Singh takes offence at his comments and tries to educate him and continues to explain the significance of why he wears a turban. Due to Pauley's comments, some of the Tommies laugh at what is being said while others stay quiet. Francis takes offence to Pauley's bigoted views and stands up and asks Pauley to apologise. Private Singh thanks Francis but assures him that he has had uneducated, bigoted fools throughout his life, poking fun, making jokes and one-liners about his identity. All he reassures Francis of is, if this Tommy who is mouthing off here, would have had some form of education there would be no issue. He would maybe comprehend other religious beliefs without gobbing off like this. Lieutenant Harvey calls Pauley aside and gives him a dressing down, and he points out this man is fighting for a country thousands of miles away from his homeland, and all he can do is make fun of him. Maybe Pauley thinks Private Singh is the fella Ludwig Koch was referring to? Suddenly, there is a slight tension due to this conversation within the cell. Private Singh looks at Pauley, who is mumbling something under his breath. He decides to offer Pauley some words of wisdom.

"My learned friend, if you let me explain something to you, I'll keep it simple, as I comprehend you resemble a simple-looking gent,"

"Someone who unfortunately did not have the same opportunities that others may have had in life and love,"

"Someone who may have been neglected as a child, beaten for the simplest of things, the error of your ways,"

"Maybe these atrocities in your life, these shortfalls, this dark hole, this void left by a maternal being maybe at a tender age,"

"I presume you now make up for this with aggression and conflict, which fuels the fire within,"

"It is your armour to protect you from these Charlatans, who really got under your skin and in your head,"

"So, in your mind, the only way you can combat this is by lashing out, with your razor-sharp tongue and your one-liners,"

"Maybe, just maybe, you should take a step backwards, evaluate the situation or surroundings before you let your mouth do all the talking,"

"I hear you say there is nothing wrong in your mouth doing all the talking, going ten to the dozen, but what of the hurt and sorrow this may inflict as it's going ten to a dozen,"

"These words you utter, simple words you think, showcase your superior vocabulary and your supreme carnal knowledge to us all,"

"I suggest you scrutinise, peer within and establish the situation is crystal clear before you comment on future conversations,"

"Do you fully decipher, what is being communicated to you here, me old China? So please, pretty please, with a Glace cherry on top, treat others kindly, you bigoted fuck," Private Singh calls out.

Private Singh stops talking and the prison cell falls into silence, it is like he had read Pauley's psychiatric file. How would he know, certain personal details about him or maybe he is a good judge of character. The Tommies are gobsmacked at what has just been said. Pauley, who probably did not fully understand what was said to him, just glares at Private Singh. Arthur jokes that this is as comfortable as the Ritz in London to Private Singh to calm matters down. Suddenly, some of the men burst into laughter at the comment.

Pauley shoots a stern glare at Private Singh, after being put in his place by the Lieutenant. Francis, with a subtle hand gesture, draws attention to Private Singh's bleeding injury. Swiftly producing a handkerchief, he deftly mops up the blood on his face. Francis then enquiries about the origin of the wounds, pointing at his own face. Private Singh recounts the encounter with the SS, who subjected him to a thorough beating when he refused to disclose any information. Arthur, demonstrating empathy, offers Private Singh a drink of water, an offer he readily accepts, taking a long, satisfying sip. The majority of the Tommies settle back into their positions within the cell, returning to where they were originally seated. Private Singh joins them, tending to his bleeding wound.

The men talk further about their plans after the war and where they are from. Francis tells the men he is from the East End of London, where he was an amateur boxer. Private Singh mentions a few places within the East End to Francis, which they talk of. Francis goes on to say that he had enormous potential to be a champion, but the war got in the way of this.

After coming to Britian from Eire, he grew up in Blighty. For some reason, he told the men he grew up in care in some boy's home where he had to learn how to fight quickly. Even though he was a big lad, the boys would gang up and beat him to steal his food due to his Irish accent. So, the only thing he could do was fight, so he did. Over the years, he shot up in height and became of stocky build, so there was no more trouble at the boy's home. This was only followed by trouble when he started work as an apprentice in a factory. He was called names due to his Irish heritage and often alienated by his fellow employees. Other men would want to challenge him due to his size. Even after joining the army, he still attracted trouble on nights out. This led to him killing a man and injuring another, hence ending up here.

He showed remorse that he did not want to kill the chap; he just wanted him to stop calling his wife names. What the Geezer was unaware of was Francis had just caught his Fiancée in bed with his GI friend. He was drowning his sorrows when this chap would not stop, provoking him. The chap kept on at him, till Francis snapped and shoved the man back with force. Francis was unaware his head would hit a table, which was flush against the wall. The chap died in a military hospital hours after the incident happened in The Loving Rose public house, Peckham Rye. He fled the scene and ended up crashing into another car, seriously injuring the occupants. Suddenly, the mood became very sombre as Francis spilt his guts about why he was now looking at a death sentence. Private Singh sympathised with this and placed his hand on his shoulder. This is before JD called out; how would he know?

For some reason, JD and Pauley had not taken kindly to this man from a different background becoming involved. The Lieutenant barked at Pauley once again to calm him down. Clive suddenly speaks up; he is one of the quiet ones within the group. He tells the Tommies he grew up in Germany. His parents worked at the Embassy, so he travelled around. He talked about how Germany used to be a different country before the Nazis came to power. He continued to talk about how he was treated differently within Blighty when he started school because he had a slight German accent, how he was bullied, beaten and had his lunch stolen most days due to being slightly different. He tells Private Singh that he fully understands where he is coming from due to his own experience.

Private Singh tells the men that wearing a turban made him a target for verbal abuse wherever he went within Blighty, how they were seen as hired help only, not that his parents were both educated people here working for the British government and military. He, too, mentioned how his school days were one of the worst he had experienced due to being different. Basic training was even worse, as one Lieutenant had really disliked him from day one. He tried everything he could to run him out of the British army, with beatings from the other soldiers, having his test scores altered, and being told he was worthless and there was no space within the King's army for someone like him. His bedding was often urinated on and even set on fire, so he would end up sleeping on the floor. How he was asked kindly to clean the latrines daily, as this is what the hired help did.

He was told he could not accept his graduation with the rest of the men as he did not deserve one. Private Singh goes on to explain to the Tommies how he saved the same Lieutenant's life after he had been drinking. His car was involved in an accident as he drove home from the pub. He pulled him free from the burning car wreckage, which, to this day, he was not thanked for. Instead, he was threatened with a Court Marshall for putting his hands on an officer without permission.

The mood had become sombre again within the cell as the men were talking from the heart. Private Singh had formed a sense of camaraderie with the group of Tommies, which was something he had not planned on doing. They looked like a straight bunch of fellas, besides Pauley.

The Major called Private Singh aside and asked him if he had seen or heard anything before, he was arrested. He replied no to the question. Private Singh told the Major a few porkies regarding how he had been arrested in some small town after he had escaped. The Major asked Private Singh, who questioned him, what sort of uniform they were wearing to fathom if he was telling them the truth or not. He described the uniforms down to a tee, as he has been around enough of them over the last three weeks or so.

He explained how the Gestapo questioned him and used electric shock treatment on him to gain information regarding the Allied landings before the SS had given him a good seeing, too. He explained he was arrested by the Gestapo at first, then passed over to the SS. They were convinced he was a spy working for the British government. He explained that because his identity was different from that of most of the British soldiers, they took some form of interest in him. Where he was originally from and why he was now fighting for the British.

Private Singh told Major Watkins that this was the truth, and that was what had happened. Minus the Gestapo interrogating him, it was more of a chat over a cuppa with the Führer and Himmler when they frisked him and tossed his room. Major Watkins seemed happy with the Sikh prisoner not being a German spy, so he opened up to him about what had taken place for them to end up here. He explained they were in the process of blowing up a power station when they were all captured.

Major Watkins felt they were not betrayed, but it was bad luck and poor intelligence which resulted in them being here. The Major explained how the 'Rum Bunch' had waded through a small river at daybreak before they made their way onto the riverbank in thick fog. The fog we talk of gave off a ghostly, eerie backdrop to what would happen next. He told Private Singh they were all gathered under a steel bridge which spanned the river. Knives were impaled into the necks of the two Nazis who stood on guard at the bridge entrance, and they exited this world. Silently killing them as the red stuff trickled from their wounds before their imminent demise. Under this cover of fog, the Tommies made their way towards a waste pipe, which led into this power station they were here to fuck up. The intelligence they had highlighted that this particular power station was going to be used to produce 'heavy water,' which is a key element in producing an atomic bomb. The Allies were fully aware of Adolf Hitler's love of new weapons, which would aid him in winning the war.

The research and development of these weapons played a massive part in the Führer's grand plan for all-out victory. The Tommies knew the havoc it would cause if Jerry lost power within the region and the loss of this 'heavy water' production facility would delay the process of the Nazis having an atom bomb. This is before the visit of the Nazi Rockstar himself, Adolf Hitler, which was originally where they were going to swap over James under the guise of the carpet bombing.

This was then changed to the town of Dieppe, where Hugo Kruger would be present for a Hitler Youth presentation. Private Singh listened attentively, absorbing as much information as possible. Unfortunately, James Hall's abrupt demise threw a spanner in the works. Suddenly, the Major realised the error of his ways and fell silent momentarily, as he had inadvertently revealed all this to a complete stranger the cunning plan the 'Rum Bunch' was here to execute. He just glared at Private Singh, who reassured the Major that he was on the same side as he sensed this. The Lieutenant looked over at Major Watkins and nodded to assure him that Private Singh was not a spy. The Major stood up and walked over to the water bucket, taking a drink and splashing some onto his 'boat-race', bringing clarity to the proceedings in hand. He stretched his back slightly before returning to where Private Singh and the Lieutenant were sitting.

"I'm sorry, but you can't be too careful nowadays, where was I?" The Major calls out.

"Oh yes, the cunning plan before I rudely interrupted my own train of thought," he adds.

Apprehension filled the air as Major Watkins looked at Private Singh while remaining silent. Suddenly he asked Private Singh straight out if he was a German spy, to which he just laughed, pointing out the fact no Nazi was going to have any form of chinwag with him due to his identity. He pointed out that V–Section would have come calling if he were. The Major still had the thought of the information Pauley had extracted from his prisoner rattling around his noggin. What if Private Singh is that man? The Major is a good judge of character as he believes and shrugged off these thoughts. But he could not answer with certitude. Both Major Watkins and Lieutenant Harvey looked at one another and after a slight pause, the Major placed his hand on Private Singh's shoulder.

"Truth be told, I'm a Nazis spy, here to extract information from you," Private Singh called out.

"Well, would Churchill trust a Sepoy like me?" he adds.

"Touché," Major Watkins replies.

As the Major nodded his head, smiling, he started to talk once again regarding who Coco was and her bevy of beauties who kill Germans for a living. Due to the nature of this attack, only the 'Rum Bunch' and some French resistance members were present. Luckily, the girls were not there, as their covers would have been blown. The Major continued the story about how the Tommies crawled up this waste pipe and into the power station while he and Clive swapped uniforms with the dead guards and made their way towards the guard room. Clive spoke excellent German, but the Major was a linguist, too. They spoke German to the guards on duty as they entered the building, making their way towards the radio room as they needed to contact London and send the message.

"Rebel calling Twelve 10," Major Watkins calls out.

"Rebel calling Twelve 10," he repeats.

The radio operator calls out for Colonel Smith, who takes over the radio handset and sits down while talking.

"Twelve 10 here, Rebel, go ahead," Colonel Smith replies.

"Seven years bad luck, Twelve 10," Major Watkins replies.

"Understood, Rebel, proceed with smash and grab," Colonel Smith replies.

"Understood, Twelve 10 already underway, Rebel out," Major Watkins replies.

"Roger Rebel, Twelve 10 out," Colonel Smith replies.

Major Watkins, with his simple reply to London had highlighted they had started systematically destroying key German instillations and causing as much havoc for Jerry as possible. Private Singh just listened and took everything on board; if only the Major knew of the fox, he had let into the chicken coop. The Major continued regarding what had happened and how they managed to radio London with the message. London had given them the all-clear to proceed with operation 'Smash and grab.'

What London was not fully aware was that the 'Rum Bunch' of Tommies had already conducted numerous sabotage missions prior to this. Now Colonel Smith had spoken to Major Watkins and given him the green light for this new operation, which they had just mustered up due to the circumstances of what had happened.

Mr X, being the cool and calculated man he is, probably had a backup plan ready to execute anyway. In case the original plan went awry, Major Watkins explained his surprise at conversing with Colonel Smith. He had been informed that they would not communicate with each other again till after the war. However, due to James's death, this unexpected encounter occurred due to the secrecy of their mission.

Meanwhile, the Tommies had strategically placed explosives in the power station's basement levels, ready for detonation. The intended course was to navigate back through the waste pipe towards the river, where they would regroup. Unfortunately, Gary encountered an engineer working at the plant, leading to an unexpected obstacle.

The Kraut asked him something, but he ignored the Geezer, who started shouting for help as he must have realised, he was not German. A guard showed up, and that is when a gun battle ensued within the basement levels of this power station; they were there to destroy. The Major explained how the Tommies held their own, but Jerry outnumbered them. German reinforcements were called in, and they watched the troop carriers arrive from their position. He and Clive destroyed the radio and shot a fair few Nazis on our way out. Clive's suggestion to plant a few explosives within the power station offices was an innovative idea, too. The civilian staff had fled as soon as the shooting started, so they had free reign of it all. Major Watkins explained how they smashed the equipment at first in case the explosives did not go off before they both slipped out of the gaff. Clive threw a few grenades into the vehicles parked outside, and just for good measure, they went up a treat, like some pukka chip pan fire in a greasy spoon.

Major Watkins continued, in the meanwhile, the boys had their work cut out due to the volume of Nazis who were now pinning them down. Luckily for them, the explosives they had used had timers on them. If not, they would all be brown bread by now, and the Major looked over at the men as he said this. A few of the men looked back over as they both continued to talk, Pauley giving Major Watkins and Private Singh dirty looks. The glare highlighted how Pauley felt he was to blame for their capture. Maybe some of the other Tommies blamed Major Watkins for their arrest, too.

The Major continued to tell Private Singh how the remaining Tommies tried to escape before the Germans cleverly poured water down into the basement area, flooding it. The Tommies were trapped, and the water level rose as Jerry poked hosepipes through the vents and turned on the water, which started to flood the basement area. They held off as long as they could before they had to swim back and disarm the explosives they had set. If they had gone off, they would have brought the whole thing down on themselves. Once they had disarmed the explosives, the water level was too high, and they were pushed against the stone vaulted ceilings of the basement they found themselves in. Surrendering was the only choice, or they would have drowned down there. The emotion displayed by Major Watkins indicates what the mission's success meant to him and his men. The Major wore a mask of disappointment, like someone who has been defeated. On hearing the story again, some of the men also looked disappointed regarding their capture and now imprisonment.

The Major paused slightly as he looked over at the Lieutenant, and then he stopped talking. Private Singh asked how the Major and Clive had come to be here, seeing they were not in the basement with the remaining Tommies. The Major replied, slightly heartedly, that they were stopped after they had stolen a vehicle and driven out of the compound. They were driving towards the main checkpoint when they were stopped and asked for their papers. He explained they could have tried to shoot their way out of there but would have certainly ended up as target practice, taking into consideration the heavy artillery which was pointed in their direction. So, long story short, that is how they have all ended up in here. Clive took one on the shoulder, which luckily only clipped his wing as it went straight through.

The Major knew this was the best thing to do, as they would face the music as one unit, as the 'Rum Bunch.' Private Singh could sense Major Watkins was very content with the issues they had caused the Nazis since landing here in France. The Major opened up to Private Singh regarding all the other attacks they had carried out previously. These simple tasks like changing the road signs around, damaging vehicles, blowing up the ammunition depot and fuel reserve and finally, the attack on the power station. Private Singh placed his hand on the shoulder of the Major as to reassure him that what they had achieved would not be forgotten. The Major first looked at his shoulder where Private Singh had placed his hand, to his surprise, as he removed it at once. The Major broke into a smile and returned the gesture. Private Singh asked him what was next; the Major just replied whatever fate had in store for them all.

Private Singh had gathered details that he could now forward to Himmler as requested. His plan of sending him in to extract information from the Tommies had worked like a treat. Similar to a Nazi sniffing out Jews hiding under the floorboards. He knew deep down they would be shot by the firing squad as no one would want to imprison them due to the Geneva Convention. The SS were renowned for killing prisoners of war without adhering to any rules of engagement. Suddenly, a German guard opens the cell door and gestures for Private Singh to come forward. The Tommies try to intervene, but the second guard thrusts a gun into their faces with intent. Private Singh puts on an act where he tries not to leave. He starts to kick and scream that he is going to be questioned again and cannot take the heavy-handed tactics of the integrators anymore. Tension filled the cell at what was going to happen to him. The Tommies tried to help, but the guards were not going to be part of any shenanigans from the Tommies.

They looked serious, as one chambered a round just to highlight, he would shoot. Private Singh asks the Tommies to stand back and let him go. He will face whatever they have for him. As he leaves the cell, he wears the mask of a scared and defeated man. He quickly says goodbye and turns to go when Pauley calls out 'that he'll be hanged in the morning'. Suddenly, Private Singh's sorrow turns to rage at what is being said here. He stops and glares at this rude individual, someone who reminds him of the bigots he has put up with throughout his life.

"So, none of those words of wisdom I offered you earlier have sunk in then," Private Singh calls out.

"I tell you what, there is no helping some lost souls," he adds.

"Regarding your last comment, not if your hung first Geezer swinging from the rafters like a proper delinquent you are," he adds sternly.

This comment really gets under Pauley's skin as the remaining Tommies start to laugh at his expense. He advances towards Private Singh, but the German guard halts him abruptly by jabbing the barrel of his gun forcefully into his chest. He calls out that the guard should shoot him if he is man enough. The two men lock eyes, and the room is steeped in tension, resembling a standoff. Abruptly, the first guard signals for Private Singh to move with a hand gesture, and Singh begins to exit the cell slowly. He turns and salutes, receiving a reciprocal salute from Major Watkins and Lieutenant Harvey. As Private Singh departs, he makes a humorous remark about keeping his dog on a lead next time, earning a smile from the Major and laughter from the other soldiers. Pauley, however, expresses his disapproval by kicking the water bucket on the floor and retreating to the corner of the cell.

Private Singh is marched to another smaller room, which looks like an interrogation room, not before he turns and looks behind him as he walks away from the cell holding the Tommies. He is told to sit down, which he does as he looks around the room. A packet of cigarettes and a box of matches had been placed on the table. He picks up the box of matches and studies them before he shakes them and lifts it close towards his ear as the guard watches him.

He repeats this on a few occasions before he breaks into a smile and places the box of matches back onto the tabletop again. He looks around the room, which has white tiled walls and flooring. A single metal table and two metal chairs are set out in this small space. Light floods in from a small window towards the ceiling, only highlighting this grotty space he is seated in. What resembles dried blood stains are on the tiles, which look like they have been crudely cleaned up, but is not sure of the offending stain. Knowing the SS and what type of facility Private Singh is within, blood is the probable answer further to some callous interrogation which had been carried out.

The Nazis were not too bothered, regarding appearances. If they cracked a few skulls mid-interrogation and the red stuff leaked out, they would simply move onto the next victim awaiting an SS-style chinwag. Placing needles under your fingernails, too-good old beatings and even extracting teeth were some of the gruesome methods employed by Himmler's boys. So, cleaning up spilt blood on tilled walls and floors was not high up on their list of things to do.

Metal hooks had been fitted onto the walls, which must be used to tie up prisoners, Private Singh thinks to himself. He notices what looks like electronic equipment sitting on a trolley within the corner of the room. It is probably used to conduct acts of torture, the art of inflicting pain on your victims. Suddenly, the door opened; to his surprise, it was Joseph Goebbels and not Heinrich Himmler. Private Singh did not expect to see him here, as he is rather taken aback by his appearance.

A lady followed him into the small room as the guard was asked to leave. Goebbels is dressed smartly in his brown suit jacket, with a Nazi swastika armband, with a white shirt, black tie and black trousers. He removed his brown visor cap as he entered the room. She looked like a secretary, dressed in a grey skirt and a white blouse, with her blonde hair plaited up. Goebbels produces a handkerchief and moves the chair holding it. You can see an element of disgust slapped across his boat, probably taking into consideration the location of the meeting. He picks at something off the table and sprinkles it away with the tips of his fingers, again with contempt at his surroundings. He starts to talk, and the female interpreter first translates his apologies for the surroundings they find themselves in. This is not up to the standard he has become accustomed to, but this is the best the SS could provide at such short notice. His critical opprobrium of Himmler and his SS was all too clear. He once again produces his handkerchief and covers his mouth, this time before he shouts and stands up. The chair drags across the tiled floor, making a screeching noise as he pushes it backwards with his legs.

"Nein, nein, nein, nein," he calls out.

He talks to the young lady, who was standing to the side of him throughout and she asks Private Singh to follow them. Goebbels calls the guard, who opens the door, and the three of them leave. Goebbels, who limps due to his club foot, slowly marches as the three of them enter a corridor, which meets another much longer corridor. They continue to walk down this corridor and into an office that has open French doors. Goebbels pulls himself up a seat as the other two sit down also. You can hear the birds singing, and the sun is beaming down, the guests can even see the maze which is set within these luscious grounds.

This is a far cry from the cell the Tommies are being held in and the room they were just sitting in. Private Singh wonders, if Goebbels is even aware why he is here, and the Tommies are in a cell within the same building as them. Maybe Himmler has kept this from him, and his chat with the Tommies. So Private Singh says nothing as he feels the game's afoot here between the two men. Goebbels starts to rant and rave, waving his hands around, which looks like he is talking about the surroundings; they had just left. The interpreter listens to him going on before she looks over at Private Singh and says something in German.

"Schöner Garten!" she calls out.

"Beautiful garden," she adds with a German accent.

Private Singh partially grasped the message through Goebbels' body language even before the young lady translated it for him. Goebbels turned and began speaking, his gaze fixed on Private Singh, who, however, was completely absorbed in admiring the beauty of the Fräulein seated across from him. Her blonde hair was neatly plaited and tied up, complemented by subtle makeup that accentuated her blue eyes. Notably, her nose added to her overall allure. Despite her charm, she remained shy and avoided making eye contact with Private Singh.

Goebbels redirected Private Singh's attention as he continued speaking, ensuring the focus was back on the conversation. He mentions the Führer himself has sent him here to talk to him about two things. Firstly, the soldiers who were known as the 'Blitzkrieg Tommies', who had been captured after their onslaught against the sons of the Third Reich was over. That the Führer wants to make a public display of them, show the world you cannot kill the Führer and his ideals. He wants the world to witness the death of these spies on film. This is where Goebbels comes into it. He suggested instead of killing them and then displaying their dead bodies in Berlin, they should incorporate this into the event regarding the 'Bayerischen Löwen.'

The Führer wanted to hold the event at the Brandenburg Gate, the object of all German hope in this conflict. He demanded one hundred French men be rounded up and with the 'Blitzkrieg Tommies' to be hung on display after being shot. The Tommies must all wear signs around their necks stating they were spies. Goebbels's voice escalates as he talks, compared to the soft tones of the interpreter who translates the conversion. He goes on to say how this would be a marvellous platform for the party and the Führer to highlight to the world, for what Nazi-Germany stood for. Private Singh listens as Goebbels talks about how only the most important Germans will be in attendance and how this gala event will eventually be viewed worldwide. It will be an insight into, Nazi-Germany's high society with its gourmet food and fine champagnes.

Private Singh continues to listen to Goebbels until the man runs out of steam due to his excessive verbosity. Private Singh applauds him for his success in the German film industry and the transformative impact he has had on German cinema since assuming control. Who doesn't appreciate a bit of ego-stroking now and then? Private Singh thinks to himself. Goebbels' self-satisfaction only intensifies, leading him to call for champagne to celebrate. He enthusiastically elaborates on the involvement of the finest German architects and designers in the creative process, with himself, of course, overseeing every aspect.

A member of the waiting staff brings over a bottle of Krug champagne and shows the bottle to Goebbels to obtain his approval. He pours Goebbels some, and after tasting it, he gestures that it is fine. The man fills up Goebbels glass and one other, which he places before Private Singh. He places the bottle on the table, which is already cold, and he leaves. Goebbels lifts his glass and raises it upwards.

"Das tausendjähriges Reich," he calls out.

Private Singh semi-understands this as he has heard this in numerous meetings with the Führer and Himmler. Goebbels is like a fat German kid in an apple strudel shop; his dark, lifeless eyes light up, and he is excited. Private Singh asks if he can propose something, and Goebbels permits him to speak with a limp hand gesture. So Private Singh clears his voice and, as he looks Goebbels square in the eyes, he suggests that this grand event will be the premiere of the new Joseph Goebbels film about the 'Third Reich'. He raises his champagne glass to salute Goebbels, whose ego is on overdrive anyway.

Private Singh suggests that the Führer would allow the British soldiers known as the 'Blitzkrieg Tommies' to be executed on camera by his hand. They would be the first British soldiers to fall under the new 'Bayerischen Löwen'. The new Indian division will be spearheaded by the Führer fighting under the Nazi swastika, upholding the 'Thousand Year Reich'. He explains to Goebbels that the apt named new division known as 'Lions' has a duel meaning. Firstly, Sikh males have the surname 'Singh,' which means Lion, and secondly, the lion is one of the official symbols of the Free State of Bavaria, with its usage on the coat of arms. So, the event to be held at the Berghof would be ideal and deserving of such an event of this cinema magnitude.

Private Singh is very vocal and confident as he speaks, delivering his argument for hosting the event at the Berghof to the best of his capabilities. He continues regarding executing the Tommies before the Führer, would only secure Goebbels's approbation in the eyes of the Führer. In her soft voice, Goebbels listens with interest as the female interpreter speaks. This is not met with any form of reaction from Goebbels to start with. As Private Singh stops speaking, there is an uncomfortable silence at first, as Goebbels stops and stares into the yonder. Suddenly, unexpectedly, it is like he is having an epiphany or something. This silence is suddenly met with loud cheers and excitement; it is like the one 'Reichspfennig' coin had dropped.

"Bravo, bravo, bravo," he calls out in a German accent.

Even the young lady is taken aback by his comments and enthusiasm towards the whole project. He picks up his glass and sips more champagne as he nods and does a fake clap. Private Singh continues about how it will cement him within cinema history, which is plagued by the Jews of Hollywood. The event must be held at the Berghof within the Bavarian Alps, considering the name the Führer originally suggested for the Indian division of the 'Bavarian Lions'. Again, Goebbels is left speechless, but Private Singh would like him to present the whole idea to the Führer as his own, which goes without saying.

Goebbels is sold on the idea hook, line, and U-Boat sinker, to the surprise of Private Singh. He asks the lady to make notes of everything that had been discussing today as he needs to present his idea to the Führer. Private Singh mentions Himmler may want to execute the Tommies within the interim, but Goebbels assures him that he will get involved, this will not take place, and they will not be harmed. Private Singh asks if the Tommies could be presented within their British uniforms as if they were on military inspection. He asks if their uniforms could be washed and repaired so they look immaculate on the day, so the footage will only be enhanced. Private Singh suggests that the Tommies could get a nice supper, taking into consideration that it was their last.

If they were happy walking into the Berghof, thinking they were being released, they would not fight? He suggests the gala evening would be much smoother if they agreed to go along. The request that Goebbels did not understand is the one Private Singh made regarding the Tommies having boot polish provided so they could clean and polish their boots. He explained that many British soldiers spent hours polishing their boots; he called it stress relief or something that could take your mind off the fighting you were participating in.

Goebbels again agreed to this, as the gala cinema event was profoundly important to the man, and he would not let everything as trivial as boot polish get in the way of something so important. So, the world could see what happened to the British when they invaded other countries and purged at will. Goebbels assures him that the Führer will be on his side, like Himmler. He tells Private Singh that Himmler has been in talks with another Indian gent who wants a similar outcome regarding the British in India. Private Singh was already aware of this other Geezer, as Himmler had previously mentioned him. Private Singh did not say anything as he was fully aware of the power struggle here. So, the wheels grind into motion about this soon-to-be pukka Nazi gathering at the Berghof we talk of.

The young lady gazes at Private Singh, a subtle smile of agreement playing on her lips as if aligned with the conversation's anti-British sentiment. Perhaps she is a committed party member, disdainful of all things British, or maybe there's a complexity of emotions towards this newfound adversary. Private Singh reciprocates with a smile just before Goebbels gestures for a third glass. As the waiter approaches, champagne is poured generously, replenishing the glasses before he discreetly departs. Goebbels lifts his glass, and the trio salutes with a satisfying 'chin, chin' clink.

"Prost," Private Singh calls out.

"Prost," Goebbels and the lady reply.

Goebbels is flabbergasted at Private Singh's handling of the German language. He jokes that he needs to keep an eye on him, especially if he is going in front of the camera lens. He has noticed how confidently he carries himself when making his point earlier.

Private Singh and the young lady exchange a meaningful look, the genuine way to toast someone. Goebbels, a known sexual predator and charismatic ladies' man, keenly observes the connection between them. He suddenly mentions he is seeing a young lady called Heidi from some small village in the mountains in the German sticks. She is of simple taste, seeing she grew up with goats, fresh air and the mountain range, so in his own opinion she has great potential as a television cook. Televisions in Germany were only for the rich, which was similar to Blighty, as only the real privileged could afford a set. Saying that, television transmissions were suspended in Blighty during the war.

Back to our German playboy, he gestures with his hands, holding them up towards his chest, to highlight she has nice assets to the disapproval of the interpreter. Goebbels has the look of a sexual predator about him. He has even filmed a pilot episode in the can, as Goebbels will promise these girls anything to get his wicked way with them. Now he is stroking his own ego, and he continues regarding another few projects on which he is working. Firstly, we have 'Frisky Fräuleins,' a show in which scantily clad ladies show off Nazi firepower. The mix of high-powered shooters with flesh, coupled with marching music, will be a Saturday night favourite, in his humble opinion. He suddenly replicates a gun with his hand in a childlike manner, making a shooting noise as he moves his hand to take aim.

Private Singh is surprised but continues to humour him by nodding his head in agreement. Now Goebbels is all worked up, and he continues to talk regarding another show, which the lady reluctantly translates. 'Fräuleins of War' is potentially a motor show in which, again, hot-looking chicks test drive military vehicles to a pounding soundtrack. He explains the section on the Tiger tank is a masterpiece, in his humble opinion. Then he suddenly remembers that some of these girls will be hostesses at the film premiere.

"Wunderbar," Private Singh calls out.

"My Cinematic Führer, bravo, bravo," he adds.

The lady translates what has just been said as Goebbels stops dead in his tracks and stares at Private Singh. He just continues to stare at Singh, open-mouthed and speechless. He then calls out that his comments are greatly appreciated and mean a lot to him. Goebbels continues to laugh as he takes another sip of champagne before suddenly interrupting his own love story. He stops again, and like some light bulb moment, he suggests that the Luftwaffe fly over to show their strength at the film premiere. He explains Hermann Göring loves to show off his new toys and over-detailed uniforms when he can. Suddenly Adolf Hitler and his four most trusted confidants were going to be in the same room with other high-ranking Nazis too. What an opportunity for the Allies. All the witches within this house made of gingerbread, cake, and cookies. Imagine blowing up this baker's delight to Kingdom Come. Just imagine a coded messaged could be sent to London, advising of this upcoming event to be held at the Berghof and who will be present.

RAF bombers could level the place with the Nazis within. Private Singh stops and stares into the yonder, mid-thought as this rattles around his noggin. Nah, he can't have this train of thought, he thinks to himself. He needs to highlight his loyalty as he wants the British out of India.

Goebbels rises to his feet, straightening himself up. Quite cheekily, he invites the young Fräulein to visit him, suggesting that he may have other pressing duties for her to attend to. She kisses his outstretched hand, his palm facing downward, exposing his bony knuckles. Private Singh contemplates to himself that it is usually a lady who extends her hand for a gentleman to kiss, not the other way around. Goebbels reassures Private Singh that this premiere will showcase great German achievement and will be a night to be remembered by all. A night which will go down in German history.

"Heil Hitler!" he calls out.

"Heil Hitler," Private Singh replies.

Private Singh responds with a Nazi salute to Goebbels's amazement. He turns and leaves with the young Fräulein following, as he makes a certain type of eye gesture to Private Singh to suggest what will happen later with this young lady.

Private Singh sits down and pours another glass of these fine French bubbles before he quaffs them down. He wears the look of a traitor, someone who is just about to slip cold steel into your gut while smiling. Maybe the prospect of what he is about to do, in front of thousands, maybe millions around the world, by killing these Tommies on camera could be too much even for him. We know he wants independence for India, but at what price? He knows Indians within Blighty and around the world will be persecuted for his actions.

This burdens him, but nothing will stop his dream of independence for India. Meanwhile, the Nazis do not unfairly treat the Tommies, to the Major's surprise. The opposite, to be honest, after their uniforms were delivered last night, they were told they were being treated to a meal. Jerry had the Tommies' uniforms repaired, washed, and even pressed, to their amazement. They were allowed to polish their boots, which the British army took pride in. This immediately got the Major's defences up. Why would Jerry want them to look their best, and why would they feed them? They were prisoners of war, after all.

His mind started to race about the food being poisoned or drugged, like Scopolamine, the truth serum. Tension consumed him as, too, what were the Nazis up to? As the men are all getting dressed for dinner, these thoughts rattle around his noggin, and he eventually speaks to the Lieutenant regarding this. Who is just as baffled as he is? Why would they go to such lengths with prisoners when the SS normally kill them rather than take them prisoner in the first place? The men laugh and joke as they get dressed. They have even been given shower faculties, under armed guard, of course. Suddenly, there is a feel-good factor among the Tommies; they all know something is up, but what?

Once they are dressed, they are led under armed guard again towards a room where a group of tables have been placed together like some buffet display. Plates of food and red wine sit centre stage on these tables we talk of. Some of the Tommies are far too eager and advanced to pick up something. That is, when Major Watkins calls out, they should refrain from doing so. Gary holds a chicken drumstick in his hand as Pauley holds a bottle of wine.

“Stop!” Major Watkins calls out.

“How do we know if this offering is safe enough for us to eat?” he adds.

The German officer who led the men into the room asks the guards to lower their guns slightly. He walks over towards the table, pours himself a glass of red wine, and picks up a piece of chicken, from which he takes a bite and starts to chew, which he washes down with some wine. Silence fills the room as the Tommie’s laughter has turned to silence after the Major called out, “Stop!” in an aggressive manner. The German officer tells them this is a gift from a friend in a thick German accent as he continues to eat. The Tommies look at the Major to obtain his blessing so they can eat, too. At first, he glares at the men before he breaks into a smile and tells them to tuck in.

With his hand, the German officer gestures for the men to eat, and the Tommies suddenly help themselves to the food and drinks on offer courteously of a friend. The men grab at different plates, stuffing the food into their mouths, not becoming of British soldiers, to the Lieutenants’ disappointment. The Major asks the Lieutenant to join in, too, who moves forward and picks up a plate, still slightly apprehensive at who is behind this. The atmosphere becomes slightly jovial, considering the silence and hostility of a few minutes ago. The Tommies continue to grab at whatever they can, stuffing it into their mouths, which is then washed down with some red wine. The German officer walks over towards the Major, who is still watching from the side, with two glasses of red wine. He passes the Major one and raises his glass. He calls out for the war to finish, and the two men salute. For that moment, they were just two men having a drink and not foes that could cause inconceivable atrocities to one another.

The next morning, the Tommies are slightly worse for wear, considering their social of last night. A hangover is a hangover wherever you are. You know what I mean: dry mouth, stomach-churning and a thumping headache. Maybe the hair of the dog is what is required. Unfortunately, these Tommies have no chance of getting a swift half-in as they are being whisked away to God knows where.

They are rounded up and transported by truck to an airfield. It is an average-sized airfield with a glass command tower with a few light aircraft which are being prepared by the ground crew. The Lieutenant takes in his surroundings just in case the opportunity presents itself for an escape. The German security seems to be beefed up for an airfield of this size, he thinks to himself. German guns are poised and ready for action if these Tommies think of testing their military counterparts.

They are unaware of where the aircraft is taking them and are oblivious to the circus that will meet them when they arrive. The thoughts of why they were fed last night, and the uniforms still play on the Major's mind. He is not stupid; he knows Jerry is up to something, but what? He knows his boys will die, too, the last man fighting for what they believe in.

They will all show self-sacrifice in the middle of insanity, as people show the most ingenuity and courage when faced with choices like they have. The Tommies are loaded into the aircraft on the tarmac as the engines start to roar into action. To his surprise, they have not been treated unfairly by the Germans. The opposite, to be honest, after what took place yesterday.

The Major's thoughts go back to the Sikh prisoner who visited them; maybe he has something to do with this. Then he realises that Sepoy soldiers within the King's army have no authority to do anything, let alone provide a banquet for them. The guards make final checks that the men are handcuffed to one another and take their seats within the fuselage. As the door is closed, Major Watkins looks at the Lieutenant as he senses something is afoot here. The signal is given for the off before the engines increase in power and the Junkers Ju 52 aircraft starts to taxi, readying for take-off. Within minutes, they are in the air, climbing into the sky.

The airfield disappears into the distance as the pilot gains altitude. The Major looks out of the window before he rests his head backwards, knocking it into the fuselage repeatedly as he tries to figure out in his mind what is taking place here. As the Tommies are being flown, they are not aware this is the day of the premiere to be held at the Berghof, Hitler's Austrian retreat.

Goebbels and his interior designers have transformed the whole place into a shrine to the Nazi party. Flag poles had been erected within the mountain, and the bright red of the Nazi swastika is clear to see as they flap within the wind, the red such a striking contrast to the surrounding countryside.

The Berghof, nestled within the Bavarian Alps, serves as the Führer's retreat. This Alpine château-type mansion stands prominently, its whitewashed walls adorned with intricate stone detailing. The structure towers over the valley below and features a patio area that offers stunning views of the surrounding mountains, becoming the backdrop for numerous parties hosted by the Führer for both guests and military advisors alike. Notably, it played a pivotal role as the refuge for Benito Mussolini after the Führer's Waffen-SS commandos rescued him from his hotel, 'Campo Imperatore', in the Gran Sasso Mountain range. However, the full account of this historical event is a tall tale for another day.

This patio area we talk of has been decorated with lights so that the event can be celebrated into the early hours. The main drawing room will be the area of this pukka Nazi gathering, where the premiere will be held, with its red carpet and wooden vaulted ceiling, crystal chandeliers, and rich tapestries adorning the walls. Goebbels' interior designers have worked their magic by introducing a selection of Nazi memorabilia, from solid gold swastikas within a leafed garland with a menacing eagle perched on it. A bust of the Führer's head sits centre stage within a glass case, cast within gold, of course, with the backdrop of the red swastika banner behind it. Other ostentatious-looking articles from the 'Third Reich' are also dotted about the gaff to make it look glamorous for this lavish event to celebrate the Nazi party.

The main window, which floods natural light into this room, is flanked with Nazi swastika banners of the 'Third Reich' too. A huge screen has been set up to play the footage of Goebbels's new film, which will be eventually showcased to the entire world. Seating has been brought in to transform this gargantuan room into a cinema theatre for this one-off screening of the 'Bayerischen Löwen'. An army of waiting staff, cooks and cleaners have been drafted in so the mastermind behind this screening could act out his vision for the perfect propaganda platform.

A young German soldier makes his way from an office towards Private Singh, who is mingling around within the main room. Other guests stare at him, opened-mouthed at who this man could be. One officer grabs his female partner's arm to protect her from this strange savage being that lingers among them. This brings a chuckle to Private Singh, who has seen it all before within Blighty. He takes a glass of champagne from one of the waiters and takes a sip. He continues to mingle, looking at a huge oil painting of the Führer on one wall. As he is admiring this piece of oil paint on canvas, a female guest walks over and stands next to him. She wears a red figure-hugging dress, which only complements her figure, to say the least. She wears her hair up with a gold metal clip, which only exposes her pale neck, with her diamond necklace around it. As Private Singh glances over, he takes her gloved hand, kisses it gently and bows his head slightly. To his astonishment, she takes it within her stride, no slap across the chops or any form of outburst that he had touched her without her permission, to his surprise.

"Evening Fraulein," Private Singh calls out.

"May I take this opportunity to comment on how you look as exquisite as that oil painting,".

"A proper work of art," he adds.

She stood, looking at the painting before this moment of intimacy; truth be told, she seemed more interested in this distinct character standing next to her. Maybe this posh German tart fancied watering down the blue blood with a bit of rough. As Private Singh is about to work his magic, suddenly, a waitress cuts between them, offering them more drinks. The German lady takes a glass of champagne and turns to be confronted by two Gestapo men. She soon realised they did not want her to speak to this man and stormed off in a rage. The two black leather trench coat-wearing Geezers paused and glared at Private Singh before walking away. They made their presence known; maybe they had been instructed to do so. The nice-looking blonde waitress, too, gave him the eye for some reason. Maybe she thought he was a bit of alright, too, as Private Singh thought he was on a winner here to himself. Another group of guests called her over, but she still looked over at him for some reason.

Singh is attired in a single-breasted black suit with a white shirt and black tie. Himmler felt his British military uniform, the same one he had been dropped into France wearing, meticulously repaired, and cleaned for tonight's event originally, would be too much. Imagine a guest mingling among the very best of the National Socialist German Workers Party wearing a British military uniform. How do you think this would go down, like sauerkraut in the Kibbutz?

Having been located by the young German soldier, he was instructed to follow him, as per Heinrich Himmler's request. Private Singh had been summoned to Himmler's private office for a discussion or chinwag. Upon a discreet knock, Private Singh entered the room, where Himmler had arranged a makeshift office to oversee the extensive security operations. The task was formidable: vetting, checking, and conducting security procedures for all vehicles and personnel involved in the event. Himmler expressed contentment upon seeing Private Singh, recognising the soldier's dual role in interpretation and operational assistance.

"Heil Hitler!" Private Singh called out.

"Heil Hitler," Himmler replies.

Private Singh salutes, holding his right arm aloft, with conviction, which impressed Himmler. This is only the second time he has seen him salute in the Nazi way since they have met. The young German starts to translate this three-way conversation. Himmler offers Private Singh some schnapps, which he pours himself. They both knocked it back, and Himmler poured another two. He tells Private Singh that the other party he has been talking to was also on board now about the plan of the German-backed invasion of India to gain independence from the British. This other gentleman has political connections within India. With this German backing, he would become the country's Prime Minister once the British left.

Private Singh is a simple man and a soldier with no inclination to rule a country. He simply requires an ally to throw the British out of his homeland. Himmler reassures Private Singh that he will be in command of the division and not this other gentleman. Private Singh asks for his guarantee that there will be no interference from this other party in the 'Bavarian Lions'.

He is meeting to finalise it next week, but he wanted Private Singh to take charge of the division, which meant a lot to him. He then surprised him by producing a 'Bavarian Lions' military uniform, which he had specially designed for him. Private Singh cannot believe that this man had gone and inconvenienced himself for him. Like a speechless child, he took hold of the uniform. He inspected the detailing and the opulence of the garment before him. Private Singh is amazed and gobsmacked, to say the least.

It must have been made by the same people who made Hermann Göring's uniforms, as it had similar rich detailing and was over-excessive within its design, but he was not going to say this to Himmler. Maybe Hugo Boss and his old pal Karl Diebitsch were guilty as charged in knocking up this razor-sharp-looking piece of clobber for Private Singh. All he knows is he will look dapper in it. The tunic is pale blue with silver embroidery and black detailing. The trousers are black, with a pale blue stripe; he even has a ceremonial chrome sword to match the uniform. To Private Singh's surprise, a pale blue cloth turban accompanied the uniform.

Private Singh held the sword in his hands, inspecting it before removing it from its scabbard. He holds the blade up and moves it around in sheer amazement at the craftsmanship. Himmler insists he wears this at the premiere later as he opens a file to show Private Singh the insignias of the 'Bavarian Lions' of the Wehrmacht. Private Singh looks at the prancing lion with a sword motif under its claws. He is surprised by what he sees, as he has never in his life had anyone put so much faith in him.

Private Singh, overwhelmed with emotion, initially moves forward to embrace Himmler but hesitates upon realising the restrained demeanour of the man, in stark contrast to the more expressive Goebbels. Instead, Singh extends his hand, and after a brief pause, Himmler shakes it, offering a smile. Singh speaks with conviction as his words are translated, regarding his reassurance to Himmler, that his soldiers will be ready to fight for the Führer. Himmler, seizing the opportunity, suggests Private Singh try on the tunic. Singh complies, removing his suit jacket and trying on the tunic. As he stands there radiating with pride in his new uniform, while Himmler admires him, recognising the favour this gesture will carry with the Führer. Perhaps Himmler contemplates the creation of an SS division, the new 'Bavarian Lions', under his own direction.

He must jostle for favour with the Führer as it's getting slightly crowded at the top, with the others all trying to catch favour with their Führer nowadays, it seemed to Private Singh. He looks at his reflection in the mirror as the silver embroidery against the pale stitching and artisanry of the uniform.

As Himmler calls out, this is far from the plain and boring-looking Khaki uniform of the Tommies. The interpreter conveys what is being said before Himmler pours himself another schnapps. There is a knock at the door and another German soldier walks in and hands Himmler a piece of paper, which he reads and places on the desk.

Himmler advises Private Singh that the 'Blitzkrieg Tommies' are in transit and should be here soon. He also takes this opportunity to tell him that he was slightly disappointed with the whole screening of the premiere and the killing of the 'Blitzkrieg Tommies' being attributed to Goebbels. Private Singh was equally annoyed with his newfound German friend, considering the new SS-unit being formed to hunt down the Tommies had been kept a secret from him. Taking into consideration Hugo is involved somehow, after what the Führer had said to him. All things said and done; Private Singh knows the Tommies would have met with a gruesome demise if he would not had got Goebbels involved. Singh, executing the Tommies at the gala event at the launch of the 'Bavarian Lion's' will only add credence to the new Indian division. He knew maybe this was not the place to bring it up, seeing Himmler was already pissed off with what Goebbels had been up to.

Himmler pours his schnapps down his throat, slightly annoyed looking. Is it due to? This gave Goebbels much more favour in the eyes of the Führer when he had originally started the conversation about the 'Bavarian Lions' and felt cheated by Goebbels. Private Singh tries to explain, that Goebbels got carried away within the meeting and assured him that he will present the idea to the Führer. What Himmler was trying to address is why it is always the Joseph Goebbels show.

Hopefully, Goebbels, being Goebbels, took all the credit for the event to be held at the Berghof and did not mention it originally came from Private Singh. There is suddenly an air of animosity between the two men; everyone knows Goebbels is a true showman and uses smoke and mirrors to achieve results. On the other hand, Heinrich Himmler is a great tactician and is the backbone of the German army with the SS. But he is a staunch supporter of the Führer and his insane ideals.

Private Singh could not understand that he was sitting here within the Berghof, chatting with Heinrich Himmler, who was throwing his toy Panzer out of the pram due to that naughty boy called Goebbels. They are like a pair of spoilt kids who always wanted their own way in life. Add Hermann Göring and Martin Bormann into the mix.

This is when you have a proper gang of little bastards who need a good hiding and sending to bed without any supper. Himmler asks Private Singh not to say anything to any of the others and takes another drink. He looks like he is drowning his sorrows for some reason or other. The telephone suddenly rings, and Himmler is being asked to investigate something regarding the waiting staff. Private Singh looks interested in hearing this while he removes the tunic before placing it onto the coat hanger again. Himmler once again requests that he wear the new uniform for the event as he hangs up the tunic. Private Singh assures him of this, and he did not want to get it creased in any way, to Himmler's approval.

To his surprise, Himmler opens a desk draw and produces Private Singh's nunchucks. He feels they should be on his person, and they would complement his new uniform, bringing an element of authority to his new look and appointment. Private Singh thanked him, as the three-way conversation continued. Himmler advised him that Göring would present him with a Nazi ceremonial dagger during the main celebration of the new Indian division later. Himmler and the young soldier leave the room and Private Singh pours another schnapps as he looks at his new uniform hanging up.

Suddenly, his dream materialised, marking his relentless pursuit to liberate India from British rule, which was soon to become a reality. Tears stream down his face as this stark reality soon sinks in, and these tears soon turn to joy. Smiling, he takes hold of the nunchucks and studies them before he looks at his reflection in the mirror. He suddenly starts to use the nunchucks violently as he continues to look at his reflection in the mirror.

In the meantime, the aircraft had landed, and the Tommies were now being transported under armed guard to the Berghof. They sense something is happening, given the visible military presence. As they drive through the countryside, Major Watkins discerns the destination. His thorough study of the landscape enabled him to recognise the mountain ranges from their flight. The picturesque scene had unfolded with peaceful mountain ranges and clear streams flowing towards white snowcapped peaks, all enhancing the beauty of the Bavarian Alps. Lieutenant Harvey had signalled to Major Watkins, who had also caught a glimpse of these breathtaking views before they had landed.

The remaining Tommies are not aware of where they are but were too amazed by the views they had witnessed. Most of the men had not seen another country till their military service. As the truck drove up the road, which snaked its way upwards, the driver had to change gears to cope with the incline and the weight they were carrying. The engine groaned as they drove close to the edge of the road. It was precarious, taking into consideration that it was quite a sheer drop downwards. After a few minutes of driving, they sense they are getting higher as the air becomes cleaner and crisper, with an altitude change to boot. As the truck struggled slightly, the driver crunched it into a lower gear and pressed the accelerator.

The engine groaned as they moved further up the winding road towards their destination. As they get closer, they see more military presence along the side of the road. The Tommies look at one another. The truck suddenly slows down and eventually stops with its escort, as do the military troop carrier and halftrack armoured vehicle. German soldiers line up, and orders are barked at them. They open the rear tail of the truck, rolling up the canvas cover, and the Tommies are forced to get out.

They are jostled at gunpoint towards the rear entrance of the Berghof. They witness waiting staff rushing around, preparing for some form of event or other, all under the watchful eye of armed guards. The Tommies cannot get their head around the number of Nazi swastika banners which are on display up the mountain, as they all flap within the wind, making a noise which is enough for you to stop and look. The Major notices that even the guards are wearing uniforms that look different from the norm. They look more ceremonial somehow, and the quality looks different.

The Tommies are led through into what resembles a storage area, where armed SS-guards are waiting. They are forced into this small space before an SS-officer arrives who tells the soldiers to bring them through to another room.

They are march down what looks like the servant's quarters and up a service staircase. As the Tommies climb this, they can see the view from small windows that run along the staircase's height. They follow each other; JD nods at Francis to check out the view. What he is trying to do is highlight to him the guests who are arriving. They looked like high-ranking Nazi officers with their significant others in tow. They only catch a short glimpse as the windows were small, and they are climbing a staircase simultaneously after all.

The Tommies are led into what looks like a meeting room, with a grand wooden meeting table and chairs around it. Armchairs are piled up against one wall towards the room's rear. There is a huge oil painting of the Führer on the wall, with two brass wall lights on either side of it. They flood the wall with light, which only highlights the painting further. The chairs are heavy, wooden-looking things, which Francis tries to move. Even though he is a big lad, he struggles slightly. The carpet is dark in colour, with a striped border running around the edge and two table lamps with oversized shades sit on a sideboard near the window. The armed SS-guards are not taking any risks with the Tommies here, as they are heavy-handed with the boys. Some of the Tommies sit down while others try to look through the window. The Major is itching to find out what the hell is happening here.

He tries to speak to the Lieutenant when he goes to get himself a glass of water. The Lieutenant has a similar thought process: something big is about to take place here, but what? Time passes as the men are confined to this room, as daylight slowly turns to early evening. Suddenly, bright lights are switched on from outside, like some form of searchlight you get at the Hollywood Gala events. The SS-officer returns to the room and recommends that the British soldiers straighten themselves up and that they will soon be needed.

The Major confronts him by asking, him for what they are required for? One of the guards moves forward, thinking the Major is about to attack the officer, who advises him that he is fine, and they are only talking. Tension consumes the Tommies as to what is about to take place and what their involvement is. The guards force the men to their feet, and they sort themselves out. Suddenly, a waiter brings in a tray of drinks, with a bottle of whisky and one of cognac, which he places down on the table.

Some of the Tommies help themselves before the SS-officer even has the chance to say anything. Trying to consume a shot of the good stuff is difficult when you are wearing bracelets. The SS-officer calls out that the drinks are complements of the Führer, Adolf Hitler. The Tommies talk among themselves as to what is waiting for them. Another few minutes' pass, and another SS-officer walks into the room, he too is dressed in a ceremonial-looking Nazi uniform, which is different to the first SS-officer. He asks the men to accompany him towards the main lounge. To the surprise of the Tommies, most of these German officers speak English. The Tommies finish their drinks and straighten themselves up; they are apprehensive at what is coming but are men of the world.

The SS-officer salutes the Major, in the Nazi way, clicking his boot heels, who in return salutes him back, as do the men in some act of military loyalty. The return salute is in the British military way, of course.

The SS-officer warns that any attempts to resist will result in immediate execution, emphasising the threat as he holds the door open. The men, still handcuffed, are then marched down a hallway adorned with overt 'Third Reich' symbols, banners, gold eagles, and Nazi swastikas. These once-shocking emblems are sadly becoming routine for the Tommies now. The entire corridor is flanked by SS-soldiers in ceremonial attire, on each side, armed and imposing they look. The Tommies proceed to line up outside two enormous, grand wooden doors. Even the Major, typically composed, is gripped by a dry mouth, fully aware that this might be the end for him and his fellow 'Rum Bunch' of Tommies. Gary, a small and emotional man, sheds a tear, making the sign of the cross on his chest. The Lieutenant, sharing a sombre moment with the Major, whispers regarding the honour of serving together. The prevailing mood is heavy with the realisation that death is imminent.

Francis places his hand on Gary's shoulder to reassure him. The Major looks over towards the men one final time and nods his head slightly to appreciate the group of men standing before him. He is proud of his 'Rum Bunch' of fighting men, of what they have achieved in so little time. What awaits them on the other side of these doors? The Major's gut reaction is that they are going to meet their marker by the looks of it. The Tommies all wear a mask of defeat; this is the end. Their senses are heightened at what they will discover on the other side of these doors.

"It was an honour serving with you, Sir," Lieutenant Harvey calls out.

"Likewise, Harvey, an honour," the Major replies.

Suddenly, the wooden doors started too slowly open. To the Tommies' surprise, they are met with a loud crescendo of noise. They hear music which starts to play as the doors slowly open. The classical music they hear is performed by some string quartet or other. Film cameras are rolling as this event, whatever it may be, will be eventually watched around the globe. People are chatting, a sea of noise of celebration and enjoyment, if the Tommies are not mistaken. The SS-officer calls the men forward, who enter the room, slightly baffled and apprehensive as they look around.

The room is fully decked out with Nazi propaganda items and has a gold bust of the Führer's head centre stage. German officers and their escorts for this event hobnob while drinking champagne. Many of these ladies are dressed in evening wear, posh hairdos, diamonds, and killer heels, not taking anything away from the hot-looking Nazi hostesses. This only adds to the glitz and glamour of the whole evening. A gargantuan ice sculpture of the Nazi swastika with an eagle perched on top sits on display. Guests are amazed by the craftsmanship on display here. An overbearing cake with other sweet tit bits sits on the table next to this. The sugary delights look tasty enough if you have a sweet tooth. How the black fondant of the Nazi swastika contrasts with the red and white of the party logo. None of the guests dared take a piece for some reason, maybe thinking it was for display purposes only, or maybe it was because this bruiser of a woman stood next to the damn thing. This beefcake, probably called Gerda, did not look like one you wanted to mess with, as she just glared at the guests.

Waiting staff and Goebbels, scantily clad hot-looking Nazi hostesses mingled among the guests while serving champagne and finger food. These hot-looking waitresses we talk of wear short little backless dresses in the Nazi colours, of course, with fishnet tights, heels and small hats which are perched on their heads. They resemble vixens of vice from some seedy German adult club or other. Sorry, back to the venue, the chairs are lined up towards the front, where a projector screen sits against the back wall. There is a raised area, which is guarded by SS-soldiers who, once again, are dressed differently than the norm. For some reason, each SS-soldier's division is dressed slightly differently, to the Tommies' surprise, probably due to the fact the Waffen-SS, Allgemeine-SS and the regular SS were all here. Then we had the Wehrmacht, Gestapo and Goebbels Reich Ministry of Public Enlightenment and Propaganda. This pukka little gathering is a who's who of the Nazi party.

What looks like high-ranking Nazi officers, are seated with their partners within this raised seating area. They resemble a night out at the opera or something. It is all ball gowns and backless dresses coupled with open-toe and strapless sandals, to say the least. The blokes do not look too shabby either; most of them are wearing what looks like ceremonial Nazi uniforms and formal dinner jackets. They quaff champagne and pick at smoked salmon and other finger food being served. The waiting staff are dressed smartly in white jackets and black trousers, besides a handful of Goebbels' scantily clad females, of course. Back to Major Watkins, who looks at the men, and there is an element of relief at what they have been greeted with, and not the death squad they had thought it would be.

The Tommies are led towards an area where they are asked to line up opposite the raised seating area. Bless them; they are overwhelmed by the grandeur of the whole thing. Most of these boys have not seen anything like this, even within Blighty. As they look around, they are all gobsmacked by what they are witnessing here. Some guests make fun and stare at them, shouting what looks like verbal abuse. Clive understands what is being said, so he makes a few comments back. The Major nods his head to gesture for him to stop. The Tommies are lined up as they are stood shoulder to shoulder next to one another. The SS-officer stands to the side of them before he signals a man who looks like the master of ceremonies as the Tommies nervously look at one another.

"This is all for you," the SS-officer calls out in a German accent.

"Any trouble, bang, bang,"

"You die," he adds.

He initiates a sweeping hand gesture, presenting the entire room to the Tommies as though this grand spectacle is exclusively for them. Then, he directs their attention towards a machine gun nest nestled in the corner. A pointed gesture singles out the Major, followed by a mimicked gun-to-the-head motion. Chuckling to himself, he signals the master of ceremonies once more, who begins to address the audience. The rather portly looking German Geezer clears his throat before extending a welcome, inviting everyone to take their seats. Gradually, the crowd settles into their chairs, and the ambient noise diminishes.

Abruptly, a hush falls over the entire room as the national anthem begins to play. Simultaneously, every person in the room raises their right arm in salute, leaving the Tommies in utter shock.

Suddenly, Adolf Hitler the Führer of the Third Reich, makes a dramatic entrance from the rear, accompanied by Heinrich Himmler, Joseph Goebbels, Hermann Göring, and Martin Bormann. All five witches within this house of gingerbread, cake, and cookies within one sitting, imagine now blowing up this so-called house of sugary delights to Kingdom Come. This thought had previously entered Private Singh's noggin when he first heard of the guest list. The Nazi Rockstar is flanked by SS-security officers, who ferry him and his cronies towards the raised seating area opposite where the Tommies are now standing.

The cinematographers all move to catch the best footage of this iconic event. In their iconic black uniforms and leather trench coats, Gestapo officers are too present as they stop the odd person as they check their papers. For some reason, they are concentrating more on the waiting staff. Maybe they have had a tip-off. The famous five are all dressed in ceremonial military uniforms, with the Führer wearing a white heavily embroidered Waffenrock or tunic, with black trousers and a matching white visor cap.

The Major cannot believe his eyes nor the remaining Tommies at what they are witnessing here. They are mere feet away from Adolf Hitler; if they could kill him now, the war could be over. Thoughts of doing in the little deranged Geezer rattle around their noggins. They all harbour the thought they will be mowed down in a hail of bullets before they even get close to him, but they know deep down they need to try something, but wearing handcuffs makes any attempt of attack more precarious.

The Major is suddenly more interested in why they are here, centre stage within this pukka Nazi gathering. Who has organised all of this, and who would want them to be here? They could have easily been done over within their cell, buried in unmarked graves, and that would have been the end of that. So why are they here? The guests cheer and wave as the party of the four men take their seats, as Adolf Hitler takes the podium. The crescendo of noise is deafening, with cheering and shouting. The Führer does his famous salute in return to his so obedient followers. He gestures for the guests to quiet down with his hands before slowly, the room falls into silence again as the string quartet stops playing too.

"Nazi scum," Pauley calls out.

"Rot in Kraut-hell! I'm gonna kill you, boy," he screams.

This is not before an SS-guard places his rifle butt into Pauley's chest, which knocks him to the floor. He is given another one just for good measure, in the boat this time, as blood starts to leak from his forehead. Slightly dazed and confused, he is helped up by the other Tommies on either side of him. The pain he suffers is clear to see as he spits blood onto the floor. The SS-officer moves towards the Major and whispers for his men to calm down, or they will be shot, even before the ceremony begins. Adolf Hitler remarks something in German. Clive translates it.

"This is the superior British race," Clive calls out.

The whole room erupts into laughter. The Tommies do not appreciate being belittled like this, and there is sudden unrest within the line-up. Major Watkins gestures to the men to stay calm as the SS-officer glares at him. Once again, the Führer must quiet the room down. As he gestures emphatically with both hands, the room falls into a sudden hush.

The Führer then addresses the audience in his customary fashion, employing expressive body movements and animated hand gestures, all accompanied by assertive remarks that resonate well with the crowd. The audience, captivated by his performance, erupts into applause intermittently throughout his speech. Seizing the moment, the Führer expresses gratitude to Hermann Göring and the Luftwaffe, announcing a fly-past that will coincide with a gathering on the patio for drinks later.

This is to showcase the air supremacy of the Luftwaffe. Glancing appreciatively at Göring, who nods in acknowledgement and raises his Reich Marschall's baton. The Führer basks in the enthusiastic cheers and praises from the audience once more. Amid the deafening noise, he skilfully signals for calm with measured hand gestures. Firstly, advising his guests that the war is going well, and they will soon defeat the inferior Allied forces. The rabble before him erupts once again, cheering and clapping. He then takes the opportunity to introduce Hugo Kruger, his Godson, and a true son of Germany.

Suddenly, Hugo, who is wearing a black Hitler Youth uniform, walks from around the rear of the stage towards the front of the raised seating area. He is displaying a wound to his head, but the other day he had no form of injuries, Private Singh notices. Is this the original Hugo who he met and saved on their first meeting? So, who was the Hugo he met within their last meeting in Berlin? His mind starts to race to what is afoot here. All he knows is Hugo is somehow, connected to this new SS-unit? Hugo turns and looks upwards at the Führer as they make eye contact. He is told to acknowledge what is being said. He steps forward slightly and salutes the Führer with conviction as his boot heels click together. He puts his arm down, then turns and nods at the guests present.

The cinematographer focuses on Hugo while the second one pans the room. Himmler gestures for Hugo to accompany them on stage, which, at first, he is slightly reluctant, maybe due to the sheer size of the event. Hugo then decides to walk over as the crowds cheer him. He is nervous which is clear to see as he walks onto the stage. He salutes the Führer and the remaining party.

"Heil Hitler!" he calls out.

"Tausendjähriges Reich," he adds.

"Heil Hitler," Adolf Hitler replies.

The room goes crazy as the Führer first salutes him with an open, flat hand and then settles everyone down with his hand gesture. He explains who Hugo Kruger is and his achievements within the Hitler Youth, how he will become a Wehrmacht officer of distinction once he is older. How he truly will be the face of the Aryan race and the future of the German people, and how they need other young men to follow his example. The guests clap and cheer as Hugo stands next to Hitler throughout what is being said here. He smiles and waves at the people who cannot get enough of him. Suddenly, Himmer walks forward and takes Hugo's arm and lifts it upwards. It is like Himmler could not wait any longer at the sidelines and had to be involved in this celebration of this young man's achievements.

The remaining three Nazis look at one another. Why would Himmler be doing what he is doing, upstaging the Führer like this? Himmler had a soft spot for Hugo, so maybe he felt it was his duty as a family friend or maybe a special friend of his mother's, hence what he did. Eventually, the crowd quietens down, and Hugo leaves the stage, still smiling and nodding with appreciation for the support from his fellow German people.

The Führer looks over at Himmler, who takes his seat once again, as do the other three Nazi Rockstars who look in his direction. As the room falls silent once again, the Führer continues to tell the audience that he has a promising future within the military and that his good friend Heinrich Himmler assured him of this.

He calls out that Hugo Kruger will kill many British soldiers before he retires an old man. The Führer looks over towards the Tommies as he says this. The room goes crazy once again as the guests start to clap and cheer. He quietens them down, and the room becomes silent once again. The Führer tells the guests that he would like to talk about a man he met from different shores who has shown him a new way of thinking. This man also saved Hugo Kruger's life and showcased humility in the face of adversity of war. If it were not for this man, Hugo probably would be dead due to injuries he sustained during the detention of the enemies of the 'Third Reich'.

He has spent time with this man and now understands other beings from different shores. So, he would like to introduce the 'Bayerischer Löwe' who will be commanding his new division of Indian soldiers. As Private Singh steps forward, astonishment ripples through the guests, encountering a being like him for the first time. The Tommies, initially convinced of his allegiance, are equally taken aback. The SS officer shakes his head disapprovingly at Major Watkins, prompting Watkins to urge the Tommies to remain calm. He understands the internal turmoil they must be experiencing but emphasises the importance of prioritising their safety. Gasps emanate from some of the female guests, accompanied by a few remarks in German. The Tommies, betrayed and angered, unleashed a torrent of verbal abuse. Hugo tries not to make eye contact with Private Singh, from where he is standing for some reason. What is the Geezer hiding, as Singh will ask questions when they meet face to face.

Major Watkins, maintaining a stern gaze, directs his attention to Private Singh. Now adorned in a regal Nazi uniform with a matching turban, Singh carries a ceremonial sword, adding an extra layer of surrealism to the unfolding scene. The Tommies are gobsmacked and cannot work out why he would defect towards the Nazis? One cinematographer again focuses on Private Singh, while the second one records the guest's reaction to this man.

"Mein Führer," Private Singh calls out.

"Heil Hitler," he adds.

He salutes the Führer with his outstretched arm with conviction and passion. The Führer, in return, raises his hand and nods at him, smiling to see him wearing a Nazi uniform. Private Singh takes his seat next to the remaining men on stage. The Führer continues speaking. He tells the guests about the "Bayerischen Löwen", which will be a fully fighting division to fight under his command and will assume arms against the British and other Allied soldiers. Goebbels gives the signal for the propaganda film to be played, which highlights this. The lights dim slightly, and everyone's attention is drawn towards the screen.

The film starts with a tribute to the Reich Ministry of Public Enlightenment and Propaganda before you see Indian soldiers being transported to European battlefields. It highlights their arrival and the trenches within France and the conditions which were faced by the soldiers. The footage shows Sikh soldiers fighting for the British during the Great War, taking heavy casualties at Gallipoli and the Battle of the Somme.

Some of the guests show their disapproval at first, as it highlights German soldiers being killed in battle, too. They soon settle down as the film highlights the wounded Tommies and Sepoys, this is suddenly met with cheers. It also highlights homesick Indian soldiers, looking demoralised and dejected under British rule.

Suddenly, the film goes on to show the new insignia of the Indian division and some Indian soldiers on manoeuvres under the flag of Nazi Germany. With the Führer's help, the Indian division would take back India and drive out the British invaders.

A map highlights the new Indian division's military tactics and manoeuvres around Europe at first, defending German-held territory against the Soviet's and Allied troops. It goes on to show them marching towards India, proud to be fighting under the command of the Führer. It highlights military conflict and images of battle before showing the British forces surrendering, with images of defeated and wounded British soldiers. The film finishes with British forces leaving Indian shores in retreat. Finally, it shows a company of Indian soldiers marching past Adolf Hitler on parade duty. They salute him and he, in return, salutes them. The song Erika, by Herms Niel, is playing over this footage, as the flag of Nazi Germany waves in the wind as the footage cuts to black, and the entire room falls into silence once again.

Suddenly, Goebbels jumps to his feet and starts to clap as the short film ends, which is replicated throughout the room with a deafening noise level. The lights go back up, with cheering, with some guests standing while applauding their Führer. The crescendo of noise is deafening as some guests call out praise for their Führer.

The Tommies try to make eye contact with Private Singh, whose vision is blocked by one of the Hitler youths, who is holding up a Nazi banner in front of him. Himmler walks over towards the podium and calls on the guests to see the 'Blitzkrieg Tommies.' The group of British soldiers who have caused havoc and destruction throughout France since they landed here with only one goal: to kill the sons of Germany. The audience suddenly starts to show their displeasure at the men who stand before them. Emotions run high as they start to hurl verbal abuse at them, with the odd item being thrown, too.

Himmler must take charge of the microphone and shout for them to stop. Goebbels is suddenly concerned that his film masterpiece and its gala night may be ruined. He signals Himmler, who in return signals the SS-soldiers to move away from the Führer's stage. They suddenly march down the steps and line up facing the guests, holding their MP–40 submachine guns across their chests in some act of crowd control.

Goebbels jumps to his feet, grabs the microphone, and asks the people to watch how they conduct themselves before their Führer. Slowly, these guests seem to calm down, to Himmler's slight disappointment. Maybe the leader of the SS wanted the night to be unsuccessful for Goebbels. Goebbels calls out the eight British spies who stand before them, only diverse to die before the Führer and other high-ranking officers of the Third Reich for their crimes of brutality against the sons of Germany.

"Is this what the German people want!" Goebbels screams in German?

"They should die now," he adds in German.

Himmler is surprised by his outburst, considering he is the head of SS and not Goebbels. As this power struggle occurs at the podium, Major Watkins continues to glare at Private Singh. There is a slight confusion about the proceedings as both men now stand, addressing the crowd. Suddenly, certain guests become aggressive and call out for the spies to be killed. The mood changes once again within the room, and people start to call out and shout; the SS-soldiers move forward and point their guns towards the guests now. By the reaction, it looks like the German people want their pound of British flesh right here and now. Tempers are frayed as the odd guest still shouts, which clearly highlights their hatred for the Tommies. This is partly due to Goebbels' speech about how these men killed German soldiers brutally. This only fuels the fire of hatred and loathing towards these eight men who stand before them.

Himmler suddenly declares that he wants to summon the "Bayerischen Löwen," for this task. He asserts that it should be Private Singh's honour to eliminate these British soldiers as a prelude to his new campaign aimed at liberating India from British invaders. These Tommies could potentially become the inaugural victims of this new division. Private Singh strides towards the front of the stage, halting to survey the guests and then fixating his gaze on the Tommies. The attendees, including the Nazi soldiers, are startled to witness this man wearing a Nazi uniform so proudly. Murmurs and discussions ensue among them, likely revolving around Private Singh and his perplexing presence.

"Heil Hitler!" he calls out.

"Tod Herr English," he adds.

Himmler and Goebbels both move for the Führer to take the podium again, with the remaining party all now standing. Private Singh salutes the Führer as he looks upwards at him, in the Nazis way. Suddenly, Hermann Göring walks over to present Singh with a Nazis' ceremonial dagger, as Singh walks up the steps onto the stage area to accept this symbol of loyalty to the Führer. All eyes are on him, as the entire room watches, which only intensifies the pressure. Singh accepts the Nazis' ceremonial dagger and holds it aloft for everyone to see. But he really wants to have a chinwag with Hugo, who he cannot see due to the crowds.

The guests once again start to clap in appreciation of what is happening, which is captured by the two cinematographers. Private Singh makes a gesture of cutting his own throat with his outstretched thumb as he runs it across his neck. The guests go wild, even though they are the crème de la crème of the Nazi party; a rabble is a rabble wherever you take them. Private Singh makes his way towards the Tommies, who all jostle and move with aggressive body language towards him as he approaches them. The Tommies have an outburst of verbal abuse for Private Singh, "traitor", "Judas", and "fucking Nazi lover" are some of the comments which they call out. Tension fills the air as Private Singh calmly conducts himself under the gaze of the whole room.

"Fucking traitor," Pauley calls out.

"Burn in hell," he adds.

The SS-guards have already shown the Tommies what they will do if they misbehave, as another SS-guard strikes Francis as he tries to lunge forward. JD spits at Private Singh in an act of defiance but soon feels the butt of a rifle for his troubles. Major Watkins glares at Private Singh, who has an element of swagger and bravado about him, as he parades himself before them. Private Singh stands before them in a defiant manner and holds up the Nazi ceremonial dagger once again. Rage builds up within the Tommies, and Pauley cannot control himself anymore and lunges towards Private Singh.

Pauley is mowed down by a barrage of bullets fired by an SS-guard who stood before him. The Tommies need to realise this will be the outcome for any of them if they try anything else. Due to the gunshots, some of the guests start to panic slightly but are reassured by the Führer to remain calm, as its just one of the Tommies being put out of his misery.

As Pauley's lifeless body lies on the floor, you can see JD is planning something similar, so Private Singh quickly moves back towards the stage where the Führer and his party are. As he moves around, a female waitress makes eye contact with him. There is a pause and what looks like a slight moment between them, as it is the same blonde waitress from earlier. No words are exchanged, but it is the body language and the way they look at one another. She walks away, and Private Singh wants the Tommies to witness what he is doing before they all end up brown bread, thanks to him. He does not want to be cheated and wants to kill them for the new Indian division. The cameras are still rolling, as this is going to be the event Goebbels will celebrate the Nazi party with.

Private Singh makes his way back towards the front of the stage. He requests the Tommies are made to kneel before the Führer and look up at him. Once translated, Himmler gives the SS-officer in charge a slight nod of his head, and he instructs his guards to do just that. The Tommies are not going to take this lightly, being told to kneel before Adolf Hitler. The SS-guards soon rough them up with a few choice punches and a few blows from rifle butts. This is just what is required, so the Tommies will do what they are being asked of.

With a few rifle butt strikes directed at chests, skulls, and midriffs, compelling the Tommies to reluctantly assume their positions, kneeling on the ground. JD spits blood onto the ground, cursing Private Singh to burn in hell. Other Tommies join in hurling verbal abuse at him, too. Major Watkins exchanges a glance with Lieutenant Harvey, recognising the gravity of the situation. The Lieutenant simply stares at the Major, nodding with a smile. Strangely, Private Singh requests the removal of their handcuffs, intending to salute the Führer before they meet their demise. Again, once this is translated it is conveyed by Himmler to the SS-officer in charge. The officer looks over at the stage slightly concerned looking, before his guards, albeit reluctantly, begin removing the restraints, stealing glances at the stage area. Himmler nods towards the SS-officer in charge again. The Tommies rub their wrists, anxiety overtaking them as they brace for the unknown that looms ahead.

The Major looks firstly to his left and then to his right at the men on either side of him. Certain Tommies are being held down by their heads with force. Maybe now their hands were free, the Nazis were concerned about an attack. Also, so there are no further interruptions to the proceedings, we presume. The Major gives them all a look of reassurance and calls out that it was an honour to serve with them all. The Lieutenant barks an order at the men, and they suddenly stop resisting and struggling. The SS-soldiers holding them down suddenly let go as they are not resisting anymore, to their surprise.

All the remaining Tommies look upwards at the stage; they know it will all be over very soon. Himmler signals the SS-officer once again, who orders his men to move back slightly, away from the prisoners. From the body language, Private Singh feels the Tommies are ready; they have now accepted their fate. He feels the moment is right for their execution before the Führer. The Major senses this, too, and looks around at the men one last time as Private Singh removes his Walther P38 handgun from its holster. He waves it around and points it at the Tommies, making a noise with his mouth.

"Blitzkrieg Tommies!" he calls out.

"BANG! BANG! BANG! BANG! BANG! BANG! BANG!" he adds.

"End of the road gents, been a pleasure though," he adds.

"Remember, cloak and dagger"

"With an element of disguise," he adds suddenly.

He looks very heavy-hearted at what he is going to do as he places the handgun back into its holster. He straightens his uniform up and looks at the Tommies one final time. Some of the Tommies wear a mask of defiance, while others look worried. Major Watkins senses something is afoot here, due to Singh's last comments? Suddenly, tension fills the air as they all know what is coming next. To the German hierarchy's surprise, he salutes the Tommies in a British military salute and hand gesture. He turns and asks the Führer to join them and witness this global event of the 'Third Reich'.

The cameras are still rolling, and Goebbels knows this is it, as he moves slightly forward within his chair with excitement. His place now cemented within German cinema history forever. As Adolf Hitler walks over towards Private Singh, he glances over at the Tommies one final time as they watch with bated breath.

Private Singh holds up his Nazi ceremonial dagger aloft, and he receives cheers from the guests. He turns and, momentarily, looks at Himmler before he turns and looks forward once again. He suddenly removes it from the scabbard and highlights the shiny blade within as he pauses one final time, making eye contact with the Tommies. Everyone within the room senses this is it; even the prisoners look like they have accepted their fate. He turns and looks at Adolf Hitler, and without any warning, he suddenly impales the Führer repeatedly in the side of the neck, like some frenzied madman or other.

STAB, STAB, STAB, STAB, STAB, STAB! The blood splashes his face and his immaculate Nazi uniform as the red stuff leaks out.

The Führer's white tunic soon turns bright red as the blood soaks in, and he gasps for air, probably choking on his own blood. Private Singh continues with his barrage of lethal blows till he is exhausted and can no longer lift his arm. He slows down his attack and eventually stops. His entire torso and face are now covered in the Führer's blood as he too gasps for air. The whites of his eyes, so noticeable as he glares at his victim. The whole room is horrified by what they are witnessing. Some people wince and pull that face you do when you've just witnessed something of this magnitude.

While others are shocked and rather overwhelmed by what they are witnessing which soon turns to aggression. Even before Adolf Hitler's lifeless body can hit the stage floor, Coco and the rest of the bevvy of beauties, who are all dressed like humble waitresses, suddenly open fire on the Nazi cunts centre stage. The horror which is about to be unleashed on the Nazi Rockstar's is evident. Himmler, Goebbels, Bormann, and Göring take the brunt of the flying lead. Major Watkins and the remaining Tommies cannot believe their eyes at the twist of fate they are witnessing before them. The SS-guards, like most of the guests, are gobsmacked at what is taking place here, too, and just do not react.

A few girls mow down these SS-guards and any other potential threat within the room first. Taking this into consideration, the girls, earlier camouflaged as waitresses, also had planted explosives strategically around the building throughout the day in case Private Singh's plot failed for some reason. The cinematographers keep on rolling as these events unfold, as this must be an Oscar in the making; Variety, watch out.

Yes, what you are witnessing is entirely Private Singh's idea; he cooked up the whole "I hate the British for what they did." His scheme was to simply drop himself and the 'Rum Bunch' into the Nazi meat grinder. It is a shame our would-be Adolf got himself killed like he did, as that would have been the cherry on the Bakewell. Private Singh had not been dropped into France and lost his unit, as Mr X and his merry men had cooked up this tall tale with him. This plot of espionage took place while savouring the subtle tones of a bottle of Johnnie Walker Black Label, with Colonel Smith being involved too, after Private Singh approached them. He was smuggled into France, and the rest was porkies too.

Private Singh had left a message at a French tavern, which was secretly used by the French resistance. The code word being "Pint of ale Gov'nor". As soon as he uttered this proper British lingo, the landlord of the Tavern, Pierre, would spring into action like some one-armed coiled viper. He would alert Coco her British date had arrived for an evening of fun and frolics. The pair of them discussed logistics and escape routes if things went wrong, with the communal idea of killing Nazis. Remember when his chaperone would be a kip, giving it forty winks and he would go out to take in the night air. Well, that is when he would meet up with Coco for a bit of "Oh la la", in the night air. The topic of discussion, the art of killing Nazis. They discussed their own cunning plan in how to rid the world of this scum.

This is how Coco and the girls knew when and where the final solution to this ugly war would be. Major Watkins and the 'Rum Bunch' were the only ones left in the dark regarding the whole mission. This was due to the fact that if they were captured by the SS, which they were, they had ways of making you talk. Lucky for them, Private Singh intervened and put a stop to this with his idea of extracting information from them himself. So, the consensus was if they did not know anything, they could not spill the Heinz beans. Private Singh wanted to tell the Major what they were getting themselves into but could not risk it within the prison cell. How their British military issued boots had hidden explosives within them and how the nunchucks were the switch detonator, hence the importance of the boots throughout.

The operation was a three-pronged plan. Firstly, we had the 'Rum Bunch' and James Hall, which was to simply swap James for Adolf Hitler. If this failed, part two would kick in, with the Major's men causing as much death, destruction, and mayhem to the Nazi war machine as was humanly possible. Thirdly, we had Private Singh and Coco's bevy of beauties. Private Singh knew of this cunning plan and devised his own cunning plan with his 'Bavarian Lion' element. So, he decided to amalgamate the first two elements and with his own. The master stroke was, gathering all the Nazi hierarchy within one expanse of space and then blowing up this house of gingerbread to Kingdom Come. "Hallelujah, Praise Ye the Lord" as some would say.

Sorry, look at me; we are getting carried away again. So where were we? Oh yeah, as submachine gunfire echoed around the room, as a mad panic had commenced, with most of the guests now trying to flee. The SS-officers all tried in vain to protect their Führer, who was now swimming within a pool of his own organ lubricant.

Within the crazy panic which followed, young Hugo Kruger, who had been hiding from Private Singh picked up a rifle and shot in the direction of all the chaos, which is where the Führer's party once stood. Suddenly, Private Singh falls towards the floor near to death, after Hugo's fine marksmanship skills had done the job.

He has inflicted a hatchet job on him, targeting vital organs, judging by the injuries. Private Singh tosses his blood-covered nunchucks towards Major Watkins, who skilfully catches them. Private Singh was well aware of the Major's time spent in the Far East and understood the potential damage he could do with the nunchucks. Major Watkins gestures regarding what Private Singh was trying to convey to him, with the pressing of the red-ruby stone set within one of the nunchucks' handles, his nod signifying acknowledgement of this.

This is not before Private Singh's near lifeless body hits the floor; he makes eye contact with Major Watkins and the remaining Tommies, as he is now at the same eye level as they are. He nods and closes his tearful eyes as he signals to the Major to press the stone set within the handle with a hand gesture. On understanding what Singh was conveying to him, Watkins salutes, while looking over at the dying Private Singh, whose lifeless gaze is in his direction. This is while Coco and the girls are mowing down Nazis, to their hearts' content. The Major uses the nunchucks to great advantage, with moves of deadly force. The Nazis did not know what hit them, as what pursued was a relentless barrage of bullets, ruination and proper mayhem as chaos erupted. Now this is what you call a turkey shoot in Provence of the Nazi kind. Blood splatters the walls, heads explode and bones shatter as the bullets do all the talking.

BANG! BANG! BANG! BANG! BANG! BANG! guns sound.

People are being crushed underfoot as others try to escape this soon-to-be barbarous conclusion of the Nazi party. The cameras are still rolling, catching all the best bits of this massacre. Hysteria consumes the guests as the uncontrollable fear of dying causes a stampede towards the doors. Like big fat black, swastika-wearing rats escaping a sinking ship, they flee. The huge wooden doors had already been barricaded by Chanel and Viv, which stopped people from leaving this evening of celebration. The guests bottleneck up against the doors, crushing people against them as others pound them with their fists in some form of attempt to open them.

Suddenly, the smell of fear is all around as you could taste it in the air, just like the millions who experienced this same fear at the hands of the Nazis. How they implored them not to conduct the barbaric atrocities against them. It's just not cricket, what the Nazis did and how they exterminated their fellow man. Now the Jackboot is on the other foot; I wonder how these Nazis are feeling as they flee for their lives. The poor string quartet too takes the brunt of the flying lead, thanks to friendly fire.

Suddenly, Prada throws a few explosives with timers around the room just to spice up the proceedings. She has placed her beret hat on and is now smoking, of course. Not before this can be out done by Louis, as this vixen has only made her way towards the machine gun nest, which Jerry had built within the corner of the room. She, being as supple as a ballerina, only climbed and swung off the rafters and chandeliers like a proper Cossack circus gymnast would, to reach this machine gun nest we talk of. This was Himmler's idea; even though it looked out of place, this advantage point covered the entire room. It would have been rude of the girls to look this Nazi gift horse in the mouth.

She pulls away the dead soldier who is slumped over the side and cocks the Maschinengewehr 42, commonly known or referred to as the MG42. She goes wild as she pumps 1500 rounds per minute into the masses of fleeing Nazis, which by now are all crowded at the closed doors. A swarm of bullets hail down onto the remaining guests within the room like this Nazi turkey shoot we talk of. Stella and Viv join in with handheld submachine guns, too. Blood splatters, women scream, bones shatter, and this killing spree of Nazi carnage continues.

By now, the SS-guards surrounding the Tommies are all piled up before them after being shot by the girl's handiwork. The remaining Tommies pick up the Karabiner 98k rifles and MP-40 submachine guns and get involved in this blood fest of bullets and butchery without the debauchery. The girls throw over a bag of grenades, which the Tommies utilised to maximum effect. Major Watkins looks over at the dead body of Private Singh. As he continues to shoot, he looks around at the remaining Tommies; the Lieutenant has been injured but, too, continues to fire. The Tommies do their damnedest to kill every one of these Nazi cocksuckers within the room. Coco throws knives at escaping Nazis and even impales Hugo from where she stands, maybe in revenge for him gunning down Private Singh. Blood gushes from Hugo's eye socket as he falls to the floor in agony before a few bullets finish him off. Prada throws some grenades into the side rooms and through the open windows at the military troop carries parked outside which explode, catching fire with some German soldiers who are burnt alive as they try to escape. Chanel helps Louis by feeding the bullets into the MG42 as she continues shooting.

BANG! BANG! BANG! BANG! BANG! BANG!

Major Watkins surveys the room, and senses it is time and presses the red-ruby stone set within one of the handles of the nunchucks. Suddenly smoke is slowly released from Private Singh's and the Tommies' military boots. A beeping noise starts, like some countdown to an explosive or other, to Major Watkins's surprise. Clive quickly removes his boots and throws them as he makes his way over towards the window area.

Gucci notices this, as she pumps bullets into any remaining SS-guards. Clive continues to shoot as he makes eye contact with the Major, who nods at him. He mows down the SS-guard who shot Pauley earlier, unloading a full clip into his face, with Gucci joining in.

On picking up a Stielhandgranate German grenade, he unscrews the base and pulls on the cord. He quickly throws it out of an open window, and it explodes soon after. The death toll continues to increase, thanks to the assault which is being conducted here. There is hysteria within the room due to the fleeing guests persist as the bullets rain down on them.

BANG! BANG! BANG! BANG! BANG! BANG!

The lifeless bodies of the Führer and his cronies are sprawled out, on the stage, rendered unrecognisable by the multitude of bullets that had peppered them. Sadly, Private Singh's blood-soaked body is slumped beside the Führer's, catching the attention of Major Watkins, who surveys the room one last time. The barrage persists, blood splattering amidst the organised chaos as the girls and the remaining Tommies persist in their efforts. Suddenly, Clive takes a bullet to the shoulder, propelling him backwards through the window and onto the canvas roof of a troop carrier.

The Major swiftly reloads his magazine, firing as he scans the room. He acknowledges that the 'Rum Bunch' have accomplished their mission and have made him proud within the process.

BANG! BANG! BANG! BANG! BANG! BANG!

The girls' MG42 spits empty bullet casings, which litter the floor as they make that clanging noise in contact with the floor. They splatter any Nazi within range as they continue to shoot. Louis, suddenly produces her pistol crossbow and impales Gerda, the beefcake, who falls face first into the Nazi cake and a few Gestapo blokes for good measure. Major Watkins suddenly notices the beeping noise from the nunchucks becomes louder and faster till it resembles a continuous tone as the timers on the explosives the girls had planted earlier all reached zero, too.

BOOM! BOOM! BOOM!

The whole building explodes, window glass shatters, concrete pillars crumble, and a huge fireball sweeps through the entire Berghof. The cinema screen catches fire, as do the Nazi swastika banners, which all fall downwards as they burn onto the guests below. The remaining Tommies and fleeing guests all perish within this fireball we talk of as they are exposed to the deadly flames. The military vehicles which were parked outside explode and catch fire too, as the whole gaff is engulfed. Numerous fulminations follow this; around the complex, even the Nazis' swastika banners outside, which flapped within the wind, catch fire too. All that remains of the Führer, Adolf Hitler, is his white visor cap flying through the air, making its way back down towards the ground, where it lands on a grass verge. One corner of it burns as silence fills the air.

FIN...

About the Author

I am a multifaceted individual whose diverse experiences and passions have deeply influenced the writing of this debut novel, Blitzkrieg Tommies. With a profound interest in the Great and Second World Wars, my fascination with military strategies and historical events is evident throughout my work. However, it's not just the magnificence of war that captivates me; it's the human stories within, particularly those of Sikh soldiers like the protagonist, Private Singh. Growing up in 1970s Great Britain as a British Sikh, I draw a lot from my own cultural identity and upbringing to breathe life into Private Singh's character, offering readers a powerful illustration of the hardships faced by Sikh soldiers on the front lines.

Beyond my literary endeavours, my passion for storytelling extends to the realm of film, where I have written six screenplays that await coming to life on the silver screen. Despite battling chronic pain for over three decades, I have found solace and purpose in my writing, using the world of make-believe as a means of coping and transcending my physical limitations. My writing has distracted me from my chronic pain, which I have suffered from for over 30 years now. My battle with chronic pain has been a rollercoaster of emotions, despair, and a feeling of hopelessness at times. The enduring love for my family, my Sikh faith and the notion of becoming an author and screenplay writer have kept the fire burning within.

In Blitzkrieg Tommies and beyond, my storytelling serves as a testament to the enduring power of human resilience, the importance of honouring the past, and the profound impact of personal identity on the course of history. Through words, I invite you to embark on a journey of discovery, empathy, and remembrance.

Printed in Dunstable, United Kingdom

71632112R00201